The Un-death of Me

Life of an Asian American Woman

Alicia Su Lozeron

Introduction

THE UN-DEATH OF ME is a life account and journey of an immigrant American woman. Avery Mingli Liang, a beauty queen and pageant winner, emigrated from Taipei to New York City circa 1990 attending Columbia University as an English Literature major. She had complete control and command of the English language, but her accent and looks exposed her to extreme discrimination, stereotyping, and insensitivity. Her understanding of history and literature rivaled great minds, yet she couldn't get past the fact she was alone, in a big city, unable to feel any level of self-worth, accomplishment, fulfillment, or true human connection.

Upon becoming a member of a well-to-do established New York City family (by marriage), she struggled to create her own identity, and to escape the trappings of what a traditional woman and wife should be. Avery Mingli Liang embodied a story of an immigrant woman, whose life journey took her through not only various parts of the world, but also high society engagements, political intrigue, and betrayal. She bolted from an unhappy marriage and existence on the road to discovery, self-awareness, and enlightenment, only to witness further scandalous incidents of both the high and the low societies.

Abbey Lori brought a fresh breath of air to Avery Mingli Liang's life. Now Avery's quest for happiness had an anchor. However, could they build on what they learned and sustain their happiness together? Or was their life together yet another futile pursuit of illusions and dreams? These were the questions Avery Mingli Liang sought to answer in order for her life to be fulfilled and come true. Her story is one of a kind because she as the protagonist reveals a unique background and experience rarely found in the literary world.

While Ayaan Hirsi Ali (the Somali-born Dutch-American activist, author, and former Dutch politician) attracts wide attention and perhaps induces negative criticism to Islamic cultural limitations in her autobiography *Infidel: My Life* -- Alicia Su Lozeron's account of an Asian American immigrant woman in *The Un-death of Me* brings about celebrations on cultural differences as well as similarities. It embraces mankind and human endeavors, proposing balanced mindsets very much needed in today's polarized societies.

I dedicate this book to Robert Alan Lozeron, my dear husband, my love, my life-partner, and my editor who provides me with invaluable suggestions. I am also grateful for my family and friends who encouraged me along my journey. Those who propel me to reflect on my inner self and the world appear as the many characters in the life account of an Asian American woman immigrant. They formulate the pillars of the world I construct. The fictional world's intricacy lies in their existences.

With them, this book comes to life.

New York, Las Vegas, Los Angeles, Vancouver, Toronto,
London, Sydney

Asia-America Connection Society

The Un-death of Me

Life of an Asian American Woman

Alicia Su Lozeron

Content

Actual happiness always looks pretty squalid in comparison with the overcompensations for misery. And, of course, stability isn't nearly so spectacular as instability. And being contented has none of the glamour of a good fight against misfortune, none of the picturesqueness of a struggle with temptation, or a fatal overthrow by passion or doubt.
Happiness is never grand.

Brave New World by Aldous Huxley

Prologue

It was in the journey of pursuit that Avery attained possibilities of joy, of happiness -- rather than giving up a quest, she searched, aimed, fired, killed what's detrimental, and experienced destruction akin to death, in order to resurrect herself to new forms of bliss. It's what went on in the world, and on the journey of pursuit that gave her peace, that turned the death of her old self into a rebirth, into the un-death of her.

Willa Cather once explained how it happened. When she found out how to take her journey, or to let her journey take her, she told stories about herself:

> *If there is one thing one can always yearn for and sometimes attain, it is human love.... You get to find your own way to dig out a heart and shake it off and hold it up to the light again. We all are.... Trying to invent our version of the story. All human odes are essentially one. "My life: what I sole from history, and how I live with it."*

Like a story Avery told herself and the world, like a story unfolding in a book -- with luck, life came true.

Chapter 1. They Were Their Own Globes

With a hint of ambivalence, Harry muttered: "You'd be the death of me, my Asian babe"! A smile pulled his full lips slanting upward nicely, glitters in the eyes.

Avery was often confounded by how culturally discriminated and stereotyped she was in America. She was unhappy about how myopic and prejudiced some people were. She was uncomfortable when she thought about how some parents were instilling cultural insensitivity in their children, because they as adults had no idea how to become culturally competent. She marveled at how America had made progress, and yet had such a very long way to go in the road to equity and diversity. She was shocked to see how Americans could murder each other simply for revenge or prejudice. Those incidents of conflicts in Orlando, Minnesota, Baton Rouge, Dallas, Milwaukee, New York, and Charlotte were alarming, disappointing, and dishearteningly recent! African Americans were discriminated against, white cops were assassinated, terrorist attacked in the name of righteous deeds, and all were made to be too black and white.

Senseless offhand comments made to Avery simply because she was a good-looking Asian woman were disconcerting. On the streets of Manhattan, a wobbly eighty-year old blonde turned white-haired grumbled atrociously to Avery: "Go back to your own country, slut"! Even more hurtful was the remark coming from one of her students in Las Vegas: "Don't tell me what to do. I can do anything in my country, unlike you"! She encountered youth insolence, to an extent she had to stand up for herself in the school district she worked in. She knew that she had to speak up and educate the kids to be the open-minded citizens they needed to be. She tried, but it got frustrating, and she suffered. In a letter to the teachers union, she detailed her dilemma:

> Starting with my evaluation from last year and continuing through this school year, I believe I am being racially discriminated against by some of my students and my administration.
>
> I had a low mark in the category of classroom management last year, but the proper procedures and supervisory interaction practices were not followed. I was not counseled or informed of issues I should have been informed of, including but not limited to, a supervisory change and a new person I reported to just prior to that evaluation. I did not have the proper amount or level of supervisory interaction or support and received the rating based on an extremely limited amount of interaction with my new supervisor. Far less than what is required to create a proper, useful, and valuable evaluation. I believe that evaluation was biased and questionable.
>
> I disputed last year's evaluation with the union and I did not receive a satisfactory resolution. I have spoken to other teachers, explained the missed procedures, and they agreed with me that this evaluation was not done properly or by the strict rules and guidelines.
>
> This year I have been working hard to discipline a select few students using the practices outlined to the teachers including: parent/teacher interviews and meetings, detentions, sending students to the Dean's office, etc. The very same students continually act up, disrupt the class, and stymie my efforts to teach the rest of the students their lessons. It seems the more I try to use the administration and the approved disciplinary practices to bring these students inline, the worse it gets. They never

come back from a Dean's office visit reformed. In fact, their attitudes are often worse because they got away with a "slap on the wrist." I continue to put up with negative and hurtful racial comments from those students. This existing system is certainly not working for the teachers or the students, and a select few students are ruining the teaching experience for me, certainly negatively affecting the efforts of the other students to learn. I believe that the same students are displaying racist tendencies, and I am not receiving the support I need to advance the other students, from the schools administration and my direct supervisor. I'm being racially discriminated against, and my administration is not instilling racial tolerance or acceptance in those kids.

Racial intolerance has fostered unjust student behavior and management mindset. The poor rating I received in Classroom Management was an unfair punishment on me. I have tried and tried to follow the proper procedures for disciplining the troubled students. I don't believe the administration is taking this seriously enough, and I continue to feel discriminated against in their lack of action about those (2-3) students. The students are racially discriminating against me and I believe the administration, in their lack of resolve and determination to "ignore" these students' behavior and "push them through the system," is failing both the students and myself.

I don't believe I'm being treated fairly by my school administration. I don't believe I'm being fairly evaluated by my direct supervisor. And I'm being racially discriminated against by certain students and the school administration. I can understand a level of racial discrimination from the students; I cannot understand or accept any level of racial discrimination from my supervisor and my school's senior level administration.

This situation is causing me undue stress, mental anguish, health issues, and fatigue. I need to see some resolve, some action. I believe this issue needs to be addressed and people held accountable for this racism and unfair discrimination.

Little did Avery realize that this challenge of stereotyping and unfair treatment carried over from her work life to her love life, ubiquitous and distressing. Her life had not come close to being true; it was full of injuries and injustices.

With a hint of ambivalence, Harry muttered: "You'd be the death of me." A smile pulled his full lips slanting upward nicely, glitters in the eyes. Did he mean he'd foresee her to be the love of his life but that rather implied his death, his reluctance to settle with any woman, or to stay in any state of being? She stared at him not knowing how to take that remark, as she had been staying too long in the relationship, or love-ship, for lack of a definitive word. She had been groping, attempting to dance gracefully around the mystery and distance he projected.

Who said it wasn't like a dance: the getting close, the withdrawing, the responding to his movements, and the taking initiatives to make him want her more? From the onset, it had been a composed ritual, choreographed. The getting-to-know-each-other was done in a month, including a cruise trip with his best friends to the Caribbean Sea. After that, he seemed to think the courting mission was accomplished, plunged back to his work, absorbed in his own world, hardly taking her to any public places anymore. It never occurred to him to arrange for a date night, a short period of quality time to be with her.

They met and saw each other, all right. They met for love-making; he'd spend the night when he came to see her. Passionate love-making was preceded by dressing-up and photo-taking sessions. Every meeting was sweet and brought her infinite joy. He probably had to work around his schedule and squeeze in a night to be with her. How it'd come to tax her such -- no companionship, no relationship, but a man that she fell hard for and did not know entirely in what way to regard -- a boyfriend, a lover, a mate, a friend with benefits -- someone she couldn't let go of in her life?

Avery broke up with Harry several times. He always found a point to come back. She could never change the ways things were no matter how hard she tried. No, love should not require her to turn her back on traditional values, her ways of living or believing. It wasn't love; it had no name.

Sent from Avery Liang to Harry Neuzil:

> Here all by myself in America, I want a substantial real sense of love -- one that accompanies me for the rest of my life. Your fantasy/demand tells what mere physical pleasure you seek from me. You know I can't settle with only that and that's why we split N times before. I asked you back because I love you and have been longing for the same kind of love from you. I cried and cried for not feeling your love or care. Please converse deeply with your inner self, to know for sure what you want, what kind of love you desire, in what way you may grow old. Think over our feelings for each other; search for a path good for both of us, a path that encompasses bliss and comfort for both. If we can only remain on a sexual level, you do not need to come to me Sunday. You

know how I love to open my door for you on Sunday --
and on each and every single day to come.

Avery

He replied:

"You are right. I am sorry. I will leave you be."

The first rule of happiness: never get with people of
different pursuits. Harry was almost too rational, too cool, and
too ready to let go of anything that stood in his way. Avery was
the one who couldn't let go. She could shut her door
temporarily only when he exhibited his outrageously wild side
that provoked her insecurity. When he laid out his all-time
fantasies about Asian women and cast his wondering eyes via a
personal ad:

There's something about.... Asian women

They drive me crazy. Dark hair, dark eyes, full lips, and
demure. If you have cute feet to go with that and look
great in heels and stockings, I'll melt;). Show me some
examples.... No, show me lots of examples:).

I'm easy to like; 6'6", trim, funny, smart, great smile,
infectious attitude. Well employed, well- traveled, and
well read. Love Sushi, Chinese, Thai, Filipino and
Korean food.

Avery's pal Mihee responded to Harry's ad, and let out
that little secret of his to her. Humiliated, Avery was convinced
that, she and Harry each had a different world, with no
interconnectivity. There were their own globes. Whatever

trajectories the two of them happened to travel to cross each other's path, there was no true connection. It would not last.

Harry was an over-aged five-star man's man, happy, honest, loyal -- honest to his own needs and ways of life! He loved to hang out with his clients, staff, and all sorts of people: family, high school friends, college friends, men and women. He traveled too much for business. He had many centers in life -- and Avery in just one of them -- off-centered center. Perhaps she could be a significant off-center, one that's not screaming for attention that he had to keep making conscious efforts to lessen its noises.

That Ad had Harry's DNA imprinted in there: VP of Sales for a huge corporation, with family businesses of brothels all over Nevada, and an alpha male, a street-smart Renaissance man, with connections in the Vegas entertainment scene that extended to a network of allies and enemies all over the Americas and the Caribbean.

Avery wanted to think that the Ad was for his family businesses, but was very aware that it was more for his own kinks. Yet, he's so attractive, so endearing, when he whispered "yes, babe" in her ears -- so distant and independent on his quest for a fun fine life of his own. He was never mean to her. He treated her with tenderness and integrity, enough affection to show that he cared for her yet not unreservedly cherishing her. He just didn't have the kind of certainty she wanted in life. She loved him and wanted to build a life with him. He did not have the mind for that. He'd go at his own pace to see her every two to four weeks, content with the ease and comfort of having a girl whenever he desired. Never mind whether she's truly happy. She'd always been elated to see him but dreading and wondering when exactly they would see each other again.

And this went on for four years. Avery was too in love to turn less demure with him; she lacked the courage to make noises. She only suffered, muffled in anguish.

9

Harry came back with a short text message, "Still mad at me?" -- and she was ready to let him in again -- a girlfriend, a lover, a mate or friend with benefits -- someone he put aside and didn't communicate with most of the time, but could be held in his arms whenever he chose to?

Avery always thought that solidarity in a relationship came from the feelings two people had toward each other, the values seen in each other. However challenging external factors could be, the inner desire for each other could rise above and bring them back together. They would always find someone else attractive and wonder whether the grass wasn't greener on the other side. But he wanted them back together, and she could be assured that the relationship meant something. Or, was she justifying being treated that way again, simply because she wanted to see him too?

It's not that she sat around all day hoping to hear from him. She was conscious of her own life and obligations. Being a school teacher, her days were full of tasks and demands, and she barely had energy to whine about love. During the summer, she worked at least eight hours a day, constructing courses, preparing for tests, taking classes to advance her crafts, and writing, traveling, living her life. Plus she was occupied with music, reading books, watching movies, and having fun....

Avery was always grateful for her love of literature; it reminded her of possibilities of life, of new territories and horizons. Of being transported out of her own existence into others'. She was proud of her secondary school English teaching job and took it very seriously. Ultimately teaching English/literacy was not what she had pictured, but it provided a connection to her passion. Literature was her life, the way she learned and saw the world; she strived to be well-rounded, mature, and self-sufficient. However, Louise Bogan would see in Avery many an impatient woman:

> They wait when they should turn to journeys, /They stiffen, when they should bend. /They use against themselves that benevolence/To which no man is friend....
> They hear in every whisper that speaks to them
> A shout and a cry.
> As like as not, when they take life over their door-sills
> They should let it go by.

In her pursuit of happiness -- of more togetherness with Harry, Avery forsook the happiness of pursuit, the contentment that came from simply living her life and pursuing her own dreams. She realized how middle-class and staid the happiness of attaining Harry's love could only bring. There was her proverbial death in his love, the inertia that he would never grant her. And she wanted to die, to perish in him; she could not help but want more of his touch and his body. She could never let him go no matter how many times she tried.

Their love-ship was not clear-cut, not "normal" and hard to pinpoint, because there's not enough sharing, not enough emotional closeness.

So with her given right of the pursuit for happiness, Avery "took life over her door-sills" and would not "let it go by." She tried for possibilities of other matches. She dated more than TEN men in a month and concluded yet again, that she loved Harry and wanted to be with him. No other men were on a par; no other men intrigued her like Harry. She contacted him to request his love back after her "extensive" search for potential mates.

In a letter to Harry, Avery wrote:

Dear Harry,

How was your birthday or holidays? Wondering why I was not with you during those blissful days, and then again when have I ever been in your life? Four years -- and you have not invited me to any holiday gatherings with your family! What am/was I to you? Would you even call if my sky should fall?

Your last words to me were: "I looked and I do not have your gate clicker." That was typical and may be symbolic of what's between us -- love abandoned; trust lost. I gave you the key to my world and feel hurt that you have not cherished it or returned my love/trust in any way. In any case, I am writing because I cannot let go of you and am seeking your help to realize that inner closure I need so badly in order to move on with my life....

Remember last year when you said you'd be my boyfriend and I didn't have to try dating so many people? Well that fell apart when you failed to maintain our communication while you're on long business trips. Were you saying all you want is a sexual partner who you relax with once or twice a month, and have no connection with whatsoever the rest of the time? That certainly is not what I wish to have out of a 4-year relationship and I am still amazed how you can justify it. I guess the problem is a lot of times we do not know what we really want. We thought we want one thing but we fall into the pattern of chasing after something utterly different, scared of intimacy, of true connection.

There, that's where you can help me. Tell me that you have passed me up, never loved me, started seeing someone else, and are utterly different than what I want in spite of the fact that I still love you dearly and cannot find a way to let go of you. Kill me -- kill the hope I might have, in other words.

The truth is I have tried to seek out a potential life partner, whose role you refuse so adamantly to take on. This sociology professor is so ready to love me and give me what I want that I have to ask myself why I am running away, not happy. I know deep down that it's because I cannot let go of you though I tried numerous times on my own. Please help me move on.

What say you?

Love,
Avery

He wrote back.

Subject: Re: SOS: I cannot let go of you.

Avery,

You put a lot into your letter. Let me see if I can add some thoughts for you.

I found your gate remote. I can drop it off at your house Monday. Sorry, my mom had been cleaning my kitchen and moved some things to new location... Moms:). I will put it on your front porch late Monday afternoon if that is ok....

You want more from me than I can deliver, and you deserve it. So anything I give you will come up shy of what you're expecting. That's what I am saying. So to be fair to you, I thought it was best if I left. As far as being a friend, I would do anything for you if your sky was falling. You need only to ask.

It's hard for me to stay away from you. You are very good to me. I do miss you. Your jumping into my arms, your lips, your calves in heels, and my mouth on yours. I love how happy we are every time we see each other. You turn me on more than I can explain.

Not sure if that helps....
Love,
Harry

She told him to knock on her door when he brought her gate remote. All conflicts or resentments went out of the door when they saw each other. Same old: he showered her with his affection, albeit metered and measured, and she wanted him back with all her heart.

"I am afraid of hurting you more. I don't want to be the reason you are crying...." Harry hesitated.

She replied: "So ready to give me off to someone else and leave me in eternal sorrow? I only wish you to communicate more. Too much to ask?"

He said: "Your request to communicate is fair and understood. It's the eternal sorrow and cast aside comments that tell me I will only hurt you."

She wanted him no matter what: "Come see me; I promise not to cry again."

He was the same old Harry: "You know how it would be, right?"

"Come over. I'm no chicken," She made up her mind.

Women settle when the man is right; men settle when the time is right. Who was she to call the shots for someone else's marking periods in life? Avery meant for Harry and her to enjoy each other when they could, for him to have her, and for herself to love him the same way she'd always loved him. She had only her own attitudes and expectations toward their love-ship to adjust. She intended not to worry but to look life in the face and seize every moment they shared.

Harry loved Avery with warmth and honesty, enough fondness and passion yet never affording reckless forces to plummet into the depth of life. Not an uncontrolled submergence of soul, a canvas of all details painted with intricate pigments. Not like Tim's love for her, but in a way more prudent than Tim's.

Chapter 2. In New York or Asia
with or without Tim

Eva was speaking so fast and confidently that Avery decided she could not converse in a similar fashion to be friends with this waspy brainiac. Jason was too smart not to notice Avery's fear, and drove her away trying to help every step of the way. Fred was super nice, a country bumpkin unable to show Avery the real NY experience. Colin was too eager to turn Avery into his girlfriend, sending her abundant flowers and notes that she found him repulsive.

Nothing was right; everything in her daily New York life posed a threat, horrendous, exceedingly agonizing.

Where was that optimistic go-getter who was determined to get admitted to Columbia University, to make an impact, and to explore and uncover the world's every secret?

Avery Mingli Liang, a beauty queen and pageant winner, emigrated from Taipei to New York City circa 1990 attending Columbia University as an English and Comparative Literature major. She had complete control and understanding of the English language but her accent and looks exposed her to extreme discrimination, stereotyping, and insensitivity. Her understanding of history and literature rivaled great minds, yet she couldn't get past the fact she was alone, in a big city, unable to feel any level of self-worth, accomplishment, fulfillment, or true human connection.

Avery needed to fight those powerful surges of fear and aloneness when she first moved to New York City from Taiwan.

She needed to merge and become a part of the Big Apple, to lose herself in it so she could find herself again. She felt like *the Native Son* portrayed by Richard Wright! And that scared her even more because she thought she would turn into this criminal creature seeking revenge on the city. But she was a "Foreign Daughter"; she was not a native black! And she lived in the modern era when civil rights were supposed to be granted to all, with all men and women deemed equal! Why on earth did she feel uncomfortable? Didn't America promise a land of opportunities? Didn't she prove that she could argue alongside her fellow graduate students about salvation and justice of the world? Foreign or native, she had not realized how alienated from society one could feel anywhere. This overpopulated island of Manhattan made her feel isolated, alone and burdened with nameless fear.

Bleak, not redeemed, not alive. Avery needed to breathe. She contacted Sophie and hung out with her.

"Maybe it would be better if you'd come live in the city for several months before you went to school."
"Yes, it's a bit overwhelming, and Tim isn't the easiest person in the world." Avery sighed and agreed.

Avery and Sophie took a train ride along the Hudson River all the way to Sophie's parents' home near Syracuse, New York. Avery had forgotten the serenity outside the city, and was amazed at its effect. The Hudson meandered and soothed a weary heart and she in turn, had an intent first look at American small-town life. They arrived on Old Hometown Day. The parade and square dance took Avery off-guard. How happy people all seemed to be in the town. Even Sophie's mom's pickled beets tasted sweet, though in reality awfully bitter with a nameless disconcerting smell.

Sophie's mom showed immense affection toward her husband and daughter. That was what family's all about. Avery forgot that she didn't belong to that family and was taken aback when Sophie's mom made off-hand remarks on the TV show they were watching together:

"How could they get someone that looks like Avery to play this role of a home-grown American girl?"

Sophie's mom could not make sense of the TV show. Her life suddenly turned disorderly when someone like Avery dropped by and reminded her of the prevailing diversity in American society. The novelty that was Avery did not suit her, and she could only understand traditional American shows that cast Caucasian actors.

Avery shrugged off Sophie's mom's fussiness and flirted with Sophie's dad who'd just turned seventy-two. She decided to make the best out of the trip, and went on country excursions with Sophie and her father. On the dance floor of the Old Town Hall, she learned how to line-dance.

"You just have to follow people's movement." Sophie instructed and encouraged.

"How, well.... Let me try." Avery attempted the move of the legs, the turn of the head, the posture of the upper body, and the whirl of the waist.

"Yyyyyes, you're doing great." Holding and guiding Avery, the friendly town folks encouraged and showed her their mastery of the country dance.

Avery had the most fun, and for the first time, she could put schoolwork and the difficulty with Tim aside after landing in the United States. She was not the most skillful country dancer, nor was she a lover of the music or dance genre. However, years later when occasions arose and she happened to be amongst country clubbers in Las Vegas, she would smile the warmest smile to herself and ruminate on the memory of this dance with Sophie in the small town of Syracuse, New York.

No one could be ultimately foreign in a land. Avery summoned her faith in the human species and was determined to make NYC her home, not knowing she would leave Tim and New York, move to Las Vegas, and file for a divorce. She had not planned to meet the lady-killer Harry in Vegas, and more importantly her future second husband Abbey, after decades of calling herself a New Yorker.

Avery and Tim met in Taipei before she came to New York to enroll in Columbia University. Tim gave up his life in Taiwan as an expat, and decided to move to NYC with Avery. Avery bought an apartment in New York and married Tim on a trip to Las Vegas after they lived together in the city for four years. She started working at a medical university after Columbia, writing Dean's evaluation letters. Things looked for a moment to be fine though she often wondered why Tim, content as a day trader on the stock market, could leave her to worry about their single-income household they both were supposed to belong to.

Tim came back to NYC after a long stay in Asia. Avery understood he'd like to have a fulltime job or paint and explore his art career in the city. For some reason, he just never started. Perhaps he's more comfortable being an American expat somewhere other than his home country.

It hurt to see Tim unfulfilled. It also hurt to think that with all the big dreams and ambitions, she ended up with a 9-5 office job that was too ordinary, too bourgeoisie, and lackluster. How come while Tim had the cause of arts to live for, she had to set aside her real passions in order to work in an office not particularly to her liking? For a while it was bearable because Avery wanted to support Tim's dreams and to give him the opportunity to live and shine. In the end, it just got too taxing to be the only person footing the bills and losing her life to the monetary chase.

Avery left her university job to work for a technology company that enabled her to travel internationally back to Asia on business. She thought she'd got a real job, dressed all executive-like and flying business class. Well that company went out of business and she had to sue her boss for not paying her salary or reimbursing her expenses that she used personal savings to cover for the company. The dot.com bubble burst in its entirety, so she stopped pursuing the lawsuit she filed against her boss to try getting her money back. Too expensive to follow up.

Avery was working for a brokerage firm on Wall Street during the September 11 attack. Shocked by the "fire" burning the World Trade Center, Avery, like most people working and living in NYC, did not realize something was seriously wrong until the second plane hit the Pentagon. Along with thousands of downtown workers, she was evacuated from the vicinity walking north away from lower Manhattan, covered in dust, tears rolling down the cheeks. September 11 killed many innocent people, including a couple of Avery's acquaintances. It was definitely the most disgusting day in her life, too gruesome and horrid for words. Numerous businesses suffered after the incident and the economy fell into a slumber. It was not pretty.

Avery's marketing position in the brokerage firm on Wall Street was probably the best paying job she ever had. However, she felt stifled by dysfunctional corporations, in which every task or project had to undergo time-consuming approval processes. Her creativity and adventurous business sense did not jibe with the Wall-Street-nese. Being just a cog in the wheel, she was afraid she might turn "brain-framed," getting too comfortable to think outside of the corporate box. She left her Wall Street job to start a business -- a coffee house where she dreamed she could realize her full creativity and make her community a better place. She was restless, impatient, and eager to live life to the fullest.

Tim and Avery had their ups and downs during the years she worked fulltime office jobs. He escaped to Asia every time they had a fall-out. Avery wanted to give their relationship the best shot, and asked him to come back to NYC to help run the business. She prayed with all her heart that a fresh start and venture would work wonders, hoping Tim would feel more settled, at home and at ease.

Avery was ambitious and gung-ho about offering a public creative space. Her press release was published in the *Village Voice*:

New Village Coffee Lounge
Unique Gourmet Choices in Art Space

A unique coffee lounge newly opened. Espresso drinks prepared with supreme foam/crema. Indy Brews featuring delicious estate grown coffees

from round the world,

custom-immersed in French Presses.

An art venue to offer a gastronomical treat, and to talk about

the caffeine punch best-of-class joys.

Village Cafe is a multimedia space that features a cafe accentuating fine coffees and showcasing the creative

work of independent artists, writers, and musicians. Wireless Access Points located throughout the space and fun collectibles add to the experience. Owner Avery Liang reports, "*Village Cafe* highlights epicurean joys as artistic acts. Beverages and foods are made from filtered water and the finest ingredients. Our state-of-the-art espresso machine produces quality specialty drinks made at precise and consistent temperatures; individually ground and brewed coffees by the pot also provide premium experience. You get to CHOOSE -- from an elaborate specialty drink, an Indy Brew, or a regular cup o' Joe (daily house brew). Village Cafe is devoted to cultivating the energizing intersection of beverage, food, art, literature, music, technology, and community."
Village Cafe, launched in the East Village, New York City, has gone to considerable effort to bring you access to the finest quality brews, espresso drinks, fresh juices, teas, health beverages, delicious desserts and light foods. Village Cafe is about YOU: your needs, your callings, requirements, and self-fulfillment. And it is about all of us in a community.

Drink up!

Avery wrote the release with high hopes and dreams -- a daring earnest young soul she was. She wanted to be happy, feel alive, and go after life like nobody else.

For a while, it was like a dream come true. Avery worked 24/7 and tried to enlist her artist, musician and writer friends to help her boost up the place, not knowing that her ultimate goal to count on Tim as the owner/manager was going to be difficult to reach. Perhaps she was just too naïve, combining business with creativity, dreaming that it would be the solution for all their problems, and the path to build a healthy life together.

Avery's good friend Andy prepared a write-up for her café to be promoted, in spite of her realization that she had just put herself and Tim in a very tight spot:

Village Café

It's an old story. "I was working in the marketing department of an investment firm on Wall Street; it was a good stable job, but I wanted to be doing things that I like and that are a little more creative. I finally decided that the only solution was to do something that I'd have done and always wanted to do, and that was to start my own business." If there is anything at all novel about this situation it is that the speaker, Avery Liang, actually carried out her plan, and she is doing it without any partners or high priced consultants. "One good thing about my previous job was that it gave me experience in business planning as well as marketing, and so in my spare time I began using the skills that I'd acquired to explore opportunities and make feasibility studies. The first thing I did was consider some of the things that I particularly enjoy, and one of them has always been coffee. I happen to really like a type called Sumatra Mandheling for instance, but I also like trying other kinds of exotic coffees, and there's no café that I know of where you can order from a selection of, say, ten different kinds of coffee." And so her idea for a need that might be filled came into being. "Then I began to think that there is a lot more that a coffee establishment could offer its patrons in terms of making their visits enjoyable than what the typical coffee bar is doing in that regard. I am absolutely convinced of that. I want to create a place where people will feel that they can spend an extended period of time because the ambience is just a little bit more stimulating than what they have at home. There will be the works of local artists on the walls, experimental music, both live and recorded, cutting edge video presentations, and free form discussions among other things. What I'm operating is, for lack of a better word, a coffee lounge."

The coffee theme will be highlighted by regularly scheduled coffee tasting sessions that Ms. Liang will conduct. "There are 800 taste possibilities for coffee as opposed to only about 400 for wine, surprisingly enough. There are hundreds of estate-grown varieties of coffee beans that we will be searching out and offering our patrons, much like the different wines from small wineries. I should also mention that we will only be serving shade grown fair trade coffees so that our patrons can be assured as best we can that neither the coffee workers nor the environment have been exploited." She went on to say, "A number of years ago I was driving through the countryside of southern California outside of San Diego, and I happened to pass a sign for a coffee roasting factory; there was no sign saying that tourists were welcome, but I drove up to the front door and knocked anyway. I don't remember quite what I said, but the next thing I knew I was invited to observe a cupping session. The roast master tried the coffee from each batch of the most recently roasted beans and in that way determined the quality of the various roasts. I was intrigued, to say the least." Indeed, she will have a small coffee roaster on the premises, and patrons will get to have something of the cupping experience on a daily basis. "We'll be offering coffee lovers an opportunity to enjoy coffee fresh from the roaster just as beer drinkers now do in microbrewery establishments," she added.

There is one more unusual aspect to Liang's endeavor, and that is that she is almost literally betting the rent on the success of Village Cafe, as her coffee lounge will be called. "Owning an apartment along with putting together a business plan was enough to convince banks to loan me enough money to get started." Unfortunately this means that the bulk of her funding is coming from one of those loans where if you can't pay it back then the bank takes your home away from you. "Well, you know," she mentioned with a smile that could make everything all right, "Helen Keller once said, 'Life is either a daring adventure, or nothing at all.'"

Andy called Avery a wonder woman. She told him that she believed she needed to either assume the right to pursue happiness, or to conform till the end of her life. All she wanted was to go at happiness, and give happiness a chance. For a while, all seemed to be flourishing. She was a busy business operator.

The business took off with monies from Tim's family estate after they got married. It was featured in Zagat under "Best Coffee in New York":

"Every hipster's 'favorite way to start the day,' dispenser of 'premium-quality espresso' and 'Indy brews' plus 'delicious' treats like the 'dream-time' tarts and cakes; just be prepared to "get in line" and step into a "Parisian café.""

The café did turn into a creative public place where jazz singers and rock musicians gathered to showcase their new tunes. The walls were decorated with local artists' pieces. And the customers often felt free to hang for hours on a cup of Joe. Naturally they did make a profit from all gatherings arranged for high-society socialites and Hollywood starlets alike.

Tim and Avery's second and third cafes were opened shortly after. They were regularly seen to sit alongside the city's government officials, judges, attorneys, politicians and lobbyists. Tim's diplomat father and French-translator mother visited from their overseas residence, and they were the ones expanding the businesses. Along with each of their visits, a facet of the coffee enterprise scored a review on a major newspaper, showcasing Tim's parents' prowess. It was about politics, about power struggle, and monetary gain. Tim was far from the owner-manager, and Avery gradually lost sight of the original purpose of fulfilling a happy creative life through her endeavor.

Avery often felt suffocated when trying to join a conversation only to be interrupted by someone bigger and more important.

"The first line of every story, be it a novel or a movie, is the most important factor of a piece of work." Jim the professor remarked with conviction.

"You're pigeon-holing, too narrow. What about actions and storylines?" One councilman pretended to be interested.

"Give some examples," hooted one beer-bellied, red-faced movie director.

The professor quickly downloaded his database and offered his recitation:

"In *The Hound of the Baskervilles*, 'Mr. Sherlock Holmes, who was usually very late in the mornings, save upon those not infrequent occasions when he was up all night, was seated at the breakfast table.'....," he earnestly continued before anyone could start talking:

"In *Frankenstein*: 'You will rejoice to hear that no disaster has accomplished the commencement of an enterprise which you have regarded with such evil forebodings'...."

"In both cases, the first sentence opens up a wide array of possibilities; it gives space to...."

Another chimed in without waiting for Jim the professor to finish: "How about the imagery and the sound?"

Avery liked to be able to mention the "synergy of all story elements," and started, "actually, what works wonders...."

"Actually there is moral in the story." Someone else finished for her.

When Avery saw that there's no real discussion going on, she turned to tend the business and found Tim training a team of baristas, instructing them to replace all the Indy brews with quick brews, to change the colors of the utensils and napkins, and to reprint the menus with his new designs. He noticed Avery watching and frowning, and told her to go home and get some rest.

Avery looked at the website and storefront she built before and after Tim's return to the US -- before and after his parents' "contribution." She saw the transformations, the makeovers. High-profile lobbyists and stars occupied her coffee lounge, to lose small monies and win big battles. With Avery's involuntary acquiescence, her creative space was created for the public, the most vociferous and visible kind.

Tim and Avery couldn't be happy running the business together. He gave negative criticism about everything she did for the shops. He left the shops to numerous managers and sat back to watch them steal. She was beleaguered. Alarmingly an illusion, the business failed to be the solution to all their problems. A door inside her was shut forever, and would never open again. She knew all along that their love was perishing, and then at one precise point, she fell out of love completely. Avery moved to Las Vegas after decades of life in New York.

Forever in Memory

Tim and Avery had sustainable yet ever-changing kind of love. From exploring the world side by side to living the daily life together, they went through the most fragile, mortal, and corruptible ways of love. Love waned and diminished with the necessities of the mundane.

Avery's love for Tim had packed it in long before she met Harry, but it also resurrected in a form akin to family love. Tim was like a brother although they never talked anymore. She had never thought that a profound love could transform overtime -- love could die, could reach a point of no return, and then trickled back gently and kindly to be with her for life, altered but gracefully part of her forever.

All-out with Tim or reserved with Harry -- perhaps all their individualities could only render their separateness: they were each their own globe. Their journeys were predestined to be lonely with only occasional significant encounters along the way. Didn't Harry's array of centers in life indicate oblivion, a lack of inner intensity for unity, for love itself? Didn't Tim's absolute exertion and subsequent failure denote futility, a lack of inner preservation for harmony, for love itself?

Marriage or no-marriage, family or no-family, sharing the quotidian or not, relationships were difficult each and every way Avery sliced them. She had yet to learn the way of the world.

Tim, Avery Liang's ex-husband, was a major part of her life, and she, his, for fourteen years. It seemed eons ago now for Avery, thinking of that night when they met on a hot summer night in her home country of Taiwan.

On a dance floor back in one of those cozy little pubs in Taipei, they snatched at happiness that was always easier to lose than to find. What she had that night was his: her little black slinky dress, her ponytail, and dainty Reebok dance shoes. He cared enough to take her all in that night, plowing into her world. They wound up spending a significant chapter of life together, on Taiwan, on the road all over the world, and in New York City.

At the end of the chapter, Avery moved out of Manhattan to live in the city where they got married and where she could divorce him -- Las Vegas. What became of love when it stretched that way, to hold so much confusion, frustration, conflict, and loss? It had to transform, and it did evolve to be something that she could still hold. Her feelings for Tim reshaped, and that sentiment would never go away, however dauntingly irrelevant that understanding would be to her present life now and thereafter.

Tim was once her husband, a friend not in close proximity any more. How she loved to have the proximity that only a husband and wife likely shared. Then honestly, she was also aware that she got by awesomely by herself, and would hesitate, even dread to have that kind of proximity again. Was it because she was transplanted and uprooted altogether from Taiwan that she longed so much to have family in her existence, though deep-down she had been a lone-wolf, with a soul wandering lonely and endlessly since childhood?

She remembered how petrified she was when she first landed in the Big Apple -- that crowded yet lonesome city. "Are you cold? Why are you shivering?" Tim asked in a mocking tone he always took on when wanting to show how in control he was. "Nope, just hungry," she announced knowing only substantial servings like red meat and potatoes could fill the shocking void in her. What's all this hustle and bustle about? Why did the cab driver speak in an accent so unlike the American language she heard from the audio tapes she used to reduce her own accent back in Taiwan? Why was the diamond of a city oozing indifference in its glistening eyes?

The JFK Airport was almost third-worldly with rundown plastered terminals. Only the travelers from all over the world convinced her that she had arrived at a cosmopolitan hub. It was ridiculous how they had to walk a long way to get transportation into Manhattan. They had not seen that kind of urban planning while traveling across Europe!

"50th Street, between 8th and 9th Ave.!" Tim told the Arab cab driver. The buildings flew by and then slowed to a still scene of a shantytown as they got to the heart of 9th Ave. in Hell's Kitchen.

"This is a one-way street. We goin to stop here on 9th." The driver announced.

That was one sunny day in August, smoldered with the city people's pregnant emotions. The sun heated up the plush seat in the taxi and seemed to cook up the Middle Eastern maqam, cacophonous with usually loud vocals. Sensing her uneasiness, Tim assured: "Sophie is a very nice lady; you will like her."

Sophie, Avery's first acquaintance in NYC, was a religious and yes, nice woman from Upstate New York -- another variance when it came to Avery's impressions of New Yorkers. Sophie lived with her bedridden boyfriend who was dying of AIDS, and yet had enough heart to put Tim and Avery up for a stay. Her one-bedroom apartment was damp, dark, and smelt of cat litter.

Avery spent the night on Sophie's couch and accumulated so many animal hairs that she turned feline in a short three days at the apartment. She had this cattiness in her when she first got to America!

"I cut my travel short to come here earlier to get ready for school, not to cook church meals." Avery said to Tim after they went to too many of Sophie's Christian functions. Tim snapped: "Why can't you be nice?" Avery felt out of her elements, smiling at church goers learning how Jesus was the Only and Absolute light in this life.

"I just don't think I should spend time around churches when I need to get ready for Columbia." She offered her explanation for needing time to herself.

"You're ungrateful."

"Label me anyway you want. I need to get my own apartment ASAP. I will find one."

They would be moving out once they found their own place. It took two weeks too long before they landed an apartment on Restaurant Row near the Theater District in Midtown Manhattan. By the time they had their own home, Tim was angry and resentful, and Avery was miserable, tired, and scared.

Avery was paying $1000 a month for a tiny high-ceilinged space, considered rent-control-stabilized. It was efficient enough with a loft bed over a study that's called bedroom, a living/painting room combined with a stove called kitchen, and the luxury of a full bath equipped with everything they needed for a dark room to develop black-and-white photos.

Avery found it inconvenient to have to commute on the subway for fifty blocks to school, another fifty back while most people lived around campus in the Upper West Side. She was anxious about learning her ways around the city, adapting to the

31

urban air, and trying to muffle her "Far East-ness" to become more American. She worried about the seminars at Columbia with all the white wunderkinds and those Middle Eastern and Indian geniuses. She divided her life in between taking up the challenges of rigorous schoolwork and trying for the first time in her life to build a life with a man, an uncharacteristic American and atypical human at that.

While the rich white students completely belonged, the Middle Eastern and Indian kids had academic gurus like Edward Said and Gayatri Spivak signifying their intelligence for them. Avery had earned her tuition running her own English language school in Taiwan. She was disappointed that Columbia School of Arts and Science entailed more of the similar battles her schooling had been taking her, with Post-colonialism, Orientalism, and Deconstructionism. Ethnicity, racial concern, and mankind's blindness or ignorance --when tossed around for mere intellectual masturbation, became kind of pointless and dry for Avery. She felt that all those topics and issues were in her reality, in her life; they were too palpable, too blatant to be tackled only in seminars and research papers. Even Shakespeare seemed fastidious and less enjoyable when Avery had to stay up and write papers that required triple, quadruple editing by native speakers before she thought they were presentable enough to be turned in to her professors.

Being the only Chinese/Taiwanese in the English Department, Avery was too different already to be hurled further away by academic milieus. She felt stiflingly nerdy, out of place, in a clumsy and self-conscious way.

Amidst the demanding coursework and onerous task of dealing with New Yorkers, Avery argued with Tim constantly.

"What did you do the whole day?" She felt angry seeing Tim lounging around in their living room, smoking cigarettes.

"Just settling in," Tim claimed matter-of-factly without lifting his eyes.

Avery resented him for not being proactive enough in getting his life started in New York, maybe getting a job, or at least, trying hard to execute his art projects. She hated that on top of her own fear and pressure, she had to confront his unhappiness and uncertainty. Arguments turned to frequent knockdown-drag-out fights.

"I held you all the way from Taiwan, Thailand, Cambodia, Vietnam, China, Hong Kong, Macau, Japan, Indonesia, Malaysia, Abu Dhabi, France, Czechoslovakia, Holland, Italy, England, Mexico, Brazil, and the Caribbean…. I held you all the way! Why are you so damned afraid?" Tim accused with rage.

"Maybe if you weren't so overbearing I'd have been braver?!" She refuted.

Then Tim left with tears in his eyes, face as crimson as the maple leaves changing colors on the sidewalk of the city. He escaped to Thailand, like times before when they had fallouts and went separate ways.

Avery was all alone in NYC, with school and life to burden her and no family or friends to lean on. She's got to reach out. She tried staying on campus after classes and talking to her fellow students. She's got to fit in.

Eva was speaking so fast and confidently that Avery decided she could not converse in a similar fashion to be friends with this waspy brainiac. Jason was too smart not to notice Avery's fear, and drove her away trying to help every step of the way. Fred was super nice, a country bumpkin unable to show Avery the real NY experience. Colin was too eager to turn Avery into his girlfriend, sending her abundant flowers and notes that she found him repulsive.

Nothing was right; everything posed a threat. The New York City that carried the symbolic glistening diamonds of her dreams

33

turned out to be menacing, full of sinister traps. With a sense of foreboding, she buried herself in schoolwork and worried to death about every detail in the strange new world. She did not have the chance to live until she stopped going to Columbia University after obtaining another master's degree. Chopping the Ph.D. program short was the right decision to make at that time. At any rate, she started working fulltime like a grown-up. She had the time and mettles to explore the employment market and change her job every two years. She acquired the wits and resources to start her own businesses. And, she came to the resolve that "Tim and Avery" would be no more. They were drifting too far apart to stay together.

Chapter 3. The Jolt

Avery flew from New York City to Las Vegas after Tim let his parents take over her coffee enterprise. She left after realizing that no matter how she tried, her love hit a point of no return, and she in turn, was shuffled out of her own dreams. Shrunken to a shy timid Taiwanese girl incapable of fulfilling a happy life she desired in New York, she moved with six bags of clothing, with the intention to reinstate her constitutional right for the pursuit of happiness.

Avery had not planned for happiness to be so shifty and evasive. Seemingly it became her life-long quest, a quest that was everlastingly intangible and elusive.

The cafés went out of business one after another after the unprecedented subprime-loan bubble, translated into housing, financial and economic crisis. Tim's parents simply transferred all their investments somewhere else. At forty years of age, with two lawsuits going against her personally, both originated from what Tim was doing or not doing in New York, Avery came to grasp the sense of calm that could only begin from within. She wasn't going to worry herself to death for the claims she could not afford to pay off. She was just going to live life to the fullest.

Suffering made Avery stronger -- what didn't kill her ended up making her stronger -- or rather, a version of her died and another updated edition of her survived. The earnest young soul kicked the bucket, surfaced was a tad bit of composure granted by the odd beast of life. Avery thought she ought to call Las Vegas home, since Confucius had taught her: "wheresoever you go, go with all your heart." Vegas would never be right if she couldn't let go of her skepticism and distrust.

Then, she met her husband Abbey Lori there. Like everything else, conjugal bliss would come with a price.

Las Vegas was a shocker. Avery had not imagined it being so American and small-town-ish, so urban yet provincial, and on the other hand, so un-American, so criminal, so shallow and flakey.

When you were lonely, you could make lots of mistakes only to feel lonelier. Avery tried breaking into the casino industry only to find that it was too close-knit for a newcomer. Besides, her temperament was not one fitting to the casino kind of hospitality. Harry was her first significant man after divorce in Vegas, but he was never around when she needed help coping with Vegas' or her own quirks. She went through another academic program to obtain her teaching credentials, and became a licensed teacher. Wasn't that what she always wanted to do -- teach and write? How come she had not thought of it earlier? She was proud to become a secondary-school English Language Arts teacher, not knowing that the journey of teaching turned out to be bumpy and challenging, and that teaching and writing were not to be ventured alongside each other. Nothing in life was easy or smooth -- it seemed particularly true for an Asian American immigrant woman who happened to be strong-willed and introverted.

Avery was very alone in Vegas, with Harry always working in or out of town, or wanting to be alone when he could spend time with her. In the end, her creditors were the ones that ever chased after her. A landlord wanted rent money to cover loss of income from vacancy after one of her cafés went out of business, and a long-distance telephone company asked her to pay an unpaid bill after she'd moved out of NY. She was sued for businesses that did not survive the financial crisis, and harassed for telephone service that she did not use. She had no idea whether she'd be able to dismiss the cases, but she was breathing. She was musing over what Paulo Coelho had to say about humans.

Paulo Coelho wrote in *The Alchemist*:

When someone sees the same people every day… they wind up becoming a part of that person's life. And then they want the person to change. If someone isn't what others want them to be, the others become angry. Everyone seems to have a clear idea of how other people should lead their lives, but none about his or her own.

Avery thought she ought to focus on strengthening up her life, instead of expecting others to act in certain ways or behave differently. She seemed to have lost control of what's happening to her, and she dared not expect more from Harry.

Was that her fate? Wasn't fate an invention of the ineffectual and cowardly? Coelho shed the light:

Everyone when they are young, knows what their Personal Legend is. At that point in their lives, everything is clear and everything is possible. They are not afraid to dream, and to yearn for everything they would like to see happen to them in their lives. But, as time passes, a mysterious force begins to convince them that it will be impossible for them to realize their Personal Legend.

It was too early to quit. Avery would not give in or let life get to her.

She aimed to resolve the lawsuits; she wanted Harry to love her more, and she hoped her life could be peaceful again. That was the desire originated in the soul of the universe to not only survive, but live blissfully being a contributor of life. It was her mission on Earth.

She recognized the good things that happened in her life every day that the sun rose, that some her capricious young students even wrote her thank-you notes: "I love you" and "I'll never have a teacher like you again; I'll miss you." She saw the marvels of the world; she needed to be contagiously happy among young souls -- among her students. She needed to teach them and guide them in every possible aspect, not only academic, but behavioral, habitual, mental, dispositional, and ideological. And eventually, she freed herself from most of the discriminations and biases from her students. Kids only needed to be taught. Perhaps adults as well?

What's in the Reconciliation?

Avery Ming-li Liang left her father, her mother, and her hometown behind. Her family was used to her being away, and so was she to her being an American. The world would reconcile their realities with her abrupt foreignness if she ceased to try changing that herself. Eleanor Roosevelt made the point: "No one can make you feel inferior without your consent." Avery had to stop thinking herself as an outsider or victim; she needed to be an adventurer again in quest of her happiness. She needed to reach out.

It was the pursuit of peace and happiness that kept one

alive. That was why no one ever got to stay happy. There's no life after every dream being realized. That was why one always wanted something more or something else.

Avery needed to get back to speak the tongue of enthusiasm, and would not dread that her love and purpose by and large, wasn't getting across to her students or the world. They would have to understand somehow, someday, her humanity, her intent, and her wish for all to be well. She would not tolerate more of the discrimination or cultural insensitivity from her students and any grown-ups for that matter; she would seize the opportunity to educate them. She would not fear how the lawsuits would turn out because she would always find ways to achieve what she needed and wanted.

She desired peace and happiness with all her heart. She would not live in either her past or her future. She would concentrate always on the present to let in joy of life.

She wanted Harry to move as free as the clouds that formulated the patterns of the sky. He enjoyed his work shaping businesses all over North America, and she would not worry his purposeful roving and distancing.

Love should not require ownership after all. She was grateful that she felt love, not fear. The fear of failure was worse than failure. She would not doubt; she would always nourish a way of being larger than life, a way that'd eternally renovate and keep her inner self alive.

At times Avery saw lights of wisdom, and she felt peaceful. There were other times she wanted to tear down everything, and leave all to destruction. Her sister Yiwen thought she was too precious to let Harry love her that way, and reminded her of the story of the Phoenix. She said letting Harry go and Avery herself die of loss was the only way for fair resurrection. She believed that love needed to grow from stable partnerships, shared experiences, devotion, commitment, loyalty, faith, and trust. She didn't see any common goal or path binding Harry and Avery's life.

Avery said intimacy warmed their lives and seemed to be the root of their love. How sturdy the root was did not matter; it could not be measured. In any case, there's got to be more than just physical elation. Why else would she feel so much warmth and spirit every time she saw Harry? And it would all fall apart as time passed. Passion did not amount to true love. Avery's traditions and values would always steer her, and she was proud of that.

Before Abbey Lori came along, Tim Rosenberg, the ex-husband, was the only person in the US for Avery to disperse assets or crises to. She got pregnant and had a miscarriage with Harry. But he was still distant, not close enough to be the beneficiary or rescuer of anything related to Avery. If he ever seized a big part of her heart, it was never meant to last. Absence did not make her heart grow fonder. Because the absence was not only physical, but emotional, Avery recognized that nothing between her and Harry would change. She had to stop seeing him.

Chapter 4. Here Came the Killer

The world's oldest profession had been legal in parts of Nevada since 1971. Avery had no idea that while escaping from her trappings in New York City, she was only stepping into another setup, ever more deceitful, treacherous and precarious.

When news broke during a police investigation, Branden Neuzil, Harry's cousin, the founder and CEO of a local porn company, had been arrested for cocaine possession. Many were surprised by the gaffe from a man who'd built his family empire on a strict code of ethical behavior and transparency. He'd been lauded in the *Wall Street Journal* and the *New York Times* for revolutionizing the porn industry and improving the communities and neighborhoods around the downtown area, his headquarters at Freemont and 4th Street.

The details of Neuzil's arrest seemed in stark contrast to his usually upstanding image -- his headquarters were found to contain large amount of drugs to be used for the filming and production of sex tapes. His family-owned brothels were also alleged to transport, store and sell some of the portions of the drugs for customer entertainment.

The Neuzil family business thrived on whatever fetish people were willing to buy, from foot worship to gangbangs to electric play to bondage. Part pornographer, part activist, Neuzil claimed that he protected those working girls' and models' rights, as well as sex/money exchange and shooting rules.

However, the Neuzil family enterprise attracted unwanted attention when working girls' pay rate was abruptly switched, and two models' workers' compensation denied. One of whom further stated she was coerced into a performance that left her with long-lasting injuries and was offered money in

41

exchange for keeping quiet about those injuries. Several lawsuits against the Neuzil enterprise had been underway and boiling.

After Avery read about Harry's family problems in the news, she was in a state of fright, but the information also shed light on why Harry had not taken her to meet his family all those years. Avery confronted him and made clear that his family did not speak for who he was. She asked to visit one of his family business sites.

Harry finally agreed and had a limousine service for them at his house, along the way picking up Mayor Joseph Lee and Chief Constable Ale Miller. Avery recognized those two politicians undergoing investigation relating to child pornography, pleading not guilty. She knew that anyone wanting to legally exchange money for sex had to get out of Las Vegas to do so. The Neuzil Ranch was in a rural desert community an hour outside Vegas where prostitution was legal, alive and prevalent. Avery wondered how Mayor Lee and Constable Miller were legal, granted, and sanctioned in their clandestine and lascivious pursuits.

The drive from Vegas to the brothel became for Avery an exploration of big empty space, parched with only ghosts of armadillos haunting passersby, barren yet charged with unknown dangers. For the men in the same limousine, the ride willfully transformed itself into sexual innuendoes stirring enough to feed their fancy. To Avery's amazement, Harry proffered for his friends in the high places, his "girl of four years."

"Good things for good friends...," he jested with the mayor.

"This one is truly a 'ciao bella'... hahaha...," the big mayor whined like a pig.

"I am afraid your guy talk has to be put on hold until we get to the Ranch where you could banter with the working girls," Avery suggested, cheeks crimson with shame and anger.

"Come on babe; we're just kidding. Have a sense of humor." Harry tried to mediate.

"Touché. Have some sense, Harry." Avery said lightly with a smile, not wanting to worsen the situation. Perhaps she was always just a sex object for Harry. How else did she deserve to be treated like that -- a commodity for vulgar display?

The driver, Carlos, was a full-time employee of the Ranch. He made the two-hour drive from Vegas back and forth a few times a day, discreetly getting customers from their hotel suites to the Ranch's front door. He had a DVD player for them to watch short ads for each girl at the Ranch, something like movie previews before the main attraction. The mayor quickly picked out a slim blond, and assured Avery that he's not into Asians. Avery averted his lewd mind and garish appearance by ignoring him. She was not very agreeable or diplomatic, and conceivably a "bad girlfriend" for Harry. She was supposed to "embrace it all," and conversed with everyone as if she belonged to their circle.

With the exception of one sign reading "Girl Girl Girl," and two loud speakers at the entrance blaring Motley Crue's song with the same title, the Neuzil's Ranch might as well be a sports bar. Avery and the three VIPs entered the Ranch and immediately had the attention of Nina, the madam of the Ranch. She led the girls to parade proudly in front of the three important men and one out-of-place tag-along that was the appalled Avery. The girls seduced with incredible knack, leisurely showing off their costumes -- leotards that carried jiggling bodies attuned to the music of sirens. They danced about to make contact with all in the audience, Avery included.

43

One girl touched Avery in her arm, and suggested that they were all going to have "super fun." Avery asked to look around the facilities -- to experience what a brothel was like and to get to know Harry's family establishment, as she requested, and took off to check out the grounds.

There's the main building that housed the showroom and the girls, but behind it was a pool and some bungalows for extra privacy. Avery stopped at the reception of the backyard "wonderland" and chatted with the girl named Brie. She was only twenty-one and first-time away from home in Idaho.

"What made you choose to work here?" Avery beamed friendly with empathy.

Brie chirped: "Nobody chose to work in this business; it just happened. It's here I got a job, and so I stayed."

"I see. What were you looking for in Nevada? Any plans for your future?" It's the teacher in Avery furtively attempting to help.

"I am a licensed independent contractor for the state of Nevada and completed an application process with the Ranch. They hired me for my great personality and even pick me up from the airport in a limousine. I have no complaints about my life."

"So you're happy here?" Avery could not believe it but who was she to judge? Brie could choose the way she wanted to live, just as Avery chose hers.

Brie introduced Avery to another girl working there named Daisy. Daisy was married with a child. She was telling the stories of how she would go home wanting to have sex with her husband because she could not reach organisms with her customers. She claimed that, in a way, that situation made her sex life with her hubby more exciting and fulfilling. At work, she was doing her job, soothing bodies and souls of lonely men -- lonely because they were gluttonous, lost, shy, disabled, or deprived. If she made them feel desirable in any way, she was successful in her line of work.

Avery understood that it all made sense to the sex industry workers. Prostitution had been around since the inception of mankind after all. Legal or illegal, it existed all over the entire world. There were porn companies and brothel owners everywhere, why would Avery reproach Harry for his family venture? But there was definitely something that was not right with Harry and Avery. What was really the core of the issue? They simply didn't want the same out of life. Avery was too fixated on the idea of love to see that.

When Avery reentered the main building, Harry was openly flirting, enticing the working girls with his cerebral musings and tirades on daily ordinariness.

"You must be tired of sitting among the commoners. You're too beautiful and regal to situate yourself there. Let me show you to my office, where you can enjoy your work in a private lounge with comfort." Half-jokingly, he wooed a good-looking girl young enough to be his daughter.

Avery gave Harry the look. Harry swaggered over to her side: "Just kidding. A man's got to have some fun after he wrote fat checks to the local government and turned the crank of bureaucracy to get all the required permits to serve food, beer, liquor, and sex. If my family can be in this business, that means we are upstanding citizens. Don't you get that?"

Avery said, "Then how come I never met them?" Eyes screaming rage and pain, she felt incredulous.

"It's all about business, nothing more. I can conquer this woman and 'hurt' her like the other two hundred I've 'dated for business.'" Harry dodged her question and quipped with an enflamed ego.

Avery walked away to look for Brie again, needing to have some fresh air to cool down. Brie was presently conversing with the Mayor about the girl he booked. Avery swerved around attempting to avoid them, but Brie was too quick at hailing Avery to join them.

"Look who is here to party!" Mayor Lee shrieked at Avery.

"So even you have to wait for the blondie?" Avery surmised sarcastically.

"I am afraid so. Why don't you fill in for her while I wait for the blondie?"

"I am no substitute, and happily employed. Thank you."

"It never hurts to have a few extra bucks, right? You don't want to waste your good looks...," he squealed in a high pitch intending to annoy the whole world.

"No, I am more interested in getting to know how you ascended to the post you hold today. Family connections? Or, all the friends in high places?"

"Then you will have to pry to understand my talents. Why don't you?" Suggested the mayor impudently, grabbing her waist to pull her close.

Avery looked at his red face and was suddenly full of disgust. She averted his embrace by pushing him away. Mayor Lee was in a rage now: "How dare you?"

He tried grabbing Avery's waist again. Brie saw Avery's dilemma and came to her rescue. She uttered in her sing-song voice: "We have got all kinds of girls here. Please leave Avery alone. She doesn't work here."

Mayor Lee shouted at both of them: "I can have whoever I want! You dumb bitch."

Brie told Avery to go ahead and seek safety in the main building. Avery went inside to look for help. When she returned to the backyard with Harry, Brie had stepped up to push the big Mayor and drag him to sit by the poolside. In the struggle, Lee had stumbled and fell head over heels into the swimming pool. Brie screamed amidst the confusion. Soon the backyard was full of bouncers or security guards, and an ambulance, on its way.

Mayor Joseph Lee Died in ICU after a Swimming Accident during a Retreat with the Neuzil Company Executive

The Metro Police say Mayor Joseph Lee drowned in a Neuzil Ranch swimming pool when he became entangled in a volleyball net that was installed just above the water in the pool.

Police identified the victim as the city's 55-year-old mayor. He was pronounced dead on Wednesday, two days after the accident at a Neuzil Ranch. The local company's executive, Harry Neuzil, was accom-panying the Mayor on a retreat at the site. Sources say the Mayor was enjoying an orgy when the accident happened.

When a security guard at the Ranch pulled the Mayor's body from the pool, he was unconscious, seemingly suffering from a heart attack.

The mayor was said to be "not good at swimming," and had gone below the surface of the water to engage in sexual intercourse with a working girl at the Neuzil Ranch.

"Drowning can happen so suddenly and quickly," said the Chief Constable Ale Miller who was also on the retreat. "And very quickly, it becomes difficult for a single person to handle. I was not nearby at that moment, and I feel terrible."

Although Mayor Lee did not drown in the pool, he was in grave condition when transported to the Summerlin Medical Center. He did not survive ICU care.

Officials said the cause of death appeared to be a heart attack triggered by an accident, but investigation was underway for potential foul play at the Neuzil Ranch. No conclusions were reached at this time.

It had been a choppy year for the Neuzil Family Enterprise, with the recent drug possession and workers' compensation scandals. Harry Neuzil refused to make comments before the media about his "plausibly" girlfriend's presence at the site, but was said to be "doing all he can to minimize the damage." The girlfriend was believed to be a local teacher by the name of Avery Mingli Liang.

Mr. Neuzil expressed deep condolences to Mayor Lee's wife and three grown children, and said very little beyond that.

Avery was petrified by what happened at the Ranch, and was distressed because she did not heard from Harry as to what would happen to Brie. She felt frightened and helpless, wanting to call Harry everyday but became even more troubled when she could not get hold of him -- as usual. When she tried calling Brie at the Ranch, they told her that Brie disappeared. No one knew where she went.

"I can conquer this woman and 'hurt' her like the other two hundred I've 'dated for business.'" With that remark of Harry's in mind, Avery knew what needed to be done -- she let her soul drift and waft, far apart from Harry.

Killer or not, in the end, what made a woman happy or unhappy was in her own device. Avery cut Harry's sordid connections; she was not the right girl to embrace all of the sways and manipulations in his world.

Chapter 5. The Quest for Happiness

Avery was alone, but free in that she wasn't needed anywhere or could been seen living anywhere. In Las Vegas, her friends Sophie (yes her first friend in Vegas had the same name as the New York Sophie) and Liz had their whole family with them. They were missed by their family when out on the town with Avery. Avery, on the other hand, was a rolling stone that gathered no moss every way she looked. She rolled and sailed, encountering all sorts of wrong guys in the world.

Edwin was six foot seven and had her heart skip a beat when she first met him. Wearing a red tie and speaking in a tone of gentle persuasiveness, he could pass for an administrator or official who had things in control and people by his side.

"You look too beautiful to be a teacher. Are you a movie star?" He sent amiable glances in hunt of her attention. She smiled, "No, I work here."

"Are you a teacher or an administrator?" He wanted to know more about her.

"Didn't you just see me teaching a class?" She jabbed with a short comment.

"That's super. I am an admissions rep from the Academy of Design and Architecture hoping to talk to your senior class!"

"That'll have to be arranged through the administrative office."

"I've done that but thank you for reminding. I'll take you to dinner for that."

A few days later, he invited her out. She was curious to see if she could find ONE person in Las Vegas to make her want to invest her time and energy. He had the imposing height and appearance she liked anyhow.

Nothing ventured; nothing gained. Avery went on a date with him. He texted her several times before she stepped into Mauna Grill running two minutes late. He was wearing a T-shirt and jeans, looking a bit stouter than in a suit. She smiled fabulously, hoped for the best, and prepared for the worst.

Mauna Grill was always crowded on the weekends and they had to wait to be seated at the bar. He was drinking profusely and asked:

"I don't know why we're sitting here waiting. Let's go to another place."

"OK, but don't you want to eat something first?" She was there for dinner, not drinking.

"Are you hungry?"

"Not particularly."

"Then let's go to the Red Cherry and dance the night away!"

So Avery went along and marveled at what the evening had in store for her. Once inside the venue, he headed straight to the nearest bar and ordered more drinks. By the time the night was on, he was too tipsy to dance or gamble or talk to her. In spite of which, he did tell her what he liked to do to release his work pressure:

"I carry my Online Gamble gadget everywhere. That's something I do to relax, during work and after work."

"How about other things? Don't you read or even watch TV?" She gasped.

"Nope, I play online slut machine games."

At 6'7" and the age of 40, his favorite was Online Gamble -- nothing wrong, but horrendously problematic to Avery's vision of a soul-mate. It would've been ok if it was some sort of ball game -- a board game or even a video game!

There went her hope of spotting another male in Las Vegas with the caliber of inner beauty that could shimmer through its outer shell, and last for more than five minutes.

She did meet Harry in Las Vegas, didn't she? She did rally up quality well-informed talented guys in New York, didn't she? They existed; none worked out to be perfect so far. But they did exist. She just had to keep trying.

Dan was a friend's friend whose extensive travels to Asia interested Avery. He was a police officer. His e-mail communications also proved that he was someone she could talk to. They decided to meet and her hopes were hyped. The moment they started talking, she knew something was absurdly wrong. They almost got into a fight over politics, over who they wanted to elect to be the next American president! Ah no, she didn't think she would go out with a guy who thought the United States would be attacked and destroyed when Obama served as the President.

John was a libertine whose interesting ideas and ways of living could only intrigue a younger version of Avery -- maybe when she was seventeen. Al was a goody-two-shoes dentist whose life she somehow thought would be too boring. And his teeth were too white! Ian's looks failed to turn her on. Dave the impersonator was fun but not her type. Ed was just a flat-out liar who lied about his age and might have some kind of psychological issues. Tony was too religiously conservative, and Justin was chain smoking like a chimney....

There were a couple of guys that survived more than one date.

Greg was a PR person and seemingly on the same wavelength. She quit the morning after she slept with him when he called at 4:30 am to say that she had to get morning-after pills to avoid pregnancy -- she didn't think his semen even traveled the kind of range far enough to claim any championship! There's no chance that she would deal with his paranoia and bear his children!

Bill gave the impression of conjuring up a deep connection, charming with his way of words and humorous inquisition about the universe. Avery never felt so close to a man before that for a while, she mistook him as someone she could spend a life with. Turned out that Bill was bipolar and capable of expressing his sentiments and desires to let Avery feel loved profoundly. He ended up marrying another girl for money after a drunken musing that at the very minimum, love would not confuse his rational or sidetrack his equilibrium. Avery had never felt loved as much, or hurt as badly. His emotions shifted from affections to insecurities so fast and so furiously that whatever feelings and pities Avery had for him were doomed, drained to thin air. Bill loved his money, his dog, his family, and then his girls -- in that descending order. Avery was saved from insanity, thanks to Bill's momentous lucidity of mind.

Ronnie was the professor who said he loved her on their third date. He was very much an intellectual equal and they talked about all sorts of things. Too bad, he loved her too soon and admired Maharishi Yogi too much. His New Age disposition didn't completely agree with her. Or Harry was on her mind; or she just didn't feel attracted -- no chemistry from her part. Too bad.

The professor diagnosed that Harry couldn't give her a real relationship, and was convinced that he'd win her over. He tried teaching her how to move on. Truth be told, she would trade one thousand nights with him for one hour with Harry. She was doomed, and she had no choice but to follow her heart.

Perhaps Avery herself was more of a commitment phobe than Harry or anyone else. She had so many worries, about losing her independence and ease of a singleton, about marriage, intimacy, family life, financial burdens, sharing a home, and merging with another's family. She worried about change. Harry had a severe case of phobia, which she understood. Or she just hadn't met the right guy at the right time -- until Abbey Lori changed everything.

Presently Avery gave up all attempts to find someone marvelous. Mr. Right was nowhere in sight. It just didn't happen for her.

Meeting up with friends became her diversion. To her, multiple frames of reference would keep her life healthy and cure her obsession with Harry. Her quest continued but transformed into a sensible thirst for interaction and care from Harry, and from friends.

Liz was a realtor turned full-time worker because of the housing bubble. She and her family often fed Avery during holidays. Avery would go to her when she needed to vent. She was very sweet and genuine.

Gina was a fellow teacher who supported her on every level, and always managed to make Avery feel assured in her life directions. She was the best kind of friend. She listened, made suggestions, but never imposed.

Sophie had been working as a casino dealer for fifteen years. Like so many Las Vegans, she was a transplant, from Maryland. You'd be amazed what kind of people you could find working in the casino industry -- not your stereotypical bimbos, but people with talents and stories. Sophie was in advertising and performance arts. Avery went with her a couple of times to Karaoke, but could never have the same kind of enthusiasm to frequent those places late into the night. Sophie was a friend to party with and keep Avery young.

Avery bumped into all sorts of people, weird ones, funny ones, somehow interesting ones, dangerous ones, and not-on-the-same-page ones. All were passersby in her life.

Then Harry posted that same personal ad for "Asian babes" again, sending Avery straight to the abyss.

Avery's super ego wanted to invite Harry over for a Fourth of July barbecue and hoped that by being nice and sweet and communicating with him, he would love her more: "Come see me this weekend. You pick the time and day. I'll work around your busy schedule, as you like."

Mihee, her Korean pal, responded to him this time:

> Don't you have a girl who loves you to death?
> Why are you doing this?!
> So, instead of finding time to be with her, this is what you do....
> What does she do wrong?
> What don't you like about her?
> Well you can brace yourself that she will never want to see you again.

Mihee got Avery's id covered with that impulsive response, and Avery's ego was quietly reasoning: "Let him go. I can do better. I deserve better. I might not necessarily want a marriage, but I could use real love and care. If he loved me, he would not have done things to hurt me. He would not think of doing such secretive things."

Harry spun her heart and then betrayed her soul. Her whole being sank and recoiled as his eyes wander and their love failed to thrive.

Values, Purposes, and Resolves

When Avery was a little child, she said "Not Me." Her mom was gossiping with neighbors about how men wandered to other women and never ceased to want more than their wives. Uncle Ming'd gone to live with a mistress and seldom went home to the aging Aunt Mei. Cousin Chung slept with a different girl every night and considered himself virile and fulfilled. Mom sighed: "See how women tolerate their men, keeping one eye open and the other shut." Avery responded: "Not Me." She swore that if she could not find the right man to love her with truth and fidelity, she'd rather be alone. She forbade herself to turn a blind eye to her values and purposes.

Inadvertently, Avery learned firsthand and from the media about many more examples of people failing to stay truthful, of transgressions and indiscretions: Mayor Lee and possibly Harry Neuzil if he ever got married, along with Bill Clinton, Eliot Spitzer, John Edwards, and Mark Sanford, and the list went on. Thirty odd years later while dating Harry, she became one of those subdued women, not objecting, nor taking any action, holding on to a slim chance of love. It might not be fair to write off those men completely because they could not keep their hands off of other women (it's not anyone else's business but their own personal tragedies). It might be presumptuous to think their women should have a clear course of action. Humans, fallen beings, suffered from their own desires, causes, and complexities. But, who could say that mankind had no way of controlling how deep they allowed themselves to fall? Who could affirm that humans had no power whatsoever to choose the right paths for them to prevent their own falls or failures?

Avery's super ego would supersede all complexes and launch a plan of attack. Harry of course had his usual cop-out -- too busy to reply to her -- until he came to terms with his lack of candor and returned to admit his omissions and inadequacies. Or, maybe he wouldn't contact her again this time. Maybe this time she could cut him loose and be able to walk away.

Then, Harry came back with a text message, a grand "Monday?" She guessed she would see him Monday.

Avery went out with Sophie to see a performer's Death Drop. It was a publicity stunt. The actor arrived in a helicopter instead of dropping himself dead as promised. Only the helicopter's landing on the Strip could redeem such catastrophic marketing. She loved Vegas for this kind of grandiose gestures, snafu and more snafu.

Standing on the sidewalk, she was amazed how quiet the crowd was -- people would have been shouting, cheering, applauding, and whooping it up in New York City. Crowds at Time Square would have embraced kitschy and utterly awesome occasions like that. There was a peculiar calmness the Vegas tourists assumed among total strangers, downright remote, withdrawn and apathetic.

Avery was whirled back to a feel of human bond by a simple text from Harry:

"Wanna come over to my place?"

She called him and left him a message, asking him to come out.

"Sorry I miss ur call phone on slient, am drunk n goin 2 bed." He responded.

Avery made sure they met Monday. He was everything she dreamed of that night -- tender, loving, and full of passion. She did not question his prowling. Lying alongside him, she was temporarily relieved from her wounds, fragile yet out of harm's way. That was how they were. That was how she was with Harry -- disregarding her own needs and wants to find worth in their relationship.

Harry would always be on the prowl, and justify that behavior pattern as "hanging out with women," "being in touch with the feminine side."

How much that revealed the true picture of their relationship Avery would not probe, as that reality would hurt. He'd actually lay it all out there as to what he could give her and what he couldn't. Was she being trite and petty getting hurt over parameters she could not alter? What kind of parameters would validate true love, mentally, physically, emotionally, and spiritually? Was she expecting too much? Did she live precariously with human limitations? What boundaries could she establish and what could be seen as transgression? Was Harry out of line? Or, did she engage hopelessly in wishful thinking, fancying that he would love her more? She could not change the way he loved her -- could she change the way she loved him, more freely and playfully? Would she still be herself, would she be happy with herself, if she compromised her values and beliefs?

You could love the wrong guy so much and for so long. A killer of the heart.

A part of Avery died, that earnest young girl, with that futile pursuit of happiness. She felt aged and grown, with a sense of stoic realization. She could live on only when unbounded from passion, unmoved by joy or grief, and submissive to natural law. She breathed on, putting herself in a state of void, and died when his touch filled her with blissful poison. There's exultation in the death of Avery Mingli Liang.

Could she lead her life vacant of ardor -- in such a Zen way of yogis, so free with stoic nonchalance? Not likely -- she couldn't and wouldn't. She should only live and die, live and die, live and die…, and in the processes, she would recognize the unbearable beauty of life.

Chapter 6. Homecoming and
the Thought of It

The sweltering long summer found Avery on a flight back to Taipei. Korean Air took her soaring into the clear blue sky, astounded by the power of modern technology. With a lightened high mind, she was all animated with the thoughts of homecoming, of spending time in Taiwan, the island full of her adolescent breakdowns and breakthroughs.

It always happened when she was on her way to Asia that she started to get really homesick. Other times, her home continent was just there waiting to be visited. She hardly contemplated how her mother's or her father's chromosomes had been developing inside her, formulating her choices and her ways of living her life on the distant continent and faraway land. How her present life could attach to or detach from their life together, their individual lives, or their life with or without her.

Avery's mother, Ciuzhi, was a tailor by trade. When Avery was little, her mom owned and ran a clothing shop. She and her siblings practically grew up in the shop. The mannequins were their playmates, and they dressed and undressed them with great enthusiasm, dodging each other playing hide-and-seek around ladies' wear, men's wear, and behind the cases where knick-knacks and all sorts of life necessities were displayed. They were too innocent to think of life's twists and turns. They were just proud that the people in their town came to Mom's shop, Lixia, to keep up with the latest fads and trends. Even Avery's school band which she handsomely conducted with a baton would come to Mom to have the uniforms made, out of silky flowery pink tops, pleated pure white mini-skirts for girls, and shorts for boys.

Avery and her siblings claimed themselves service clerks of Lixia, especially when Mom went out of town on a fashion-merchandise-purchasing spree. Avery's two older sisters were Xiangyu and Yiwen, and her younger brother, Weicheng. They all lived in different parts of the world now, but they were close-knit as children. Xiangyu would lead all of them lining up in order to greet customers -- Laoda (the oldest), Laoer (the second oldest), Laosan (Avery -- the third and youngest sister), and then Laoyao (the youngest, their little brother). They put on the most delightful smiles and asked their customers how they might be of service. When the customers wanted to try on dresses hung on the top niche of the display panel, they would get Auntie Ah-ying to fetch the long stick-with-a-hook-at-the-end to retrieve the piece of clothing back to life, purchased and put on live bodies of their customers. They proceeded to help with the negotiation and point out how a particular piece of merchandise was worth the money. Then, they retired together into their shared 20x20-meter huge tatami mat to play with their "treasure boxes," or to bicker for the sake of bickering.

Their brother Weicheng's treasures consisted of toy cars, warriors, and pieces of cardboard which he utilized to construct an airplane along the doorway to their backyard, often hooting and booing to try making the plane take off. Avery and her sisters had in their treasure boxes paper dolls, rubber dolls, rag dolls, dry flowers, colored fabric scraps from Mom's sewing machine, and precious collections of notes, maxims, proverbs, quotes, drawings, pictures, bookmarks, hairclips, and barrettes, and so on and so forth.

Some of Avery's treasure boxes also held lots of her certificates of awards, for pageants, beauty shows, composition contests, academic performances and achievements. Her family teased that she could not hide them along with all the romance novels and world classics she started reading hiding under her quilt in fourth grade. So the certificates had ended up being posted on the shared bedroom wall to hint that she might just be the one who would get away, as the neighbors said: "What's the use of all the awards if you do not show them far far far off to prove you can amount to something?" Her sister Xiangyu said that the neighbors were just awestricken and did not know what else to suggest. She said Avery Liang would not go anywhere far, and she would always be near her.

The House with
Two Neighborhoods

The Liangs had two sets of neighbors, one set from Mom's Lixia storefront, the other from the backdoor alley. Lixia faced the busiest street in town, Chonghua Rd., and their backyard led to a small alley where you found a grassy slope to climb and dream on, a vegetable garden, several pigsties of their neighbors', an elementary school nearby, a garbage dump, and even a little brothel further down the lane, where lonely men lingered and frequented.

They got along famously well with their storefront neighbors who were also business owners: a hotel, a salon, a dumpling house, a bookstore, an auto dealer, a bakery, a fried ice cream parlor pioneering bubble-teas, and a butcher selling meats and groceries. Their storefront neighbors seldom met their back-alley neighbors, because their house was rectangle-shaped, so elongated length-wise that a couple blocks actually ran perpendicular to it. You could ride a bike from their front door to their back door through various streets in about fifteen minutes. The fun part was that they seemed to have one house with two neighborhoods. To this present day, Avery still had dreams about that house on Chonghua Rd. and on a nameless alleyway, that one house with two completely different neighborhoods, and two sets of neighbors.

Avery, her brother and sisters couldn't have played on the busy Chonghua Rd.. It was the little pathway beyond their backyard that stored vivid memories of her childhood. They raided the garbage dump for anything valuable to them, a broken arm of a Barbie for making and trying on ornaments for their healthy dolls, a bright piece of candy wrapper for constructing Origami thingies, and a wood box to be washed clean to hold more of their jewelries or treasures. They plucked flowers and vegetables stealthily, and then ran from their enraged neighbors for their lives. They watched and fed the pigs in the sties and often imitated how they snorted and nuzzled. They sauntered down the path to parade on top of the school fence declaring themselves free from and immune to all disciplinary plans. They hunted and ran around the little Japanese hut on the other side of the slope that had legendarily preserved the historic marks of Japanese imperialist control over Taiwan for over 200-300 years during the Ming and Qing dynasties until the end of WWII. Avery got the shivers and quivers when recalling how perfectly her grandparents could speak Japanese, as if they had been strangers or oppressors just like the Japanese persecutors. Taiwan was in fact under Japanese rule for fifty years, marking a period in history when the island was literally a colony.

The little brothel further down the alley was mysterious and the Liang kids were too little to really understand what it was; it's just a place where funny women with painted faces lived, and where lonely men like Laoxiangs frequented. Laoxiangs referred to the Kuomintang soldiers, veterans of the Chinese Nationalist Party who came to Taiwan around 1949. Taiwanese people called them Laoxiangs because Laoxiang literally meant Old-Home-Towner. It was supposed to be a friendly term of endearment, but it also indicated what conflicts simmered underneath, in between the Bensheng (home-province) people, and the Waisheng (outside-province) people.

The House with Two Neighborhoods

Home and Beyond

Bensheng people were the Taiwanese/ Chinese people who had long resided on the island of Taiwan since as early as the 13th Century, perhaps during the Yuan dynasty, long before the Portuguese discovered and named the land Formosa in the 16th Century. Waisheng people were the Chinese who fled to Taiwan during the Chinese Civil War between the Nationalists and the Communists. For better or worse, these two groups of people coexisted along with the indigenous tribes of the isle, and so the political situations in Taiwan always centered on the integral process of making the country one homeland to be or not to be recognized on the international stage, to be or not to be part of the People's Republic of China (PRC, the communist China or Mainland China), or to be or not to be its own, Republic of China (ROC, Taiwan as a country, a state, or as a province of China).

Both Avery's parents' families had been in Taiwan for generations from God-knows-where in China. Some said the northeast and others assumed Fukien Province because most Taiwanese people were from there. Avery did not see herself to be any more or less of a homegrown Taiwanese than the Waishengers (outside-province people). But there sure was a lot of problematic tension brought by the new influx of Chinese migrants and the Kuomintang government -- even till the modern times. Looking at the pro-Taiwan-independence DPP (Democratic Progressive Party), one would discern how history often had a way of getting to you. President Chen Shui-bian was enormously disappointing, as he broadcasted Taiwanese independence, but in the long run, was just as corrupt as the Kuomintang government preceding him. Taiwan continued the status quo with the Mainland China, to be the China hardly acknowledged by the world. Taiwan, The Republic of China, was scarcely a part of international engagements after the People's Republic of China replaced the entity to be a charter member and one of the five permanent members of the United Nations in the 1970s.

Most Taiwanese civilians cared more about economic prosperity than a corrupt independent Taiwan. If Avery had felt any animosity toward the Waishengers (outside-province people), she would have understood somehow the ways she was regarded in her adopted new country of USA.

Avery was often confounded by how culturally discriminated and stereotyped she was in America. She was unhappy about how myopic and prejudiced some people were. She was uncomfortable when she thought about how some parents were instilling cultural insensitivity in their children, because they as adults had no idea how to become culturally competent. She marveled at how America had made progress, and yet had such a very long way to go in the road to equity and diversity. She was shocked to see how Americans could murder each other simply for revenge or prejudice. Those incidents of conflicts in Orlando, Minnesota, Baton Rouge, Dallas, Milwaukee, New York, and Charlotte were alarming, disappointing, and dishearteningly recent! African Americans were discriminated against, white cops were assassinated, terrorist attacked in the name of righteous deeds, and all were made to be too black and white.

When would mankind progress enough to cease senseless killing? When could Avery stop being bothered by small offhand comments about her heritage? When would she be free of judgements and presumptions?

Avery could not foretell what her future held. More scrutiny, more unfair treatment, more stress. She kept faith and tried her best. She had to at least, educate her students to fight against hatred, to learn to understand people who were different, like herself. She was aware that only quality of care for her students could turn things around for her. She was determined to provide just that: quality care and teaching. It was all she could do, at her work, in her personal life, and with her pursuit of happiness: one day at a time; with each effort, one little step forward and one inch closer to happiness.

Avery's father said that the Waishengers (outside-province people) had raped and slaughtered Taiwanese when they came to the Taiwanese island, and that was as terrible as the Nanking Massacre. History, either pertaining to the Japanese, the Waishengers, or the natives or minority groups in the US, should have taught not hatred, but enough love to prevent similar gross mistakes. It should have taught plenty of lessons. But, could humans ever learn fast enough to avert tragedies? Could any values, reasons, or resolves ever deliver adequate forces to induce progression?

Avery's first boyfriend of six years was from a Waisheng family of Jiangsu and Shanghai origin. Xiangyu's husband was from a Canton family. Yiwen was happily married to a man whose family's from Hunan. Her brother Weicheng had a son with a woman from one of the numerous aboriginal tribes in Taiwan, and two daughters with his wife of Hakka origin. Avery's ex-husband was a Caucasian American of German and English descent, and her husband Abbey Lori, Swiss and Irish. There was a running joke in her family that they all wound up tossing themselves far and beyond to show off what materials their family members were made of. Whenever someone in her family wished to get away, he or she would hold the chopsticks at the far ends away from the food. And then, with the measurement of the chopsticks, came a self-fulfilling prophecy.

They were just a big melting pot of a family. Whose family wasn't a version of the United Nations? Why would humans insist in fighting otherness? Was it because they were too afraid? Too small to grasp the bigger picture of mankind? Too bigoted to embrace the unfamiliar, the foreign, the new, the different or the unknown?

Avery's sister was right to say that she would be always near her. No matter how wide the world was and how faraway they lived from each other -- her parents, sisters, brother, and the house with two neighborhoods, were forever and ever treasured in her heart, tugged away to fill holes when that corporal organ of hers called heart needed serious lifts to be restored to a functional level. On more than one occasion, Avery had to Skype or Line her family all over the world to regain her bearings. They were always her ultimate support.

A Father Too Far and Unsung

Avery's father, Chengte, didn't come into her life, at least her memory of life, until when she was in fourth grade. Before the fourth grade, she would call her mom's brother "papa." Her uncle papa came visit the Liangs once in a while to be a father figure, and she liked to pretend that she had a father around her. Before that, the memories of her father were composed of railroad trips to the county jail, of his heartfelt humor in showing magic tricks to both Mom and the children, and of the times when Mom and Dad would disappear behind some structure in the jail courtyard to be all alone by themselves and reemerged, faces blushing and eyes, of the wild. Their children would wait quietly and no one would ask where they went or what took so long.

Avery's Taiwanese countrymen liked to joke about how they were all castaways from ancient or recent China, just like Americans, criminals from the British Empire. There were makings of rough lives and hard earnings that made those country people distinctive. Avery's father was a survivor in shackles. How he went to the jail exposed unnamable red tape that was deep-rooted on the small island of Taiwan. He'd only bought a batch of Acer rubrum logged off of a wrong zone in a forest to try raising a family, making ends meet. Black market or not, his involvement with the forestry and logging industry only designated him to be the unsung hero of his clan, one who charged forward in the front line to explore and define possibilities for his people. He was an honest straight-shooter to all his family, friends, colleagues, and associates.

When Avery's father returned home, his children would follow him everywhere in the house, to the bathroom, to the storefront, to the backyard, to the shop, to the barber, and to his friends' houses. They simply could not let him out of their sight at any moment. They loved him to no end.

Avery's father came back home starting over to embark on a career quarrying precious stones. His whole family moved to Taipei City, and that marked a transition of Avery's childhood. Many times in her new middle school, she wondered about her friends and playgrounds back in the small town on the eastern coast of Taiwan by the Pacific Ocean: how the neighborhood kids were growing, how the floods might came back, and how the geckos in the house with two neighborhoods all seemed to disappear as she grew. She missed her friends who she played dress-ups with. She missed holding tiny babies born in her old neighborhood. She missed the paper boats her siblings folded and floated down the stream during a flood. She missed the candles her family lit at night when the electricity went out. She even missed assuming lots of attention, being the one getting pushed down the steps and ending up with an arm in a sling. She missed the bickering, laughing, and sharing in her childhood house.

Mom, Geckos, Buddhas and Future Husbands

Avery's mom once told her in the old house, while she lay wide awake in bed refusing to close her eyes to sleep: "Geckos would travel into your ears and plug up your system if you fail to fall asleep after midnight." Later when Avery needed to stay up and prepare for all kinds of entrance exams, high school, college, graduate school, she thought about how the geckos were actually helping her because she was highly aware of her body's operating system. She made the geckos work their wonders to her best advantage.

Avery's mom or dad never actually gave the children any pressure about getting into a good school or something like that. They were kind of laissez-faire, busying themselves with new endeavors in Taipei's intricate city life. Her mother took up Mahjong, and her father studied the lottery circuit boards to try hitting it big. They had fierce fights at times, but their marriage never fell apart. Of course after ups and downs and losing their family home and business to gambling, they realized all the Buddhas her mom prayed to would only bless people who help themselves. The odds would be better if they all quit risky undertakings and believed that their life together amounted to the most precious prize they could ever win.

Avery's mother resumed making her children six-course-plus-soup meals every single day, and her father researched and studied Chinese herbal medicine. After they grew old and retired to their ancestor's house, they were happy growing vegetables and taking care of their family land in the countryside. Off all the good and bad and what was, Avery's parents' ways would leave indelible marks in her past, present, and future lives, however undetectable those marks might be. She was grateful that her parents gave her life, showed her how to be resilient, and taught her to take the bull by the horns, being an entrepreneur and adventurer of life, not a mere opportunist.

Avery's parents imparted upon her valuable survival mechanisms. She managed to rise above circumstances because of the ways they exposed her to how the world could be interpreted and understood. Her mom determined that the best dowry for Avery would be the wisdoms in the books Avery collected and loved. She would gaze at Avery's certificates of awards and say: "Mingli, mei shemma geini -- we have little to give you, and these will be your dowry when you grow up." She would go on to remind Avery: "Always finish every piece of rice in your bowl, otherwise you will marry to a husband with rice freckles all over his face."

It's true that Avery's parents had always allowed her to explore all opportunities and educational undertakings, never opposing to the "useless" literary field or to any career path she marched on. So it was in the name of education they married their daughter into America -- along with all the tacit approvals they provided her for whatever she wanted her life to be. She was left alone to pursue her purposes and wander all over the world. She was able to earn her way through life. She was obliged to become independent and self-sufficient.

Avery's father absolutely believed that she would be fine everywhere she went, and whatever she took upon herself. That belief was his best gift for her. Her father had narrated in detail how life should play out for her, sounding intense on the phone when she was in any kind of trouble or triumph. Her mother habitually asked if she knew better to take care of herself. Their finest quality remained in the way they loved her, so beyond mundane words, yet with such firm endorsements in all regularities and irregularities of her being. Her parents made Avery Mingli Liang out to be the most precious cut of an unpolished hidden jewel in the whole world, no price tags attached, not for sale. Her radiance would shine luminously when held dearly to one's bosom, provided one was lucky enough to uncover her, appreciate her pricelessness, prize her, and cherish her to death. One day, that one wise man, that lucky man, would come.

The Dear Ones

Growing up there were other significant people who Avery held fond memories of: Auntie Ah-ying, Grandma Great-Aunt-Tigress, and many mentors as well as her childhood friends, Wenlian, Jingling, Ailian, Yuwing, who she hung out and played dress-ups with all the time. They were the unforgettable dear ones.

Auntie Ah-ying worked alongside her mom in the clothing shop, Lixia. Ah-ying was her second mom when her father was away. She disciplined the children and fed them morsels of foods that she meticulously chewed and pre-processed. She even gave them each a nickname that would stick to them for a long time: Xiangyu was Sanbasong since she was outspoken and vivacious; Yiwen was Pojiaowo since she often needed patches on her knees from crawling around too much, Avery, Mingli, was Laokuyan since she had the tendency to wear her pants and skirts too low and expose her belly; her brother Weicheng was Kanglong since he liked to show off his martial arts kung fu, flying and bobbing around like a "headless dragon-not-chicken."

Auntie Ah-ying continued working with Avery's mom after Avery's father returned home from the county jail. In fact, Ah-ying met her husband, Uncle Ah-chiang, through the kids. The Liang children were playing too late into the night at a neighbor's house where Uncle Ah-chiang and his brothers stayed as one of their routine truck stops. Auntie would come and fetch them home but hung about to talk to the brothers. One night, Uncle Ah-chiang took lodgings at the Liang family's tatami mat, instead of their neighbor's house. Avery remembered catching glimpses of them smiling at each other, and afterward, her father's raging tirades leading to their prompt marriage. Aunti Ah-ying married into the trucking business; for thirty years and counting, they thrived on their enterprise as well as their marriage. Avery had three cousins from them.

Grandma Great-Aunt-Tigress got her name because she told stories of a Great-Aunt Tigress to the Liang children when she came to visit and stay with them. According to Grandma, Great-Aunt Tigress was a tigress incarnate. Disguised as a kind great-aunt, Great-Aunt-Tigress would visit children at night to tuck them in, but would gnaw on their bones when she transformed into a tigress involuntarily. To the tigress, you've got to eat when you've got to eat, and there's no telling when Great-Aunt-Tigress would call on a household and reveal her blood-thirsty beast self. The best policy was to watch one's doors, not letting any strangers or distant relatives in.

Grandma Great-Aunt-Tigress told the tales of Great-Aunt Tigress with such animation that Avery and her siblings sometimes suspected that she was the tigress incarnate herself, with the same high cheek bones, the curious flickers in the eyes, and the inevitable baring of canine teeth. But when Grandma Great-Aunt-Tigress went months without visiting the Liangs in their house with two neighborhoods, they would beg their mom to get hold of their grandma, so Grandma could come pay them another visit. They loved Grandma Great-Aunt-Tigress and her stories. In their eyes, she was the best storyteller, the greatest living bard of Taiwanese folklore of all time.

In another story of Grandma Great-Aunt-Tigress's, a newlywed bride was suffering from her husband's infidelity. And here formed the rhyme the Liang sisters took into account whenever they encountered boy problems:

> Bridegroom, bridegrung,
> Eyes plastered with dung.
> Queen erred as Concubine,
> Urgh Concubine, creepin' woodbine!

Toward the end of the story, the bridegroom aka bridegrung, turned into a pesky fly rushing around singing on top of its teeny lungs in hopes of a chance for redemption:

> Hum ah hum, hum ah hum.
> Officer ordered me to sell betel nuts,
> If you want to buy betel nuts,
> Do receive some in the huts;
> Otherwise, betel nuts, betel nuts,
> Stay spoiled
> Stray away from the sweet sweet guts!

The bridegroom/bridegrung turned insect wandered farther and farther flying aimlessly, not knowing when it would be able to see the wife or its home ever again.

Avery and her siblings believed that Grandma Great-Aunt-Tigress's teachings helped them see through the core of a bad man. If a man would not come back, he was never yours to begin with. If a man came around, you needed to see what he's made of and love him accordingly. The Liang sisters were never to settle for men with no spines. They were to seek integrity, courage and character.

As a matter of fact, Avery wasn't allowed to date any boys until college, let alone settling. Her father would go into a rage every time a boy from school called her up. She had no ideas how the boys got her house phone number, but she was pretty popular and was dubbed the "school flower" in her hometown. Rumors had it that the boys would compete with each other to be the one to talk to her on the phone. She never did date any of those boys. Her father was her firewall.

Middle school and high school flew by while Avery was acing English and Chinese all over the place, but having nightmares about math tests many a night. It's not that she couldn't give you the sums of some additions using an imaginary abacus by heart (she was an expert at abacus, on the contrary). It's not that she didn't love geometry. She just didn't think she had time to do the math problems. Her teachers called her an over-achiever in the language arts, yet a philosopher in numbers. She simply focused on ideas and minds, refusing to be subjected to the diversion of all the formulas, calculations, and functions.

When Avery required her American students to share their learning experiences in English classes, she meant to draw out their interests in learning as well as their metacognitive reflections. Avery came up with her own account and provided a writing sample to share with her students:

> Those who inspired thoughts of endearment stayed with me. Memories of English classes returned with three excellent teachers' voices telling intriguing stories, speaking about life, and inciting critical thinking over issues in society.
>
> In Taiwan, English skills had been exceedingly emphasized to an extent that it took precedence over the majority of courses. In other words, I had to excel at English to be of any academic success, and of value in society. Tests, quizzes, practice questions, and examinations consumed most of my school-days. English teachers taught curricula geared towards the High School or the College Entrance Examination. For each lesson, I was taught to memorize all vocabulary words, grammatical rules, idioms, phrases, expressions, and to recite selections of texts by heart.
>
> I viewed the study methods of English in my secondary school years as mechanical and pressure-ridden. However, I also realized that the building blocks were constructed very systematically. Like most secondary school kids in Taiwan, I strived for the best grades, and studied hard to advance to higher education. School, to me back then, translated into numerous tasteless days and sleepless nights. Every so often, I would even have hideous nightmares about failing a test.
>
> Whose adolescent life was not revoltingly bleak and difficult? I was fortunate not to have to deal with gangs, drugs, sex or violence as much as our American kids nowadays do. However insipid those tests, quizzes and exams were in my school years, great learning did take

place. I was particularly inspired by my three favorite English teachers: the storyteller Mr. Zheng, the soul searcher Ms. Xu, and the critical thinker Mr. Decker.

Mr. Zheng was my sixth-grade English teacher who possessed unparalleled skill at telling exciting warrior stories. His depiction of hundreds of feudal lords in the Three Kingdoms, such as Liu Bei, Guan Yu, and Zhang Fei, brought to life the many battles in the tumultuous era towards the end of the Han dynasty in Chinese history. Sir Gawain and the Green Knight also came alive as chivalrous as they could be, while King Arthur became every boy's and girl's beloved mascot of the class. Little did I know until much later that those legendary tales arose from a late fourteenth-century Middle English alliterative romance, and that sites and places had been identified as "Arthurian" in the twelfth-century. King Arthur, Sir Lancelot, Sir Gawain, Merlin, the Knights of the Round Table, and many other Chinese warriors, LIVED in our classroom, right there in a small town in Asia. Those heroes and brave men drove me to correctly spell "brave," "heroic," "valiant" and "courageous"!

Ms. Xu was my freshman English teacher, a lady of enormous talents. Her English class was memorable because she shared her life stories and had each and every student keep a journal. I remember being always eager to get my journal back from her. She read my accounts very carefully. She made comments that often occupied more pages in my journal than my own writings would. She saw a star in me. She cared about me. She expected me to grow to be the best human I can be. I would not have been as diligent about memorizing idioms as I was if she did not connect with me at a significant level. I wanted to share my daily stories with her, and I wrote in the verbiage that I acquired in her English classroom.

Mr. Decker was my senior English teacher who was capable of delivering about five hundred hugely challenging, thought-provoking pieces of information in as short as five minutes. He was an American and could speak Mandarin fluently -- you would not believe he was a "lao-wai" ("gringo" in Mandarin) if you only listened without seeing him. He was always enthused about what he was teaching and what we would ponder in every single lesson, be it a newspaper article, a poem, a novel, a play, or a text that simply existed in our English text book. He could turn any tedious reading into something interesting and attention-grabbing. He connected our lessons to our society and to what was happening around us. He asked meaningful and testing questions. He gave fascinating and captivating messages. Reflecting back, I do not think that I could have successfully gotten through that trying final year of high school if Mr. Decker was not as stimulating and magical as he was. He made College Entrance Examination, SAT, TOFEL and GRE all purposeful! As I continued to pursue many more years of higher education (four years in college and five years in graduate schools), Mr. Decker was there in my mind and heart compelling me to be an independent thinker and critic.

I could conclude my learning experiences in English classes stating: during my secondary school years, I became an English writer. I had been a little Chinese writer in grade school, earning many awards in writing or composition contests. In middle school and high school, I continued attaining recognition in writing and wrote in English as ardently as I did in Chinese. I know

I have to thank those three grand motivators, those three English teachers, who exercised their "intellectual emotions" as well as their "emotional intellect" to so immensely benefit me. I loved English then and I love English now and forever. Mr. Zheng, Ms. Xu and Mr. Decker formulated an English major/reader and lifelong learner out of me.

And perhaps Mr. Zheng, Ms. Xu and Mr. Decker have also instilled an English teacher in me. On the journey of English teaching, I will always build upon what I have learned and keep gaining new ideas and strategies. I will always remember the elements of engagement and thoughts of endearment endowed by those who enthusiastically teach, who genuinely help, and who have the mind and heart to guide young souls. In turn, I only hope that my students' journeys can be rid of unnecessary thorns and blocks, and their lives be filled with meanings, ideas, values, and good choices.

Avery's students wowed and ah-ed at her description. One minute they would love her and admire her, calling her the smartest and the most beautiful. Next minute, they would gang up on her, making racial and disrespectful comments. Avery recognized, and acknow-ledged, her students' developmental processes, full of angst, lacking developed emotional depth. She only hoped that some of them could learn to love stories and grow with reading. Although teaching in the public schools was far from being lavished with wisdoms of all the classics and great works she grew up with, Avery urged her students to convert their love of digital games into understanding of intrinsic benefits of the language arts and literature.

Avery understood the needs of her underprivileged student population. She came to acquire teaching aptitudes similar to parenting skills, where encouragement and redirection of behavior worked far better than punishment. She stopped sending students to the Dean's, and instilled in them that she would never ever quit on them. However challenging her students were, she was determined that each child could be reached and taught. She would do whatever it took to get them where they needed to be.

Growing and Heritage Licenses

Growing required essentially an acceptance of the reorganization of family and friends. Change was the one and only eternal law of the universe. What held the world inside her at its entirety would have to be the legacy her identify and culture mapped out for her. A line from a well-known Chinese poem described this "oneness": "If only people mean forever, from near and afar, savoring together the gracefulness of the One Same Moon." She might not see all her family and dear friends as often as she liked to, but in her mind's eyes, she would always behold their kindred spirit, their memory, and their celebratory act.

Avery's heritage granted her countless licenses which she sustained to overcome difficulties and challenges in life. She could look for the Moon Lady on the 15th day of August in the lunar calendar, and never failed to find her and converse with her. She could put on Cheongsams (Chinese dresses) whenever she felt like, and praised to the mirror how delicate it looked. She could conjure up all the geckos in her system to work wonders when she needed to stay highly alert. She could consult with her Family Book of Astrology and tell her monthly fortune based on the first day of each monthly menstruation. She could refuse to buy any shoes for her husband or to share any pears with him, because Fenli (sharing pears) was a homonym of the word that meant separation in Chinese, and giving shoes as presents was just going to drive one's spouse to walk out. Her husband would pay her one penny for each pair of shoes she bought him to break the spell.

She also chanted the names of the Buddhas in her house altar her mom prayed to and sensed a medicinal relief: Guanyin, Guanshiyin, Nanwu Guanshiyin, Nanwu Guanshiyin Pusa, and then Guan Yu, Guang Gong, Guan Di, Guan Sheng Di Jun. She could think compassion from the Goddess of Mercy who conveyed encouragement and kindness to her with an image of a holy lotus. She could feel honor and justice as tangible items when the figurine of the Saintly Emperor Guan shielded against her demons for her in the darkest of nights. Attested by her mom, Guan Yu/Gong the legendary warrior turned god-like figure and Guanyin the merciful goddess were her godparents, and they would never stop looking after her however nonreligious she was. She said to herself that she was a tough cookie, biting her lips to endure any pain, always heading forward like a gallant horse that was her zodiac sign. With all those licenses, she could do no wrong. She would sail through life unscathed.

Chapter 7. What Happened in Vegas

Prostitute Involved in
Mayor Lee's Accident Feared to Be Dead

Police are investigating whether a man killed by a prostitute in Charlotte, N. Carolina could also be the prime suspect in four cold cases in Las Vegas, among them the death of Brie Frawley, the prostitute involved in Mayor Lee's accident at the Neuzil's Ranch last year.

Richard Weller, 40, was shot and killed according to Charlotte chief of detectives, Lt. Nickolas Crabtree.

Authorities are investigating links between Weller and four Las Vegas-area prostitutes' death -- Linda Jones, 23, Judy Lopez, 19, Susie Davis, 21 and Brie Frawley, 22. Frawley admitted pushing Mayor Lee into the swimming pool in self-defense at the Neuzil Ranch, and subsequently went missing for months before her body was found near a dump near Lake Mead in Las Vegas.

The Charlotte murder incident began when Weller and the woman, whose name is to be kept confidential, met for money/sex exchange. Weller went to the woman's house, and pointed a pistol at the woman's chest to threaten her life. The woman struggled and grabbed the gun and shot Weller in the head, killing him instantly. She told 911 dispatchers that Weller told her to "live or die" as soon as she opened the door. He warned that she had the option of rape or murder, and either way, he would be getting laid without paying her. Weller's car was found to contain five sets of handcuffs, an ax, a machete, trash bags, two gallons of bleach, a bulletproof vest, several knives, and handcuff keys. Based on the sheer brutality of the assault, along with all of those suspicious items, the police suspect that Mr. Weller has been involved in other violent crimes in different states. The case file was shared among law enforcement units across the country. That includes the North Las Vegas and Henderson Police Departments.

Henderson Department spokesman Randy Johnson stated that the police have been investigating Weller as a suspect in the four prostitutes' murder cases. North Las Vegas police spokesman Adam Gonzalez said a connection between Weller and the Nevada women appears possible. The two local police departments were collaborating to find a possible nexus. Those four cases remain open.

Avery felt weary about the news, about the tragedies across the country. Conflicts between men and women, among different races, beliefs, and cultures had proven to be fatal, too disparaging to grasp. She found no escape from the dismaying soap-opera-like calamities that took place all too close to her surroundings. How ironic was her flight from New York City, leading her to more menace and dejection. Bleak, skeptical and uncertain was how she felt, and there seemed to be no end to the misery and quandary.

What Happened in Vegas

Chapter 8. How She Carried On

As Avery figured, the wise man was impalpable, nowhere in sight. That's a fearful reality, yet dreadfully significant. She was alone but rid of phony happiness; she was not lonely but craved a deep sense of sharing. She realized how she needed to teach others how she should be treated, to men, her students, and strangers. She planned to carry on with dignity, to carry out what should have been achieved with adjustments from her own part.

Avery valued multiple channels to happiness, and saw value in different social interactions. She did not believe that marriage or romance translated into one single channel. A narrow constricted life would lead to misery. She would love one man deeply and uniquely, meanwhile having profound affection for her family, friends, students and fellow human beings. Her goal was something larger, somewhere beyond her present environs. Her purpose was not her security, but intensification and refining of knowledge about life, about humanity and man's wellbeing.

She knew she had to strive for a larger self; she had to be heard, be heeded.

Avery's ex-husband Tim was fantastically sharp, but seemed to be all wrapped up in his own world. He never stepped back into American society. That was the biggest problem. He wasn't in touch with the framework of practical matters, an atypical white male preferring chess games and art museums to football games or TV shows. In many ways Tim was one right guy, but their relationship turned out all wrong.

Perhaps that's why she picked Harry, an all American boy, in innumerable ways the opposite of Tim. Harry loved all kinds of sports, and was an NCAA player in college. He's one of those athletes that had it all. He never played chess with Avery, cut out articles from newspapers for her, cooked for her, accompanied her, explored the world with her, or showed her off to his family or friends, as Tim did. Harry had no intention to share. She needed to teach him how she'd like to be treated and listened to.

With Harry, it's like the ax was bound to fall at some point and she was just waiting for that moment so she could walk away with no regret in her heart.

He's working, traveling some-where all the time, while Avery went to Taiwan to visit her family and friends.

"Where/how r u? I'm alive back in the States after visiting Taiwan." Avery tried reaching Harry upon her return.

"Glad you are back." He replied.

"How's work?"

"In MN till Tues. PGA Championship,

Chaska, Minnesota."

Ten days later, Harry came to see Avery. She was pleasantly surprised. And then the pattern continued. He disappeared. He materialized. He disappeared. He materialized yet again.

Another month later...

Harry texted Avery:

Harry: how r u. been thinking about u.....

Avery: Let "us" perish please since you don't want me in your life circle. We want different things. Won't work – I'm worth more than a few moments. Best.

Harry: I know. But wanted you to know that I was thinking of you. That's all.

Avery: Thanks. I bet a construction worker thinks of me more than you do:(

Harry: Doubtful! I'm trying to leave u alone.....Please understand.

Avery: Pls do. Good luck.

Harry: I've erased your #. You won't hear from me anymore.... Sweetheart, you asked me to perish! So I am.... Having your # only tempts me to text you with my naughty thoughts of you! Erasing your # stops me from doing that and having you tell me construction workers think of you more than me.... Not trying to hurt you but since I recognize I am. Don't want to perpetuate it.

It didn't matter how Avery chose to carry on; her relationship with Harry ran its course and died away. If she had validated Harry's deliberate distancing or insouciance by desiring him so before, she was teaching him and showing him how she wanted to lead her life. It didn't matter how Avery elected to regard her difficulties from her business's lawsuits in New York, or from her whimsically loving and hating pupils; she lived her life safely and soundly without having to waver her principles for anyone but herself. Her lawsuits were dissolved by the fabulous judges who saw no grounds in the cases, and her students turned out to be moldable in any case.

Creatures lived, mated, reproduced and died, they came and went. They would go their own ways, of their own accord. Occurrences in Avery's life had similar ways of finding their own places, in their own time. Or rather, where there was a will, there was a way. All was well, and would always be well.

Avery died -- a long, long process of coming undone from one's brazen, former self. And then, she let life in.

Chapter 9. The Happiness of Pursuit

Abbey Lori was a breath of fresh air, yang to Avery's yin, and the best of Tim and Harry combined. It took Abbey a whole year of persistent contact for her to start seeing that fact. And when it was right, things were never too difficult to work out. There was no teeth-pulling, no futile suffering, only the truth of life and fate unfolding.

Avery agreed to meet with Abbey again after a year of dormant love life. During the year, she focused on selling her upside-down house and purchasing another house that made more financial sense. Learning of the judgements that ordered dissolution of the lawsuits in New York, she started to breathe life again. She had time to wonder about Abbey who kept trying after their first date nearly one year before. She thought: "Why not give that guy a try"?

Abbey was at first blocked from Avery's world due to the fact that he's some sort of VP of Sales like Harry. Then his entry to Avery's life was further deterred because of her life circumstances. She simply had to sell her upside-down house and move to another one before she could think about getting involved with someone. She did not expect Abbey to be there when she was ready to let life happen.

Abbey must have really liked her. Why else would he keep trying after a year of no response from her? At any rate, he happened to contact her again after she remembered to breathe again. It was fate that it all just happened. Life just happened.

A Big Man with Immense Love

Abbey and Avery met for their second date one year after their first. At the Golden Biersch in Boca Park, Avery was prepared to confirm Abbey as another workaholic, to tell him flat-out that's not what she's looking for. It turned out that they stayed up that whole night, he playing his guitar telling stories, she admiring his ingenuity. A VP of Sales playing guitar rocking away with soulful tones! There was something more than an energetic sales executive in Abbey. Avery was convinced of that. She had to find out more about Abbey, about what made him so charming and magnetic, full of charisma, too multifaceted to label or resist.

"This tune I composed when I was fifteen; it's called 'Girl of Mine,'" strumming his acoustic guitar, Abbey introduced and sang with a beautiful sonorous voice.

"That's really incredible. When did you start playing the guitar?" Avery tried getting to know him.

"Since I could hold a guitar. My mom was a piano teacher, and my dad played every instrument you could think of." Abbey beamed in his reminiscence.

Then he changed his acoustic guitar to an electric one after numerous songs he said he used to play and sing with his brothers. With the electric guitar, he rocked away like a super star. Indeed, he played in a band professionally many years before his career in sales. Avery could anticipate more stories behind that simply genuine manner of his, and there was nothing she loved more than a few wonderfully told narratives, tales and accounts.

Abbey turned out to be quite different from any corporate-ladder climbers Avery had met previously. He showed her off, he took her to his business conventions and family gatherings, and he yearned for time with her. He was kind-hearted: a humanitarian suggesting western companies to take part in assisting the poor around the globe, and a devoted father working hard to support his two children from his first marriage, financially, intellectually and emotionally.

Abbey was always readily offering help to people in need, anyone and anywhere. Abbey gave napkins to a young man sorting out shopping carts and spilling juice over his own arms at a grocery store. Abbey stopped to help strangers stranded with their cars broken down on the street. Abbey dropped change for a street performer or musician on the sidewalk, but was frugal and hesitant to spend five dollars on himself. Abbey opened doors for elderly people, said hello to everyone in his neighborhood, and played with every child who came near him. Avery saw the type of men she could share life with in Abbey, in a man so practically and imaginatively adept. A responsible human being living his potential,
happy, optimistic, loving, and giving.

On a Christmas card Avery made for Abbey, she typed up a quote from Melville to capture the image of the man she saw in him:

> It does seem to me that herein we see the rare virtue of a strong individual vitality, and the rare virtue of thick walls, and the rare virtue of interior spaciousness.
> Oh, man! admire and model thyself after the whale!
> Do thou, too, remain warm among ice. Dou thou, too, live in this world without being of it.
> Be cool at the Equator; keep thy blood fluid at the Pole. Like the greatest dome of St. Peter's, and like the great whale, retain, O man! in all seasons a temperature of thine own.
> --*Moby Dick* by Herman Melville

Avery admired Abbey's breadth and depth, and hoped for some day, she would attain a sense of self so sure and happy, so calm and so strong to match his.

Abbey and Avery had their share of turmoil having to moderate the initial ecstasy and passion of two people so very taken to each other, to turn into a form of normality, a mode of proper sensibility to function and regard each other in their daily life. They had their love rituals and momentums, and in time, they learned about each other, with each other, and alongside each other.

Avery's insecurity and uncertainty creeped up now and then, particularly when she felt her pursuit of a life by her own design was jeopardized. On an occasion she communicated to Abbey via email:

I can pretend that I am emotionally fulfilled, and that my wants and wishes do not matter at the moment. And your phobia will be miraculously cured someday. But how realistic is it? I am willing to wait but can't be on the back burner all my life. Shucks! Wasn't this something we had to consider before we got involved? How naïve of me to believe that love rules and our inner demons will all perish!

Abbey, while I have no regret in loving you and enjoying the time with you, I am not sure how to proceed, except for being completely honest with myself and with you. I don't and can't play games.

How would you look at a wedding chapel and exclaim that if I want to get married, we can now? Those things are not to be taken lightly. You know your kind words and mindless remarks did give me hopes and mayhap in reality, false and illusive! How could you look at me and say, "Sex and food, that's why I keep you around"? How could you joke and ask me, "Do I know you; my girlfriend is tall"!? You know your man's talk and cruel witticism can be offensive.

You're the best bachelor in my life, but I want a life-partner! I love you and I can't change you. It's not you or me; it's just the timing. I understand there're things that are hard for you to let go at this juncture in your life. I understand your priorities, but it's hard for me to be an add-on, when you try sorting out your obligations from your previous marriage.

Putting up with a romantic partner who does not honor and cherish my essence is a thing of the past (no matter how in love I am, and boy, you're charismatic). I learned and I still have faith and believe in a mature, happy, true partnership. People get stuck in a rut, in the relationships you see and dread. But don't you think one should have the mind and power to take initiatives and change life conditions for the better, such as being considerate, communicative and loving to the one person you are intimate with? Don't we and shouldn't we all learn and grow up enough someday?

I am sorry if I have brought up matters that you were not ready to handle. It's just that things are not always easy though I am trying to give you time and space. I am trying to operate from a place of love.

I certainly don't feel happy when unwanted for matrimony, though jokingly so. Mind you, I am not in need of a piece of paper but surely value the commitment and bond that a marriage brings. I am not looking to get married; marriage is never a goal but a natural outcome of a fruitful love-ship. I have been on my own all along and do not need that validation two years into our relationship.

A relationship does take time to solidify, and without a solid foundation, no one should vow into such a bond. But isn't that bond, trust and closeness what we all desire in the long run? It's hard to swallow an utter rejection. Do you understand? My body follows my heart; I need to feel loved.
I live and let live. And love you dearly.

Have a great week! -- Avery

Abbey wrote back:

OMG Avery. I had no idea you had all this stuff bottled up inside you. I just read your e-mail. All I can say is I'm sorry if my little jokes hurt you, that was not my intention, I'm sorry for everything, I'm sorry for all the trouble I've caused you, and I'm sorry for making you feel like "food and sex are all I keep you around for." I never meant that by the way. I'm sorry you feel that I could never love you, and I'm sorry you felt that I could never marry you. I never said those things, and I don't know why you feel that way.
I have a job which has been very taxing on my time and energy; I have a son who I'm raising and that keeps me busy. No excuses, but it's clear to me that we need to take a break. I'm too disappointing for you by far!

Best Regards -- Abbey

Avery pined for the whole week when Abbey did not see her. Then he surprised her showing up at her door one evening, telling her how he missed her. They loved each other and made each other feel youthful and alive in ways they never felt before.

After that, they had more heartbreak and rapture, and then more blissful and hear-warming time together.

Abbey and Avery were married four years into their relationship. Avery became his second wife and his kids' stepmother. Ill-equipped throughout the process, Avery was agonized every step of the way. She went from a woman trying her hardest for her step-children's understanding, to a neutral person realizing those children would never be hers to love.

She never cooked as much and spent as much for any children in her life, only to be unappreciated and antagonized more. She never shopped and planned as much for any children in her life, only to be turned down and pushed away for no apparent reason other than that she was the woman who married Abbey, their father. She gave up trying to be friends, established the boundaries, and only hoped for her own life's peripheries to stay intact.

It Was Never Easy

At first Avery was determined to treat Abbey's children as her very own, only to be excluded and rejected in every way like an outsider, or worse, as a second-class human being.

So, discrimination, stereotyping, or insensitivity was yet again, infringed upon her -- in this instance, by Abbey's grown children, who were supposed to be her new family. It was even more heart-rending and perturbing than any she had experienced from her adopted American country fellowmen, from her students, or from people in a world that she loved and trusted with patience and faith.

So they said there's a price to everything. Avery's conjugal bliss with Abbey came with conditions she was not fully prepared to cope with.

Something had miraculously happened after Abbey returned to his high-paying job. His daughter, Claire, who had not wanted to talk to him for the longest time after he married Avery, returned to assert that "a daughter's love for her father is forever." However, Claire would still hug every friend and relative around the table at a gathering, yet not acknowledging Avery and bypassing her physique as if a yellow colored person could be completely invisible. Moreover, Claire would aggressively rival for her father's attention whenever they got together. She would be sure that she was talking, working, shopping, and playing with her father, excluding Avery. She would even violate Avery's home, dry her clothes on every piece of Avery's furniture, and went through Abbey and Avery's closets to find her father's clothes for her boyfriend and herself to wear, as if she had been the keeper or possessor of everything Abbey and Avery owned.

"Dad, too bad it has to rain when I visit you. I got rained on. My clothes are all wet, and I dry them in your living room." Claire presumed and stated "her right and rationale" to put her bikinis and shorts up for show in Avery's house.

"Ok. Put them away by the end of day, so our house can be back to normal." Abbey said good-naturedly.

"And dad, I am going to make a cake for Ethan. Do you have a bundt pan?" Claire asked Abbey, not acknowledging that she was staying at Avery's house and using Avery's kitchen. It never occurred to her to confer with Avery about anything. Whether intentionally by design or accidentally by negligence, Avery was forever invisible to Claire, feeling like an outsider in her own house.

"I don't believe we do. I can go out and get one." Abbey readily offered.

"Great, and don't forget to get some brandy, too." Claire further demanded with her bossy approach to everyone and everything.

Avery did not agree with Abbey's way of letting his daughter bossing him around. She did not condone for Claire to use the same attitude on her -- if Claire was ever to discuss or speak to her about anything. Claire never did. Avery was eternally, deliberately ignored.

Avery raised hell when her life was encroached upon, and always felt uncomfortable with Abbey's kids, with letting them visit, stay or live in her house. She talked to Abbey about keeping the boundaries, about not slaving for or mothering his kids, about being reciprocated in sharing, and above all, about tough-loving his kids to make them become more independent, responsible, and less sanctioned to childish or malicious behavior. So, she was to never pamper Abbey's kids like an accommodating mother-figure. And, being a non-mom or stepmom -- was never easy.

Abbey had repositioned himself to a mid-level job when he first married Avery. The couple had sold Abbey's old house and saved the money as part of their retirement funds (then he was too bored and returned to his old executive position after two years). Abbey's son Ethan lived with them at the time, as he had not finished high school and very much needed to stay with his father. Ethan took over Avery's whole house soon after he moved in with them, leaving dishes everywhere in the kitchen, playing music late into the wee hours, inviting friends over to eat, drink and party, and making loud noises and unbearable clutters.

Ethan behaved as if he owned Avery's entire house and had a sense of entitlement teenagers assumed: he tagged on the walls, altered closets and shelves, and broke household items amazingly more often than not. Avery tried having Abbey teach good habits. Ethan remained his lofty self, too narcissistic to think from others' points of view. Both Abbey and Avery were frustrated, and many times argued over something Ethan did or didn't do.

"Ethen would not listen to me. YOU need to urge him to think and form good habits." Avery told Abbey.

"How about you also help him grow into manhood?" Abbey was hopeful of bringing his wife and his son together.

Avery had never cooked so much in her entire life. Avery offered help whenever Ethan needed, grocery shopped and prepared meals like never before, only to have him make caustic comments in order to guard his own sense of loyalty to his birth mother:

"Why are the shrimps cooked with the tails on?"

"Do Taiwanese people always have so many sculptures in their backyards? Are they like you or what?"

"When I become famous, I will have a huge mansion and my father can live with me. You can come too if you want."

"Do Chinese make food all the time? You cook all kinds of foods, but I rather cook for myself."

"Why does anyone want to be a teacher? Las Vegas is an awful place for teachers and students. It's ironic that you're an English teacher, isn't it?"

"It probably was easy for you to buy this house because it was cheap when the housing market crashed."

"When I have my own music studio, it will be full-sized, high-tech, and has the best sound."

. . . .

In the end, Avery had Ethan move out upon his turning eighteen years of age. Knowing that Abbey was not quite himself looking to adjust his life, Avery made Ethan move out to save all three of them. She was probably the best thing that ever happened in Ethan's life. She made him learn. She forced him to start facing life challenges on his own.

Abbey resumed his guitar-playing after Ethan became more responsible for himself, trying to make a life of his own. He and Ethen met frequently after Ethen moved out. Ethen called Abbey ten times a day, asking for advice aka attention, hoping for his father to pay for whatever expensive whims he fancied. They occasionally included Avery in their daily conversations.

Ethan also expected to come back to the house to dine, play and be entertained like before. Avery developed an aversion to his behavior and refused to cook for him like an old maid ever again. Only during traditional holidays, Avery found her equilibrium and good spirit to invite Ethan back again.

Abbey showered Avery with weekend getaways that allowed for couple's quality time. He tried making up for their interrupted love and life together. Often their trips were delayed or rearranged because Ethan called his father for help.

"My car broke down. The battery died. Can you come get me?" Ethan said on the phone, sounding pretty distressed and desperate.

"Yes we are driving our motor home to Lake Mead. I will come get you when we get off the highway." Abbey assured. Avery waited in their motor home which Abbey left in a parking lot -- for eight hours while Abbey went rescuing his son. Although she was "home" waiting, she couldn't resist the thought of getting away from it all. She wanted to just leave Abbey and put all the aggravation behind. She was not sure whether any alternative way of resolving Ethan's problems other than "Dad" could have easily done the same job Abbey did for Ethan, and taught Ethan a better lesson of being responsible and careful for himself.

Then the next day while Abbey and Avery rested in their motor home by the lake, Ethan called again.

"My car is back from the shop, but I lost my key."

"You will just have to have your buddies drive you for the day." Abbey was annoyed and feeling Avery's discontent by this time. "We'll be back in the house tomorrow, and you can come get my spare key then."

Ethan made copies of the spare key, and learned to keep another extra copy of the key in a secret place for emergencies. So hopefully his father would not be the only source of solutions he could have in life. Hopefully he learned not to lose his keys and to safe-guard his belongings. And hopefully his car headlights were off when they needed to be, his apartment door was secured and locked, his dishes and clothes were laundered and put away, his relations with his roommates were affable and cordial, and his mind and soul would grow and mature to take him on his journey to manhood. Hopefully, Avery could feel comfortable or loving again towards Abbey's kids one day.

Traveling, became not only her passion, her favorite way of learning about the world, but her escape from mundane challenges, and her precious time alongside her husband to appreciate the bigger picture of life together. Traveling, provided Avery with spaces and channels in which she could process her thoughts to ascend to a happier place and realize what treasurable aspects of life she needed to retain and reinforce, and what despicable patterns of living she wanted to diminish, deescalate, and discard.

Avery was often humored by the fact that she was welcome everywhere she traveled to, treated as a five-star VIP simply because she was spending, happily contributing to a country's economy. Furthermore, she could pass for a local in many places she visited because she always explored every corner of a town or a city to the extent that her efforts to mingle and learn earned her many dear friends and helpful allies.

In dire contrast, she could not get past the fact that she had to deal with discrimination and mistreatment in the city she called home! Perhaps Avery's global interest and open mindset was more agreeable with people who were also concerned with humanity, who were curious about mankind as a whole. She was not a typical Las Vegan, New Yorker, American, Taiwanese, or of any particular nationality. She was most comfortable living outside the box, looking in. She was a World Citizen. She loved traveling with her husband Abbey.

There was no other way to put the sparkle in Avery's eyes than a mere suggestion such as: "Let's go on a road trip this weekend.... We need to plan for our winter/summer trips." And so Abbey and Avery went on numerous road trips and flew to countless exotic locales over many weekends, spring breaks as well as winter/summer vacations. Their life together was full of adventures and learnings. Avery could not find a better partner in life; she was immensely grateful for everything her husband brought to enrich her life. Even the difficulty with her step children seemed miniscule in the grand scheme of things.

Chapter 10. The World with Abbey

As world citizens, Abbey and Avery traveled to the Bahamas, Belize, Mexico, Costa Rica, Ecuador, Peru, and Brazil. They toured through the European countries of England, Ireland, Scotland, Belgium, Hungary, Spain, Greece, and Italy. They went further to the Southeast Asian countries of Thailand, Laos, Vietnam, Cambodia, Malaysia, and Indonesia. They circled back to Japan, Korea, and China. Avery welcomed a sense of purpose, a mission to find an ideal mental and physical place. It differed in intent from the youthful roaming thirst during the travels with her ex-husband Tim. She was young and had no home then; she matured and had a charged sagacity of a homemaker now. Would she and Abbey find that ideal place together through life's journey? Would they combine and merge their worlds to build a healthy life together?

Would they march onward and upward through trials and tribulations in life? Would they reconcile their intrinsic differences as man and woman, father and step-mother, Westerner and Asian? Were they in their own globes or were they fortunate enough to share and converge? What had they learned? What had they taken away with them to the world? What kind of settings would they leave behind and what kind of home would they build? Would it be a better, improved place? Or, would it be another world to cast their injuries and successes in? Avery had faith, and she could only sail with her heart to face fearlessly whatever came her way.

The Americas

The Hogs, the Butterflies and the
Pirates of the Bahamas

Americans and Canadians frequented the Bahamian islands as if they were playing and reveling in their backyards. A short distance from Florida, the Bahamas were nonetheless exotic, vivid as dabs of motley colors on an artist's palette. Indeed, since Christopher Columbus discovered the limestone landscapes in 1492, the islands' became active and alive with pirates, fugitives, smugglers, and explorers carousing for centuries. The country's 700 islands and 2400 cays had 400,000 inhabitants, with over half of the population in Nassau. While some islands were uninhabited and could be up for sale to some tycoon or celebrity, downtown Nassau's beachfront shopping and Paradise Island's over-the-top Atlantis resort became the centers of tourist attractions.

Abbey worked mobily on their trip, and so liked to relax by the pool with the backdrop of gorgeous, mesmerizing azure.

Avery walked the streets of downtown Nassau, dodging the jostling jitneys and cabbies, haggling with vendors and shopkeepers. She acquired straw fans, straw handbags, and expensive souvenirs from Paradise Island. She learned about the extravagant beachfront mansions, as well as the 2.3 billion new Chinese investments in the country. Hoping to catch the country's Junkanoo beats and folk arts, she strolled to the rundown areas of the island.

"It's so expensive in the Bahamas, more than the States. How do local people get by?" On the way back to the hotel, Avery asked a cabby named Donald.

"You stay away from the hotels, you budget. We know tourism is our bloodline, so we budget in the low seasons." Donald explained how people got by.

"Who owns the beautiful beachfront houses all over?"

"Some locals, mostly timeshares. On Paradise Island, the cheapest house is 4 million. There's no road there because the rich people want privacy."

"So they fly their helicopters in?"

"Yes something like that. Paradise Island used to be called Hog Island. No one wants to visit hogs, so it's Paradise now with Atlantis and everything." Donald pointed out the gap between the rich and the poor.

"Looks like the hogs are here to stay. There's offshore banking and there's money laundering." Avery had heard stories about famous people manipulating and storing their wealth offshore in the Bahamas to evade taxes, dues or debts, claiming multiple bankruptcies.

Roaming recklessly, Avery deemed her exploration worthwhile when she found the Poinciana trees of her childhood. She returned to the hotel to show Abbey how she and her childhood friends in Taiwan had made butterflies out of the Poinciana trees' flowers.

"We call these Phoenix/Feng-huang trees because of its flowers' flaming red color like the bird, and in English you call it Royal Poinciana, Flame tree, Flamboyant tree or Delonix regia." Seeing the familiar trees of her childhood in a foreign soil, Avery had looked up its names in ecstasy. She could not wait to show her Poinciana butterflies to Abbey. "You take two feathery petals to make wings. You take two filaments from the stamens to make antennas. You scratch the inside of two sepals to make them sticky, and then combine them together to make a butterfly's body. With the body, you insert the wings and antennas to position them properly and form a shape of a beautiful butterfly. Each flower is good for two butterflies because there are 4 red petals, 4 sepals and plenty of stamens in a Poinciana flower. You keep them in books and press them." Avery was making the butterflies as she explained excitedly.

"They are gorgeous. But how did you have these same trees in Taiwan?" Abbey was curious now.

"Taiwan is on similar latitudes as the Bahamas or Florida, and so I am not surprised to find these trees everywhere here on the island." She realized these fiery flowers grew everywhere on the Caribbean islands as well.

"That's great."

Abbey was appreciating the butterflies while the phone rang off the hook.

"Can I speak to Abbey Lori? I have his passport." A male voice announced.

"What?" Abbey was dumbfounded.

"Yes I have the passport of Abbey Lori."

"How did you find it? Can you please deliver it to my hotel where I stay?"

"A passenger found it in the backseat area of my cab. I remember taking you and your wife to your hotel."

"Good, thank you for calling. Please if you can, deliver it back here. I will be waiting right here."

"How did you lose your passport in a taxi?" Avery wanted to know how Abbey could leave such an important item in a taxi.

"I didn't. Someone must have taken it. The driver handled my luggage. And there were two other passengers sharing the cab, as you know." Abbey was sure someone had reached into his laptop case and got hold of his passport.

Abbey and Avery waited in the hotel for hours and there was not a sign of a returned passport. The taxi driver finally came after Abbey called him back and announced a reward of one hundred US dollars. Abbey's passport was lost to some modern-day pirates, and could only be regained after giving in to the gritty vibe of a pirate land. The Bahamas were exotic, all right. Abbey learned to be extra careful on the road after the incident.

Across the Caribbean Sea in
Extraordinary Belize

There truly was no place in the world like Belize. Its extraordinary location at the convergence of five diverse eco-systems allowed a mixture of cultures: Mexican, Mayan, Caribbean, European, Spanish, and American. The diversity made the country seem so alive with possibilities.

Abbey and Avery stayed on mainland Belize, and were able to easily explore several of the Maya sites: canoeing down the Macal River, hiking in the jungle, and doing cave tubing, zip lining and horseback riding in the natural wonders. They explored the magnificent coastline hugging the Caribbean Sea with more than two hundred offshore islands. On the twenty inhabited islands, the golden and white-sand beaches were readily accessible, beckoning for them to visit, such as Ambergris Caye.

Reading up Brazilian history on the beach, Avery learned that in the 1600s, British pirates roaming the Caribbean found this little haven, discretely tucked inside a great barrier reef. The pirates used Ambergris Caye as a safe port to hide-out and stash their valuables. They eventually used the Bacalar Channel to transport their treasures to mainland Belize. Ambergris Caye supposedly got its name during that period. It was believed that the pirates collected whale excrement, called ambergris that washed up on shore of the island. The oil from this ambergris was sent to Europe where it was made into perfumes and became very valuable.

The island was twenty five miles long, made up of three main areas: mangrove swamps, lagoons, and sand. The lagoons were to the western (leeward) side of the island. The Barrier Reef lay about a half mile to the east of the island, running the entire length, the reef and the land touching at the northeast of the island at Rocky Point. The sand reached a height of three to five feet above sea level, to a maximum of ten feet at San Pedro Town, where all the tourists, bars, restaurants, and activities were located.

Abbey and Avery visited his brother Jason and sister-in-law Gena, who had chosen Ambergris Caye as their retirement haven. Their neighbors were the British born Taylors living precariously with their African and mestizo house-workers.

"Millie Taylor has ten servants. That's a form of modern slavery." Gena, an aboriginal Canadian from one of the First Nations, had been quite a union activist before she retired. She had traveled worldwide to help with causes of human rights and justices, and was still a humanitarian on all fronts.

"The Taylors are loaded. They can do whatever they want." Jason wanted to be neighborly. "We are coming over and I hope you're not gonna talk about Esmeralda's wage or Teresa's living arrangement," he forewarned his wife.

Avery thought the Taylors' beach house was enchanting. A beautiful teak terrace wrapped around and led directly to the beach. A living, dining room and kitchen extended seamlessly with the open terrace, blending the outdoor elements into the indoor spaces. The beautiful infinity pool that looked over the beach was spectacular, so were the numerous bedrooms, workrooms, and playrooms beyond guests' reach.

The Loris joined the Taylors to sit and watch birds sauntering along the sand, boats dotting the horizon, and people playing in the sea. Teresa, the chef, prepared a full-course dinner with her three assistants and was ready to line up the dinner feast.

"Yo'al shud come eat nau." Teresa summoned her masters and their guests in her Pidgin English through an intercom built around the many rooms in the house.

"We will take another forty minutes. And I make the call, not you. Understand?" Brian Taylor stated loudly and irritably with authority to the intercom.

"I don't mind going inside for dinner now, do you, Avery?" Gena defied Brian's con-descending attitude.

"I am easy. Whenever everyone is ready." Avery tried not to escalate the situation.

Millie backed up her husband Brian: "Teresa, you can use another forty minutes. Make sure all the silverwares and utensils are polished before you they put them out."

Teresa stayed at her living and working quarters and took orders from the intercom -- the Taylors' servants were not allowed to show their faces to the guests.

Gena told how she would see these servants circled around the side of the Taylors' house until no one was around so they could travel to and from the house. The Taylors explained that their workers were not to be treated as the beach residents, and so they should not mingle with the people in the community. They were there only to work and serve the Taylor couple, nothing else.

Gina and Jason felt they shouldn't have brought Abbey and Avery to the Taylors and exposed them to their neighbors' attitudes towards domestic help. They apologized after the gathering. As a matter of fact, Gina had, behind the scenes, supplied used clothing and other necessities to the Taylor's household servants. She was held in very high regard with the locals.

The Loris rushed through dinner after the intercom incident, cutting the gathering short to return next door. Abbey and Avery learned to choose which houses to visit on the beach front. Only after they found the right people to hang, did they start appreciating the lovely life of the retired Jason and Gina.

Avery and Abbey mingled with the tourists and locals alike. The place was truly a diver's paradise. They cruised around the numerous neighboring cayes, saw the incredible barrier reef that sat on the bottom of the ocean, along with huge schools of wondrously colored fish, all in a mere six feet-eight feet of clear, warm water, wearing only goggles. Even Avery the bad swimmer could easily navigate alongside her husband, speaking with the friendly sharks, feeding stingrays carefully with their breakfast left-over bread. She never snorkeled or dived, and yet she got an unforgettable first view of the beautiful sea-world -- carefree, unlike the paranoid little girl too afraid to swim on the island of Taiwan.

At night, they enjoyed lots of music mixed in a family-type atmosphere. No sex industry in sight, a welcome relief from the bombardment of images in many cultures and resorts of today. Avery loved the quiet and charming little town.

On Another Trip to Mexico

Mexico was America's distant neighbor, physically close but miles apart in culture and economy. Abbey and Avery's road trip to Tijuana ended with a quick turn back to the US Border Patrol after they realized their SUV was an easy prey. The swarming street peddlers were common throughout the country. They saw them in Ensenada, Mazatlan, Los Cabos and even the ritzy part of Cancun. But those hawkers in the border town of Tijuana were some different kettle of fish. They gawked, gestured, and purveyed, all with an alarmingly persuasive act of a mime.

Mexico's sharp class and social divisions were apparent. A small upper class controlled much of the country's wealth while the majority lived in poverty.

"Buy a key chain, a souvenir....This one is nice, see?" A peddler urged.

"How much are the little figures?"

"Five Pesos."

Avery bought eight figurines for forty Pesos. The two US dollars Avery paid, average Mexicans could spend two days to earn. Many of them migrated north to America for employment. Las Vegas certainly contained a fair share of the Mexican population. Along with the colorful piñatas, melodious mariachi tunes and wonderfully spicy cuisines, came the steep cost of drug abuse and juvenile crime.

Avery compared notes with a local teacher she met in Guadalajara. Alejandra was pleasant and helpful, a thirty-year-old 7th grade science teacher in the inner city.

"After my class I can show you guys around." She offered to be their local guide.

"That will be wonderful. How are your classes? How are students here? Are they behaving and learning?" Avery was curious about the kids.

"Oh they are ok. I hate the class right before siesta, because most of my students want to get out and can't sit still. I am ok with wearing uniforms because they give a feel of order and unity."

"I guess they are as unmotivated as the US children a lot of time. The difference is Americans mostly do not wear uniforms, and have way more exposures and choices." Avery observed with concern.

Alejandra seemed to think that her students were indolent, where Avery found them well-mannered. Juvenile delinquencies or not, they appeared to be polite and agreeable -- in comparison. Though Avery met many wonderful students of Mexican descent in her school district, she also encountered students who were placed under house arrest and attended school with GPS trackers, needing constant watch, far from respectful, or compliant, or law-abiding.

Abbey surmised that sometimes too much modern technology and media contact was detrimental for kids. When they stopped by a brick-maker's home to watch the family work, Abbey affirmed his point based on how happy the family managed to be without one tenth of what the Americans had.

"Los materiales deben ser mezclados correctamente. (You have to make sure the materials are mixed properly." The father trod on the mud-like substance in their front yard before molding and shaping it on a home-made device, no machinery involved or needed.

"How fascinating. Can I try?" Abbey was excited to see the ancient technique.

At the end of the tour, they each tried making bricks, none of them fitting as building materials. However, they felt elated as if they were skilled masons.

It's remarkable how a Mexican household lacking running water could make bricks for a living. It's also startling to learn how many U.S. expats there were in Mexico -- one million and rising. Avery's Hispanic students back in the US had expressed discontent in the wake of the election, and swore to move out of the States should some American president rub them the wrong way. For Abbey and Avery, though the expat population was likely to grow in Mexico, they stayed in the touristy parts of the country, and spent too much buying knick-knacks in order to feel charitable to the poor Mexicans. They avoided the authentic Mexican towns, hoping to reduce their chance of crossing paths with the cartels. Mexico was close by, yet so far away.

Epic Tour across Costa Rica
to Little Yolanda

Throwing caution to the wind, Abbey and Avery flew to Costa Rica and toured across the country. "Samara is like the black hole for paradise seekers." More than one expat mentioned the charm of the place to the newly arrived couple. Avery could see how people could stop here on vacation and never leave. But "never" was over-stretched, even for Avery who had the tendency to want to live in every country she visited. On the surface, Samara was easy-to-navigate, offering a three-star crescent-shaped beach spanning two rocky headlands. Underneath Samara's palpable comfort and tranquility was an undercurrent of opulence and overindulgence. Abbey and Avery left after one week of stay. The personality of the place didn't jive with the scenery -- too many pretenses and hot airs.

North of Sámara was Playa Barrigona, equally famous for its pristine beach as for its celebrity resident, Mel Gibson. Abbey and Avery couldn't come near the beach where the star and his entourage were having their important summits and conferences. The expensive beachfront resort was not quite the minimal natural preserve to their liking. They took to traversing Costa Rica through the natural wilderness of the Central Valley.

Their crossing took them on bike, foot, raft and kayak. The trails were often slippery and poorly demarcated, with several river crossings. They came across indigenous settlements hidden in the cloud forest and had glimpses of rare wildlife and birdlife. The views and terrains varied greatly as they traversed the mountainous backbone of the country.

Their journey took them into the depths of the Pacuare River on one of the world's classic whitewater experiences, where they undertook an exhilarating rafting trip with class 2-5 rapids through a series of spectacular canyons. In between the powerful rapids there was time to absorb the superb surroundings and the tropical rainforest. They left the rapids and gorges behind as they eased their way by sea kayak along a much slower moving section of the river, through plantations to their final goal, the pacific coast of Costa Rica.

Costa Rica's northern Pacific coast, near the border with Nicaragua, was a popular destination with established expats communities. It also sheltered many of the country's 20,000 refugees with over forty different nationalities. The increased immigration created tension and conflict, adding to the country's xenophobic complex.

Abbey and Avery sat in a restaurant ordering food from their Nicaraguan servers.

"How would you like your steak cooked?" Miguel asked politely with a bright smile.

"Medium, and please add a baked potato, loaded." Abbey craved the red meat he could rarely have crossing the Central Valley.

"Do you know what to tell the chef about 'loading' a baked potato?" Avery overheard Miguel's Costa Rican manager, speaking condescendingly to his subordinate.

"Yes, Sir. I have been working here for two years." Their server replied.

"I'd better tell the chef myself. No point ruining an order, porque eres un idiota." His manager doubted him, and seemed determined to make him look bad.

Miguel became Abbey and Avery's friend after their many dining experiences at his workplace. He told them how he was always treated as a second class citizen. His brother had died during a drug deal gone south, and the police had refused to help his family find his brother's murderer. On top of that, Miguel had been interrogated brutally with physical torture, for his brother's case that had nothing to do with him.

Avery wished bigotry could be less damaging. She wanted to see Miguel's children obtain equal education and opportunity to grow to be successful individuals. It was alarming and heartbreaking to hear Miguel's twelve-year-old daughter Yolanda talk about her school days.

"No one at school wants to play with me. They say I am not white, and I can't work with them," with tears in her eyes, Yolanda reported her difficulties.

"Are you trying hard for good grades? They will work with you if you do have good grades." Yolanda's brother Jesus encouraged her to work hard.

"No. Because I still have to work after school at Mama's factory."

"No excuses. You just have to stay up like me." Her brother found her a solution.

"But I also have to do house chores." Yolanda beseeched him to understand. "Help me do the dishes."

"That's a girl's job. Get to it." Jesus refused to let go of his machismo, or relieve his little sister.

Avery helped Yolanda with her school work, meanwhile trying to get Jesus to help his little sister. With the first woman president in 2010, Avery trusted that Costa Rica was more progressive of a country than what Abbey and she had seen. If equity and diversity was a long road to travel, every step further would count, and any support would be worth striving for.

Ecuador Impressions

With weighty thoughts and musings, Abbey and Avery headed for Ecuador. Abbey had left Miguel's family a small donation for their kids' education. They had to relax in a resort for days before they could stop thinking about little Yolanda's dilemma. The surprisingly pleasant climate of the country was a big help.

Rich with historical and ecological dimensions, Ecuador made a strong impression on Avery. More remarkable was the widespread presence of Chinese businesses in the country. China had invested billions in Ecuador, using its economic power to win over the country as a diplomatic ally and secure natural resources. Water pipes were set aside near where Ecuador wanted a Chinese oil company to build a giant refinery, outside the port of Manta. China was lending $7 billion for the construction of the refinery, which could make Ecuador a key global player in gasoline, diesel and other petroleum products.

At the Andean foothills, approximately 1,000 Chinese engineers and workers had been pouring concrete for a dam and a 15-mile underground tunnel into the Amazon jungle. The $2.2 billion project would feed river water to eight giant Chinese turbines designed to produce enough electricity to light more than a third of Ecuador.

China had a lock on nearly 90 percent of Ecuador's oil exports, which mostly went to paying off its loans. As the country's energy minister Alberto Acosta foretold, Chinese imperialism had in fact replaced its Western counterpart:

> The Chinese are shopping across the world, transforming their financial resources into mineral resources and investments. They come with financing, technology and technicians, but also high interest rates.

With China's notorious record when it came to worker safety, environmental standards and corporate governance, Avery feared to see the worst practices exported to magnificent places, including one that she and Abbey could stay for a while in.

Avery was afraid that the cost for Ecuador would be steep. Issues had already surfaced a few miles from the site of the hydroelectric plant, where the Coca River vaulted down a 480-foot waterfall and cascaded through precipitous canyons toward the Amazon. The tallest waterfall in Ecuador might suffer -- when the dam was complete and the water was diverted to the plant, the San Rafael falls would slow to a trickle for part of the year. As climate change decreased the Andean glacier that fed the river, the popular tourist spot might not have enough water to generate even half the electricity predicted. And an underground river had burst into a tunnel at the site. The high-pressure water engulfed the powerhouse, killing 14 workers.

The incident was a wake-up call to ponder the consequences of overlooking environmental conservation and labor safety. What Avery read in a brochure about Ecuador was tinted with solemn reality:

> Ecuador is home to great weather, scenery and jaw-dropping low prices.
>
> The country offers perennial springtime in the mountains...a land of longevity in Vilcabamba...and Spanish-colonial charm in Cuenca...all of which can be enjoyed on even an extremely modest budget.
>
> This beautiful and diverse country offers you the chance to retire in style on as little as a social security budget -- a maid, gardener, dinners out.
>
> A natural wonderland...from the famous Galapagos Islands...to the cool Andes mountains...to the deep lush Amazon rainforests.
>
> In Ecuador you'll find some of the best value health care in the world, at a cost of only 10-25% of that in the United States.
>
> Ecuador also offers premier retirement visas for foreigners, complete with perks, including discounts on utility bills.

Seeing Ecuador for herself, Avery knew that the cultural divide barely began. Few of the Chinese workers spoke Spanish, and they lived separately from their Ecuadorean coworkers. When they left their camp for lunch, they walked down the main street in separate groups.

At night, they also walked in separate groups up the hill to the local brothel. (Prostitution was legal in Ecuador.) The workers sat at separate tables drinking bottles of the Ecuadorean beer, Pilsener. A Chinese influenced, segregated Ecuador would pay the cost for its ecological footprint.

The Appeal of Latin American Authors
and a Spymaster

For Avery to choose between Peru and Columbia was not easy. She wanted to go everywhere and see everything. She had always been partial to authors of Latin America: Octavio Paz, Julio Cortázar, Jorge Luis Borges, Gabriel García Márquez and Carlos Fuentes among numerous others. Her studies on Italo Calvino and Umberto Eco had taken her to Italy's cities. Another visit to a beloved author's birth country would have similar inspirations.

Abby could not stop the ever-wandering Avery from strolling into every ritzy area or shantytown of a city. He worried to no end while he stayed behind to take care of business back home as well as their itinerary arrangement. Avery realized the quandary her wander-lust induced, and picked the easy Peru en route to Brazil.

Peru's Nobel laureate Mario Vargas Llosa, a leading member of the Latin American Boom, was enough to lure Avery to the country. It also had the Mayan ruins, topped with intriguing Afro-Indo-Chinese influences. Avery was happy to see that Peru upheld a wide variety of festivals and traditions to pay respect to its cultural heritage. A never-ending succession of jubilees and events throughout the year brought cheerful colors and flavors to everyday life. From vibrant dances to profound religious acts of devotion, Peruvians celebrated with passion and with glee.

Abbey and Avery read about some of the customs before they hit the legendary Machu Picchu. Erected high on a mountain, Machu Picchu was an Inca city with temples, palaces, paths, and water channels. It's amazing to observe how an ancient civilization built with huge stone blocks, without any cement, but with great wisdom. The citadel, which lived in harmony with nature, represented a single expression of the fusion between mountain and city. Due to its important historical legacy, Machu Picchu was declared a World Cultural and Natural Heritage site in 1983. According to research, Machu Picchu was built in the 15th century by the Inca Pachacútec. It provided one of the best examples of Inca architecture. Set in the middle of a tropical mountain forest, the city appeared to have been sculpted from the rocky slopes. Savoring the spectacular landscape, Abbey and Avery had fun exploring the endemic biological diversity in flora and fauna.

Among the most impressive details of its construction were the stone walls, perfectly shaped and juxtaposed without cement, as well as the channels' system and water sources. Machu Picchu was interconnected with the entire Inca empire through the Qapac Ñam, the network of Inca roads, which Abbey and Avery walked to in wonder. They also learned that access to the city had been previously prohibited by rural communities and local inhabitants, as its location was a state secret, protected by the deep ravines and wild mountains. Abby and Avery felt privileged to walk the site, taking in the artifacts in awe, immersing themselves in the rich culture.

Apart from the colorful festivities, they also witnessed grime, child labor and corruption. Peru had undergone an extended period of political unrest and economic turmoil. A twenty-year civil war against radical insurgent movements had made it difficult to sustain its economy. Mining for decades had accounted for over half of Peru's exports, but was not properly regulated to protect the environment. The natural resources could be depleted beyond repair, and corrupted government officials might just be paid off to evade concerns of human rights or poverty.

Peru's fugitive spymaster Vladimiro Montesino had been exposed giving congressmen over $15,000 or a Judge a $10,000 month salary to sit on as the head of the electoral board.

President Alberto Fujimori was re-elected in 2000 as a result, while economic and environmental regulations remained ineffective. Montesino was said to have escaped from the country on a yacht and sailed the Pacific to Ecuador's Galapagos Islands, then on to Costa Rica and Venezuela. He was last sighted having plastic surgery at a clinic in Venezuela. His frozen Swiss bank accounts contained $70 million and a dozen gold and diamond-encrusted watches.

Peru's corruption and scandals had died down, whereas the cheerful Peruvians rebuilt with jovial festivals and celebrations. Abbey and Avery took too many pictures and bought too many souvenirs. The county's stamina and resilience was what they would always hold dear in their hearts. However untrustworthy some politicians and government officials remained, Abbey and Avery loved the ways the country's people persevered and rejoiced.

The Marvelous City of Carnivals and a Suspected Policeman

Flying into Rio de Janeiro, Brazil, Abbey and Avery were greeted by golden beaches and lush mountains, as well as samba-fueled nightlife and spectacular football matches. Standing atop the 710m peak of Corcovado, they felt they could forget the entire world's wearies and problems. Rio the Cidade Maravilhosa (Marvelous City) offered delightful experiences they would forever treasure.

Verdantly forested mountains fringed the city; shimmering beaches traced the shoreline, and a string of tiny islands scattered along the seafront. After enough hiking, cycling, sailing, surfing, rock-climbing, and hang-gliding, Abbey and Avery were excited about Brazilian carnivals. They let their hair down to enjoy the city's glitters and splendors.

Cariocas were downright partiers, with joie de vivre, lebensfreude, or lust for life. Rio had many occasions for celebration and revelry -- celebrations after the big Flamengo (or Vasco, Fluminense or Botafogo) soccer match, weekend samba parties around town, baile funk parties in the favelas and boat parties on the bay, not to mention major holiday festivals. On the legendary Copacabana Beach and Ipanema Beach, Abbey and Avery fell in love with bossa nova starring Tom Jobim and Vinicius de Moraes. The Girl from Ipanema was mesmerizing and alluring; she was alive not only in the lyrics, but also on the backyard of Rio. Music often came with endless enjoyment in the form of football, volleyball, surfing, snacking, drinking or simply watching the passing people parade in assorted colors. Abbey and Avery adored the spontaneous and good-natured spirit. The urge to live life to the fullest was endearing.

Atop Corcovado (meaning 'hunchback'), Cristo Redentor (Christ the Redeemer) gazed placidly over Rio, captivating and redeeming all walks of life. At night, the 38m-high and 1145-ton-heavey statue was brightly lit, visible, majestic, and awe-inspiring. Nothing could go wrong in such blissful and joyous atmosphere.

Avery didn't mind even the dilapidated houses in the favela of Complexo do Alemão in Rio. At a distance, the coloring of the slums looked like hillside cottages to her. With Abbey, she toured the favelas with fervor, and learned to love the way locals fared.

There were close to 1000 hillside favelas in Rio, home to 20% of Rio's population. Riding the minivan through the area, Avery noticed the complex and multihued architecture; amidst it were vibrant commercial activities and friendly people going about their daily life.

"Welcome to our school." A samba dance school master greeted the tourists.

"Wow! Look at all the costumes and masks. Quite stunning." Someone in the crowd muttered, drawing everyone's attention to the display around the walls.

"Yes, we train most dancers that participate in the Carnival parade here in the favelas." The drummer Demetrio said proudly.

"So the people here can make a decent living performing in the parade?" Abbey asked.

"Not bad. Remember the Carnival takes place only once a year." Demetrio pointed out the seasonal industry's limit.

"So what do the musicians and dancers do the rest of the year?"

"We prepare for the Carnival all year round. People are poor so be careful of your wallets when you walk around the favelas." Demetrio warned half-jokingly.

Rio Carnival, a wild five-day celebration, at the beginning of Lent during the forty days before Easter. Roman Catholics and some other Christians traditionally abstained from the consumption of meat and poultry; the term "carnival," from carnelevare, "to remove or literally, to raise meat." Visiting the samba school gave Abbey and Avery a vivid picture of the revelry. And they were extra careful walking around the craft centers and establishments, heeding Demetrio's warning.

Ironically, Abbey was mugged later that evening, sauntering with Avery on the hip, upscale Ipanema Beach of Rio. He was robbed of the 170 Real he carried in his pocket, still a nuisance though his wallet was safe kept in the hotel room. Oddly the aggressor looked to be a uniformed security guard or policeman of some sort. The couple found out from the locals that it might very well be true that the robber was with the law enforcement. The community people generally feared the corrupt and violent police. Therefore, the Ministry of Justice created the National Public Security Force to respond to major emergencies and crises instead of the local squads. It's mind-boggling not knowing the good guys from the bad -- confusing, the system was.

For Abbey and Avery, Brazil's presence in international financial and commodities markets overrode its poverty or crime. The country was one of a group of four emerging economies called the BRIC countries, along with Russia, India and China. Avery thought that the word Ipanema was too romantic to encompass its indigenous meaning of "bad, dangerous waters." However perilous it was, Abbey and Avery played with the strong undertow and oversized waves crashing on the shore, with exuberance and enthusiasm like little children.

Europe

From the Roman remains of Hadrian's Wall, to the serene countryside of a classic seaside resort, and to London's remarkable theater, museum, and music scene, England was full of astounding variety. Abbey and Avery re-lived the most stimulating historical moments, laying their hands on the ancient megaliths of a 5000-year-old stone circle, walking the battlements of a medieval fortress, visiting the sites of the legend of King Arthur, Shakespeare's sonnets and the palaces of royals. They had a dose of modern architecture in Manchester, and explored the world's largest green house at Cornwall's Eden Project. They meandered through the hustle and bustle of the cities and got a little confused by the local Cockney accent. However varied the land was, they felt history emanating from every corner. That aura of its towns and villages, castles and cathedrals grown organically over many centuries, created for Abbey and Avery, myriads of calming settings for contemplation.

A Broken Society of England

Like all societies, England had its fair share of problems and issues: poor urban environments, drug abuse, teenage delinquency or pregnancy, family breakdown, welfare dependency, educational failure, the loss of traditional values, binge drinking or alcoholism. Tony Blair in 1995, called it "a broken society," and urged for a new civic society with everyone contributing and doing part. With the new development of Brexit where a 2016 referendum drew the legal framework for the country's withdrawal from the European Union, Abbey and Avery were curious to know what their London friends took away from the vote to leave.

Abbey and Avery questioned Joshua and Jess, the Londoners they met on previous travels in Central America, about Brexit.

"England is paying too much out to the EU, and not getting the return we need to see. Why remain when there's so much at stake and so little in return?" Joshua affirmed.

"Besides, the EU member states are vulnerable. Look at France, Belgium … it's scary. I don't think the EU plays a significant role for England's national security in any case." Jess added.

"It looks more like England needs to take care of domestic needs of democracy and economy." Abbey observed.

"I seem to see the EU becoming a benign power, and England itself faces the challenges from Scotland and Ireland...." Avery looked at what was happening in reality.

"The challenges are always there, and there's no sight of an economic downturn -- perhaps just a delay of spending." Joshua reasoned and speculated.

They concluded that Brexit was more like a symptom of European political and economic strains. The precipitous drop of the British Pound and England's financial uncertainty remained to be ridden out. All similar issues would have surfaced if Remain had won the vote. It was time for Joshua and Jess to focus on their homeland and worry about their own country's unity, whereas the world, waiting to see how the Great Britain could survive this wave of impasse.

The Scottish Tales of
Grey Friar's Bobby and
the Loch Ness Monster

Scotland was compact and stunningly beautiful with many treasures -- historic castles, enigmatic legends, great authors, spectacular wildlife, superb seafood, and hospitable people. The lochs, mountains, and every corner of the country bore stories and myths of their own. Avery particularly loved the Loch Ness Monster and the Greyfriar's Bobby. She appreciated how the tales of the magical monster or the loyal terrier were told from generation to generation, and still held so many meanings, brought so much inspiration for children in different parts of the world.

Abby and Avery spent a whole day at the tavern named after Robert Burns, appreciating everything that signified

Edinburgh or Scotland: the Royal Mile, the festivals, the haunted closes, the whisky, the witchery, tweed, and tartan -- although after sampling, they determined that haggis, neeps, and tatties were "acquired tastes" -- too Scottish for their American tastes.

They roamed the streets of Edinburgh and found gems everywhere. The Scottish parliament building was designed by Catalan architect Enric Miralles (1955–2000). It represented a "flower of democracy rooted in Scottish soil," and was strikingly noticeable. It's different. It's pleasant -- and like the whole city, it's entirely Scottish and strikingly captivating.

Lyrical Ireland

Ireland's unvarnished lyrical quality earned the country its much-deserved reputation. The Irish people were informal, poetic, welcoming, and ready to share moments irrespective of where one's origin was, what one's politics were and how one worshiped. A small country with the biggest heart, it manifested its own national identity with timeless landscapes, good spirits and humanities.

Taw fall-cha row-at, "You're very welcome." Or, more famously, céad míle fáilte, "a hundred thousand welcomes." Those were the phrases Abbey and Avery treasured and tried to master. They discovered that Irish camaraderie was infinitely complex, it was moderated and expressed in an altruistic manner that brought about comfort for all involved. Abbey, being of Irish and Swiss descent, connected really well with the Irish fellowship, and Avery loved the age-caressed literary scene. James Joyce's depiction of the Dubliners, Oscar Wilde's theater, and Seamus Heaney's poetry, spoke not only of the Irish spirit and soul, but also generosity of spirit that validated universal wisdom and insight.

Throughout their travels in Ireland, they were overwhelmed by the cultural choices the country had to offer: a play in Dublin, a music session in a pub, or a gig on the sidewalk. Trinity College, founded in 1592 by Queen Elizabeth, was home to the gloriously illuminated Book of Kells. They observed in awe how this institution continued to make its mark in the 21st century. The architecture of the Dublin Castle or any random building engraved in them a slice of the truly candid Ireland. Awash with feeling and thoughts, Abbey and Avery took their understanding of a people and culture all to heart.

France's Artistic Pedigree

France had a familiarity that derived from instantly recognizable icons such as the Eiffel Tower and the Avenue des Champs-Élysées, along with exquisite cuisine, stylish boutiques and priceless artistic assets. Abbey and Avery sauntered along the Place de la Concorde and the Place Charles de Gaulle, where the Arc de Triomphe was located. They soaked up the blend of history and modern living, visited numerous art nouveau cafes along the Seine, and stayed a whole day with the gargoyles, relics, artifacts, and saints and spirits of the majestic Notre Dame Cathedral.

Among the flawlessly prepared and presented food and wine, Abbey was particularly taken by the delicious patisseries of all sorts. Avery as always, loved to browse emerging or established boutiques and flagship haute couture, and found many fabulous buys at concept stores, quirky shops, malls, flea markets, as well as art nouveau department stores. They each discovered their favorites and enjoyed this seductive city tremendously.

They both valued the country's artistic pedigree -- Picasso, Van Gogh, Renoir, Rodin, Monet, Manet, and Dalí. The Louvre was splendid not only because of the exceptional impressionist collection inside, but of the ingenious work of its Chinese American designer, the renowned architect I. M. Pei. The Centre Pompidou's industrial appeal was incomparable, with a trove of modern and contemporary art that reminded Avery of her days spent in New York's art studios, cocktail galleries, exhibitions, performances, cinemas and all sorts of entertainment venues. Former French President Georges Pompidou wanted an ultra-contemporary artistic hub, and prize-winning architects Renzo Piano and Richard Rogers magically presented this premier cultural center in 1977. It provided an enormous public space, full of life and energy.

Abbey and Avery learned that Gustave Eiffel designed and built the 320m-tall signature spire of Eiffel Tower as a temporary exhibit for the 1889 World's Fair. The tower was so popular that it survived to this day and became the most important icon of Paris, or France for that matter. Then the same architect and civil engineer was commissioned to design the magnificent 1836 monument to Napoléon's victory at Austerlitz in 1805. All the symbols and icons had so many enlightening stories behind, that Abbey and Avery felt immensely inspired during each day spent in France. With gratitude and awareness of the beautiful world they lived in, they left Paris for Brussels, bracing for more cultural nourishment.

Belgium's Quirky Mannekin Pis

The fact the Belgium had sixty-plus UNESCO (the United Nations Educational, Scientific, and Cultural Organization) sites, gave memorable impressions about the country. The strong social support systems afforded liberal attitudes, a vibrant theatrical and artistic life, divine beers, and fabulous food. The City of Brussels, capital of Belgium and administrative center of the EU, charmed with its Flemish and French community specific authorities, united in the embodied essence of a European city: historically profound, culturally rich, and intellectually stimulating.

The road signs in both Flemish Dutch and French took Abbey and Avery to Brussels' most iconic landmark: a tiny statue of a boy urinating (the Mannekin Pis), which they had made acquaintance with via a replica in front of the D Casino in Las Vegas. The D Casino's Belgium born owners were apparently advertising their country people's attitude to authority. Abbey and Avery were very fond of the enduring deadpan humor, and enjoyed much of the city's contradictory mishmash. In a quirky Victor Horta type of Art Nouveau building, Abbey and Avery found the historic context: the World War II devastated capital, built with rampant postwar redevelopment. They only hoped that the city would fortify itself to withstand, the unchecked assaults from ISIS or any underhanded intimidations.

From Brussels, Abbey and Avery journeyed to the UNESCO World Heritage-listed city of Bruges. Medieval Bruges boasted charming canal ways, cobbled streets, and centuries of history. They started their walking tour by the delightful waters of the famous Minnewater (Lake of Love), and lingered at Our Lady's Church -- home to Michelangelo's magnificent 16th-century marble statue, Madonna of Bruges --

and the Market Square with its grand Belfry. They loved how tranquil and beautiful the place was. The traditional European cafes along the winding alleyways kept them wander for hours, before they were willing to conclude their visit, and depart the country of Belgium with tender mind and soul.

Belgium's Mannekin Pis

The Legendary Paprika Country
of Hungary

Hungary's unique cuisine or landscape had an overall European feel, yet distinctive in its own ways. Hungarian food was more than goulash, and it involved the most sophisticated styles of cooking. According to Abbey and Avery's Magyar friends, there were three essential world cuisines: French, Chinese and their own. True or false, one had to give credits to the country's world-renowned wines -- from the big-bodied reds of Villány and white Olazrizling from Badacsony, to honey-gold Tokaj. All varieties tasted delicious and uniquely Hugarian.

As legend had it, Hungary was an architectural treasure trove, with everything from Roman ruins and medieval town houses to baroque churches, neoclassical public buildings and Art Nouveau bathhouses and schools. Budapest, Szeged, Kecskemét, Debrecen, and Sopron, all had very impressive architecture. Abbey and Avery learned that Hungarians had being utilizing 300 thermal springs since the ancient times, for therapeutic, medicinal and recreational uses. The hot spring venues ranged from authentic bathhouses dating from the Turkish occupation and Art Nouveau palaces, to clinical sanatoriums, or facilities where clear chlorinated waters in organically-shaped pools that bubbled, squirted and spurted at different rhythms and temperatures alongside the requisite wellness center offering a myriad of treatments and services.

Abbey and Avery took their thermal baths, and hung out at pools in the northern end of City Park, the Széchenyi Baths. The place was unusually immense (with fifteen indoor pools and three outdoor); its bright, clean atmosphere made the water temperatures of up to 38°C viable and wholesome. They played chess on floating boards while snow dusted the treetops in City Park. They chatted with the locals and tourists, and found the city's inhabitants surprisingly consisted of varied people from all over the world.

Ohannes and Taguhi moved to Budapest from Armenia to operate a business in the tourist industry upon Hungary's capitalist transition in 1989. Their son Saam, as a hotel concierge, helped Abbey and Avery with many travel details, while Saam's wife Idella, sold merchandise to Avery in Budapest's fabulous Central Market Hall. Chatting up with the old Armenian couple, Abbey and Avery learned about their struggle in the country.

"When we first moved here, there were no jobs. We used everything we had to run this hotel." Ohannes recollected.

"It's never easy. See now our three grandchildren have to work in Austria during the day, and drive home at night to the bordering city of Sopron in Hungary." Taguhi stressed that the economy in Hungary was failing the young.

"It's ok for them to see other parts of the world and be responsible for themselves." Avery suggested, the teacher in her preaching independence and self-fulfillment.

"Soon they should earn enough money and experience to become real business people." Ohannes was still under tremendous stress after all the years of operating the hotel.

"You are doing very well compared to the Roma people, who had already moved hundreds of times before they came to Budapest." Abbey reminded Ohannes of the much discriminated population in Hungary. Roma people, aka the Gypsies, were persecuted, underprivileged, and discriminated against throughout various parts of the world for centuries.

Yes, compared to many people in the world, Abbey and Avery felt very fortunate and grateful that their life's journey had taken them through so many countries and allowed them to meet wonderful peoples and learn precious lessons of life. They spent numerous evenings with the two generations of Armenian couples, telling their life adventures and picking one another's brain.   Very much cleansed and rested, they enjoyed the relaxation Hungary had to offer, and prepared themselves for the exotic and exciting Southern Europe.

Danube River, Budapest

Gaudi's Architecture, Spain

What Spain Taught Avery

Barcelona and
La Sagrada Família

Sophisticated, and lively, Spain was more diverse than Avery imagined, like many other European countries. Avery caught herself illusively expecting a homogeneous Europe. Her presumed image of Europe failed to filter in the substantially increased immigration. On a postcard with pictures of La Sagrada Família, she wrote to friends back in the US:

> Barcelona certainly is vibrant, full of culture and life. Here's Gaudi's famous architecture; you'll have to see the details yourselves -- it's striking! Although Spanish and other unfamiliar languages spoken here were not the most elegant singsong to our ears, we're enjoying saying 'No comprendo' to strangers. People here are busy, not all cordial or friendly but bearably polite. We're staying in the city for another three days and headed to Madrid to see more art and architecture. From there we may take a jaunt to Bilbao for Frank Gehry's Guggenheim Museum, and hopefully taste a bit of the Spanish country life....

Avery realized that she needed to learn to appreciate that element of cacophony and diversity in Barcelona, just like much of the world needed to see her as she was, a US citizen, albeit an immigrant woman from Taiwan. If she couldn't be comfortable as she was, who would? If she herself was confused about her own identity -- how could she tell her stories as they were? She knew that she must adjust and grow her mindset, so that she could live her life as it was. She recognized that she must embrace all countries and all peoples as they were, so that she could revel in whatever the world had to offer, wherever she traveled to, whenever life unfolded for her.

Avery visited La Sagrada Família with a newly acquired sense of clarity and joy. Abbey shared her frame of mind and joined in to examine the architecture with awe. They were mesmerized by its sheer structure, in the style of the medieval cathedrals. It's still under construction after more than 100 years. The Temple Expiatori de la Sagrada Família (Expiatory Temple of the Holy Family) became Antoni Gaudi's all-consuming obsession. Gaudi saw it as his holy mission: to build the temple as atonement for the city's sins of modernity. For Abbey and Avery, Gaudi's mission was accomplished, through the reverence and devotion his majestic endeavor inspired.

Madrid and
the Ancient Towns

Flying into Madrid, Abbey and Avery watched a beguiling city coming alive and learned how to live among its exciting streets. The Passion in the fabric of daily life was palpable, with music and art in its veins. Its open arms to people from all over the world manifested in the phrase: "if you're in Madrid, you're from Madrid."

Abbey held Avery's hand through buildings of artistic pedigree that formed the backdrop of the city life, from medieval mansions and royal palaces to Spanish contemporary architecture, from brickwork and slate spires of Madrid baroque to the extravagant belle époque. The Museo del Prado, Centro de Arte Reina Sofía and Museo Thyssen-Bornemisza all housed impressive collections that took them days to explore. They felt reprieved when done with the jangles of a big city, taking day trips to the ancient towns of Chinchon and Toledo.

Chinchon and Toledo,
A Timeless Spain

The small town of Chinchon was pleasantly full of tempting and beautiful restaurants in its main plaza, the gorgeous Plaza Mayor, which despite the name "main square" was actually surrounded by lovely green and white facades and small balconies that formed a round circle. Abbey and Avery walked the narrow streets leading off the plaza and found each home decorated with charming saint medallions on the front door. They sauntered up to the old clock tower to view the entire town, admiring its sweetness and tranquility.

Toledo was the monumental ancient city of Spain, a captivating UNESCO World Heritage Site. Abbey and Avery were determined to find their way in a labyrinth of winding pedestrian streets, to discover important historical landmarks in the country. The legacy of the past was embroidered everywhere on the stone buildings and cobble streets, on the dazzling array of churches, convents, synagogues, mosques, palaces, and fortresses. Avery bought too many souvenirs with art works displayed -- including metal charms and wooden coasters that were supposed to help her take home pieces of the city's churches, convents, and the renowned El Greco Museum.

Spain's landscapes were as diverse as the peoples of the country. Abbey and Avery hit the wildly beautiful cliffs of the Atlantic northwest, as well as the charming coves of the Mediterranean. They saw pleasant villages of a timeless Spain everywhere, perching on hilltops, huddling in valleys, or clinging to coastal ridges. Roman ruins, cathedrals, and Islamic architecture revealed that a great civilization had risen, fallen, and made indelible marks.

Abbey and Avery loved the tapas dishes that signified Spain's varieties and ranges. It became their tradition back home in America to visit a restaurant every Wednesday for happy hours and tapas. Additionally, Avery adored the rebellious and creative spirit of Spain's great masters: Francisco Goya, Salvador Dali, Pablo Picasso, and Antoni Gaudi. They were past and present, they were the future, and they were front and center in the country's public image, one that was modern and at the same time, deeply rooted in history.

Greek Cities of the Titans
and their Predicament

Greece was one of Abbey's favorites. With his dark hair and features, he had passed as a Greek spending his youthful days along the endless coastline, rambling through sun-bleached ancient ruins, sipping ouzos at local restaurants. With his company, Avery quickly became acquainted with the melancholic throb of rembetika (blues songs) and the longtime anticipated ancient sites of mythical gods and giants. Together, they encountered thought-provoking modern art and vivacious contemporary music, stumbling across galleries, live music, and impressively modern museums in the least expected places.

Abbey loved the tang of home-made tzatziki and the aroma of grilled souvlaki. With basic ingredients like feta and olive oil, the Greeks made any regional dishes and styles of cooking a culinary joy. It's particularly astonishing for Avery to witness the details of the Greek life, as she had valued how important of a contribution the country made to modern cuisine, democracy, politics, philosophy, literature, arts, and sports. The Parthenon, not only epitomized the glory of Ancient Greece, but also represented for Avery, a sacred image that bred civilizations. Her World Literature class would not have been appealing without her showing the marble-white structure and telling stories of the Titans, gods, goddesses, and humans who intricately weaved the myth of western civilization, ever-pervading and intertwined in a remarkably beautiful world.

Parthenon, Greece

Once the cradle of civilizations, Greece nowadays faced many problems, its economic predicament, most unsettling. Abbey and Avery watched eight university workers going on strike to oppose the dismissal of thousands of administrative staff. The Education Ministry's measures had fallen short of the principles of a democratic society. Abbey and Avery found it unnerving and struck a conversation with the inhabitants of the city.

"Why is this happening? So many people are losing jobs and health insurances?" Avery asked the friendly locals.

"The school officials did not give the government a list of people to dismiss. And now the government is taking legal action against the staff." A man named Nikolos replied tersely.

"What is the staff's story?" Abbey wanted the details.

"The strike is directed at plans to increase the country's property tax. The tax applies to many workers. People are having a real hard time in this dire economy."

"We heard that hospital workers are also opposing the dismissal of employees and the closure or merger of hospitals."

"Our health system is already on the verge of collapse. Hospitals lack the most basic materials, and 40 percent of workers in Greece have no health insurance." Nikolos frowned and signed, his melancholy eyes searching for support and understanding.

"We have borrowed so much from the IMF and ECB that they needed to see massive downsizing." A young student named Kora explained, looking distraught.

"Greece is very cheap for tourists now. Do you see an increase of visitors?"

"It's always a popular tourist spot. The country would not save itself from a bankruptcy because people come or don't come now." Nicolos suggested.

"What do you think the country needs to focus on?"

"Everything. Agriculture, tourism, banking... fixing redundant administration and officials...."

With unemployment rising to a rate of over 25 percent, Greece was in a really sticky situation and needed more emergency loans. According to calculations, Greece would experience a shortfall of at least €6.6 billion (US$8.9 billion) between 2014 and 2016. Abbey and Avery could discern the tragic outcome of Greece's dilemma: the authoritarian tendencies of the state apparatus. Systematic development of the fascist Golden Dawn party by the police and army was under way. The Greek government justified its forceful measures of suppressing protests and demonstrations, as well as Golden Dawn's organized activities. It wasn't pretty -- Avery feared for Greece, and prayed that the crisis would lead to opportunities. It's time to seize the opportu-nities to turn things around, to cleanse and improve this ancient, ill-faring regime.

When Soul Awakened in Italy

Italy was an extraordinary feast of arts, cuisine, history, and landscapes. This land of Dante, Verdi, Titian, Michelangelo, Raphael, Botticelli, da Vinci and birthplace of the Roman Empire and Renaissance was coveted beyond the galleries, museums, cathedrals, frescoes, paintings, and life as art itself. It was also home of fashion labels like Prada, Armani, Fendi, Salvatore Ferragamo, Valentino, Versace, Gucci and many others. Its geography offered remarkable diversity: from the north's frosty Alps and glacial lakes to the south's volcanic craters and turquoise grottoes, with stunning cityscapes and country villas in between. Abbey and Avery tasted this nation of Gualtiero Marchesi and watched its splendor and flair furnish in every way of the Italian bella vita.

The Breakup in Rome

Rome was so overwhelming and thrilling with rich history and culture that Abbey had to invite his children to join them on the trip he called the "journey of magnificence."

"My kids are coming; I am excited." Abbey announced to Avery out of the blue.

"Oh, you didn't tell me. Was it planned? Ethan called two days ago." Avery was surprised to hear.

"Why did Ethan call you?" Abbey seemed to want his children to himself and was insecure about losing their affection to his divorce.

"Oh because you were occupied with work and he could not get hold of you. I didn't know your kids are coming though. They didn't tell me." Avery was taken aback.

"Yes, they are coming to join us. Hope you don't mind." Abbey intoned.

"Of course not" muttered Avery, feeling a bit confused.

Thanks to Rome's many World Heritage Sites, Abbey and Avery dived into the fascinating Pantheon, into its massive dimensions and magnificent dome, before any more confusion infiltrated or tension surfaced upon Claire and Ethan's arrival.

Pantheon, Rome

Colosseum, Rome

Avery praised the wonderful structure: "The ancient Romans' cupola was the largest in the world -- until the 15th century that was."

"See how symmetrical it is -- its diameter is exactly equal to the Pantheon's interior height of 43.3m." Abbey pointed out.

They met Claire and Ethan at the entrance of Rome's gladiatorial arena, the 50,000-seat Colosseum. Avery tensed up at the sight of Abbey's two grown children screaming "Dad, Dad," and running in full speed toward Abbey to embrace him.

"We wanted to change our hotel to yours. Could you do it, dad?" Claire announced immediately after she hugged Abbey.

"Yes when we finish visiting this place, I can do that." Abbey proposed to tour the site first while they were there.

"You don't like where you're staying?" Avery tried making conversations with Claire and Ethan -- so that she could feel less embarrassed and uncomfortable about the way Claire talked to her Dad, ignoring Avery.

Claire, not looking at Avery, stated: "It's better we are in the same hotel so we can take some family photos of me and you and Ethan all together."

"It's nicer over there at your hotel, Dad." Ethan backed his older sister up.

Avery felt Abbey's children's intention to leave her out, but kept her pleasantries: "Look over here...." She was interrupted before completing her sentence.

"Look inside. Tiered seating encircled the arena, and down there they caged animals and prepared stage sets. The fighting took place right here." Claire expounded rapidly and led the party of four to a tour guide who she had commissioned to explain details of the arena. Abbey and Avery went along and listened to Giovanni the tour guide:

"Titus held games that lasted 100 days and nights at its inauguration. Some 5000 animals were slaughtered. Trajan later held a marathon 117-day killing spree involving 9000 gladiators and 10,000 animals." He depicted the gory picture with a loud clear voice, as if cheering for the games of carnage.

"The Colosseum's outer walls have three levels of arches, framed by decorative columns topped by capitals of the Ionic order at the bottom, Doric and Corinthian orders at the top. Covered in travertine and marble statues, the columns fill the niches on the 2nd and 3rd levels. The upper level, laced with windows and slender Corinthian pilasters, supports the awning over the arena. The 80 entrance arches, known as vomitoria, allow spectators to enter and be seated efficiently in a matter of minutes."

With attentiveness, Abbey learned the Roman architecture from Giovanni. He thanked Claire for arranging a guide: "Thanks to my smart darling daughter -- we learned a great deal today."

When the four of them arrived at Abbey and Avery's hotel room, Claire urged Abbey to change hers and Ethan's accommodation arrangements. Meanwhile, their luggage had been moved to the room, and they went straight to showers and to bed. "Dad, we are very tired. Going to crash in your bed. Good night."

Left hanging with the room changes and phone calls to make, Abbey spent hours talking to travel agents and hotel bookers. Avery, startled to learn her husband's way of adoring his children and obliging their requests, waited and wondered how she would call it a night with Abbey's two grown children sleeping on her bed. She started to straighten up the mess of laundry Claire and Ethan left on the floor of her hotel room.

Claire suddenly talked in her sleep: "Shhh... those are my clothes. Don't you dare touch them."

Avery halted not knowing how to respond or what to say.

Abbey intervened: "Don't worry about the clothes. They will do their laundry when they get up tomorrow morning. Don't put them away, please."

"Dad, did you find rooms for us yet?" Claire demanded.

"I am working on it." Almost sheepishly, Abbey indicated his efforts and busied himself with more phone calls.

"We need the rooms by tomorrow morning because I have a photo shoot arranged for me, you and Ethan in the city center tomorrow afternoon. Have to freshen up properly." Claire further mandated, and then went back to sleep.

"I will read downstairs in the lobby." Avery started feeling edgy, ready for a breather.

By the time Abbey came down to get her, Avery was well into page 143 of her book. She looked at the clock in the lobby: 3:00 in the morning. Waiting for Abbey to explain his children's sudden appearance, Avery hoped to hear that her husband would advise his children to include her in their arrangements of activities in Rome.

"Well I finally locate two rooms for these kids. Damn these hotels. I don't understand why it's so hard to make changes." Abbey pronounced his victory over hotel red tape.

"It's last minute. They have to go by the bookings." Avery said matter-of-factly.

"I should be able to make changes I need to. It shouldn't be this hard."

"You mean your children should be able to…, and they should…."

"What? Do you have a problem with their visit?" Abbey was oversensitive and defensive.

"No, it's just that they butt in like that…." Avery still hoped to be comforted and reassured in some way.

"I am happy with their visit, just so you know." That was Abbey being offensive.

"I know. So where are we sleeping tonight?" Avery wanted some relief from the day, and was slightly annoyed by her husband's leniency. He would do whatever his children asked him to do, right or wrong, good or bad.

"I don't know. But parents sacrifice. That's what parents do." Abbey further indulged in his love for the children.

"Claire is 24, and Ethan 19. Don't you think they could be a bit more responsible for arranging their travels?" Avery was baffled and became ill at ease.

"I have no problems helping out my kids when they need me." Abbey justified.

"Ok how about our itinerary tomorrow?" Avery desired that Abbey could stick up for her and teach his children how to regard her. She felt rejected and excluded, although in reality, she would rather explore Rome than worry about them.

"I can use some time with my kids now that they are here." Abbey claimed, nearly exploding when his kids were not indulged as precious Prince and Princess.

Abandoned and devastated, Avery suddenly needed everything and everyone to disappear. She needed herself to vanish, to dissolve, into a destruction that would have to happen to enable her and her husband to face each other again.

"I will go to Florence and the rest of Italy by myself." Avery made up her mind.

"Why? You can't give me one day with my kids?"

Abbey went off with an acerbic comeback, as he usually got wary when he wasn't exactly sure how to mingle his wife and his kids. Avery would have felt much more comfortable if she was informed of their visit, and so was prepared for the change of her travel itineraries or arrangements. It bothered her that Abbey often went behind her to arrange activities and expected her to go along with "the family" or to feel fine left alone by herself without notice.

"No please go ahead enjoy your time with your children." Avery mumbled, but screamed in her mind: "Yes, love your children, your family. Forget your wife, who is not quite as important as your blood family, right?"

"If that's what you want, I will cut my trip short and return to the States to work earlier." Abbey was vindictive at this point.

"Ok." Avery made a terse sound, shut down and speechless about the turns this conversation took.

Wiped into a realm painfully nameless and undefined, Avery was humiliated, devastated, and annihilated by her husband's anger and her own indignation. She went on to Florence and Milan with a broken heart, thinking she would not return to Abbey -- at least for a little while.

The Magic of Florence

Standing on a bridge over the Arno River, Avery's mood calmed and her view loomed large on the cradle of the Renaissance, Florence (Firenze). So striking and magnetic was the cityscape that she cheered up considerably. Florence's magic imparted upon her the ability to forget the pettiness of her family problems. She admired how the coloring of pietra serena, pietraforte and pietra bigia could render such rich hues: pink, green, white, red, brown and gray on the Florentine palette which at a distance, painted a picturesque masterpiece too sublime for words. She lunged into the city's intricacy with gumption and resourcefulness that could only be gathered when she was alone by herself.

Covered with Filippo Brunelleschi's red-tiled cupola, Duomo was a staggering edifice whose breathtaking multi-colored marble facade and campanile towered the medieval landscape with grace and preeminence. Architect Arnolfo di

Cambio began work in 1296, and it took 150 years to reach it consecration in 1436. Avery examined the interior frescoes by Vasari and Zuccari, which presented fascinating ever-changing visuals through the lights from the stained-glass windows. She felt she could rise to a limitless space through those ethereal lights, flying freely to the sky.

The U-shaped Palazzo degli Uffizi gallery was another awe-inspiring structure, built between 1560 and 1580, and now housed Renaissance art collections and government offices. Avery had to see the famous Piero della Francesco's profile portraits of the Duke and Duchess of Urbino, and the masterpieces by Sandro Botticelli, Leonardo da Vinci, Michelangelo and more. She spent a whole afternoon viewing the paintings, and left for the rooftop cafe with a divine sense of revelation, too magical for words.

Fresh air and marvelous Tuscany vistas allowed Avery to recollect her thoughts. She thought about what qualities of Abbey she appreciated and what traits she disliked -- what in her attracted Abbey and what might push him away. What needed to be cherished were their similar virtues that converged and made them fall in love and decide to have a life together in the first place: compassion for others and generosity of spirit. She had shared and given much of what she could for Abbey and his children. Her open heart was forced to lock away when ripped with much antagonism and rivalry, sealed along with her initial attempts to treat Abbey's children as her own. They were not hers and would never be.

She would express her opinions, state her standpoints, and let Abbey be the kind of parent he needed to be, but she would not lose herself in playing a role she could never win approval for. She would give space and stay at a distance. She would focus on herself and what she hoped for her own life. Only when she took care of herself, could she attend to others' needs and wants. She would not permit her world to turn topsy-turvy and she would treat herself well and show the world how to treat her. She needed to be selfish and love herself first in order to remain generous or magnanimous. She needed to stay in the course of her purposes -- she needed to enjoy her trip and return to Abbey with certainty.

Growth from Destruction, Surviving Milan

So with growth from destruction, Avery went to Milan and lived to tell the tale. The internationally recognized arbiter of taste in fashion and design was seething with vitality matched by few other cities. Avery seized the serious sense of a presence beneath the veneer of glamour and wealth. She visited the grand Gothic cathedral, the Duomo designed by Giangaleazzo Visconti in 1386, and found the power that drove the city of Milan. Adorned with 135 spires and 3400 statues on the façade, the cathedral was very much a symbol of Milan's ambition and extravagancy. She also went on a shopping spree, and attended an opera at La Scala, the prestigious mark of Leonardo da Vinci's virtuoso and ingenuity. At the end of her stay in Milan, she was exhausted with the elaborate details. And, she survived -- she survived the sulfurous phony play of the world; she grabbed the core of life and gave the rest its peace. She would forgive; she would not hold grudges. She would let Abbey be. She would let her brand of a family be.

Venice and
a Mural Remembered

Awaken with self-awareness, Avery would not leave Italy without visiting the city of Venice. Venice had been in her list of places to explore since Tim her ex-husband painted a vivid mural of the city on a closet door of her New York apartment. In the city of marble palaces built on a lagoon, everything was tantalizing and fascinating: produce, seafood, spices, garden islands, and cicheti (Venetian tapas). Avery took in the scenery and architecture along the Grand Canal, and was particularly fond of the narrow backstreets where tourists gathered around neighborhood churches to observe local creations and customs beyond Roman or Venetian influence.

Italy was too brilliant and exceptionally beautiful for Avery to stay in a sour mood. She returned home to Abbey with joy and love, and her husband, in turn, gave her the warmest heartfelt welcome home. He said he missed her and would always love her deeply. They went out to Avery's beloved neighborhood restaurant and had a candle-lit dinner that was so romantic and wonderful that the staff had to assume it was their wedding anniversary and sent them a lovely cake on the house. They would go on another tour to Asia together the following summer. Life, with each other's sweet companion, continued to entail pleasant discoveries and meaningful pursuits.

Chapter 11. Home in Asia

Over the years, Avery's parents moved out of Taipei, the city where Avery spent her youth. Her parents lived in Hong Kong for a while, and then returned to their ancestors' home in western Taiwan. Avery's oldest sister, Xiangyu, moved to Canton, China with her husband; Yiwen, the second oldest, in central Taiwan; her brother Weicheng, in the southern tip of Taiwan, and Avery, her husband, her step-kids and her students, in Las Vegas in America. Grandma Great-Aunt-Tigress passed away some fifteen years before, and her cousins from Auntie Ah-ying were all studying in New York, whereas her nieces, nephews, and Abbey's family, in California, Ireland, Canada, and Australia. It's never easy to have a reunion with her family, or to see any of her childhood friends. Wenlian was working at an art gallery in Taipei last she knew of, and Jinglin, a happy wife and mother of two in Hualian.

It would take Avery to travel back to Taiwan to see her parents. Before she married Abbey, her trip to Taiwan was lonesome, and often brought memories of old wounds and hurts. She had to find the conduit to let it out and heal.

Things at home weren't always pink and fluffy. The freedom Avery's family bestowed on her could be deciphered as something completely different, at times when she felt helpless and ousted from her adopted home in American. She wondered if whatever she did ever mattered to her family at all. She was competitive by nature and wanted to be the best in all aspects. Perhaps that temperament stemmed from a deep root of insecurity -- she thought people around her would love her more if she did well and really proved herself a winner in all contests.

Escaping the Metamorphosis

Avery's mother called Avery "arrogant" when she earned more certificates or awards, putting them up on the wall. Avery would never forget how she was in tears of anger when her mom and her second oldest sister Yiwen made fun of her, and how she was always criticized: the way she dressed, the way her eyes were too big and un-Chinese, the way her features and coloring denoted foreignness of a halfie, or the way she slouched to show her "cockroach-flat" belly. It seemed part of her culture for parents to communicate negative feedback in order to push their children to do better. Whatever Avery had accomplished was never enough or was commented with indifferent or unconstructive remarks.

She realized why she often had this trodden feeling inside her; it was as horrid as the isolation and vulnerability Herr Gregor Samsa in Kafka's *The Metamorphosis* experienced. There she was, like a clumsy flat-bellied bug failing to please her mother, or fulfil the filial duty of being humble in front of her. Ever since then, she's had a phobia of cockroaches like no one else. She took off screaming all the way to the streets when she spotted a cockroach on the twentieth floor of a building; she covered her eyes running and begged anyone nearby to get rid of the bug -- as if by keeping it out of sight, she could somehow escape the damnation of a metamorphosis.

Uproars and Thunders of Sentiments

Avery's father was poetic yet militant at the same time. He would punish his children when they fought, having them stand facing each other to take turns slapping each other's face, until they burst into tears or laughter and then made up. He would have them all kneel on their knees for hours on end, or do lots of jumping jacks until they begged him to release them. His children worshiped him when he was in good spirits, but exercised extra caution to shun away when he drank rice wine and cracked peanuts all by himself. They could sense a perfect storm coming when their father cursed in fervent and profane terms to beat the uproars and thunders of sentiments within him. They knew very well that oftentimes he wasn't really drunk; he was just jiejiu zhuangfeng, fanning craziness in the name of rice wine.

Avery's father was not usually in a dandy mood about her little brother. Her brother Weicheng was perpetually falling out of a tree, stepping barefoot on broken pieces of glass, and once nearly split his head open, hanging, tumbling upside down from a shelve. He was often grounded for not doing his homework right. Weicheng always cried and smeared his workbook too scrappily to have any clear ideas what he was doing with his schoolwork. He got punished for that but he was never chided for bringing home assortments of teenage girlfriends -- and later, girlfriends at different stages. While Avery and her sisters weren't permitted to even talk to boys prior to college, Weicheng got away with his promiscuity. Her parents, like many older generations of Chinese people, considered daughters to belong to others' families upon marriages, and sons, encouraged to experience as many love interests as they could in order to choose their best mates. Chinese parents all had to have sons, and deemed it necessary for sons to date around to pick the best daughters-in-law. Daughters were not expected to see the world, travel far, or have their own ways of life other than how their fathers or husbands chose to live. In China, some even killed or abandoned baby girls to ensure their sons survived the one-child policy from 1978 to 2015. Avery considered herself lucky to be born in Taiwan, the "alternate version" of China.

The One Who Got Away

Avery got away as the neighbors from the house-with-two-neighborhoods predicted. She traveled the world before she landed in New York City to attend Columbia University. She held different posts before settling to being a teacher. She divorced Tim her first husband to pursue a life without putdowns. She dated various men before she found her second husband Abbey. She escaped the metamorphosis or the sentimental uproars and thunders imposed upon her. She refused to be treated like a second-class citizen by her step-kids, her students, or anyone else -- grown-ups or children, to be or not to be educated. She demanded fair attention and an honest share of a good life. She learned, progressed, and would always seek growth, warmth and love from the world that she so faithfully treasured and valued.

On the trip back to Asia, Avery fought off her homesickness by talking more than usual to her fellow travelers. However ambivalent she was about her home of origin, she knew she would cry if she didn't try distracting herself from the thought of it. She had to chat up strangers and occupy herself with gossips to halt her train of thought.

Nibil was a French Moroccan sitting next to Avery on the flight from Seoul to Taipei. He worked for a shipping company as a Trade Line Manager and lived in Shanghai, soon to be relocated to Florida. He was readily available for a chit-chat with her.

Traveling for his job to Taiwan, he said, "It's impossible to have a stable relationship when you immerse so in the job and travel that long and frequently."

"You're young, and will have plenty of time before you settle," Avery suggested.

"How about you? Are you married?" Nibil wanted to know more about her.

"Once divorced, and too agonized to settle or marry for now."

"Well, there goes my chance of a future wife!" He flirted with Avery, eyeing her pretty face and figure.

"Just bide your time. You will find the right one." She proffered optimism.

Avery told Nibil about Taiwan, about how it's much more westernized than China and how the people were friendly and open to western ideas, though rooted in Chinese traditions. Feeling almost like a civilian ambassador of both Taiwan and America, she was glad to show hospitality and cordiality to the fellow traveler.

Nibil emailed Avery later when he got back to Shanghai, telling her about how he had a good time in the places she suggested him to visit in Taiwan and how he looked forward to visiting the United States and maybe meeting up with her.

Avery's second oldest sister Yiwen and her husband were coming to pick Avery up at the Taipei/Taoyuan Airport. Avery wondered how Yiwen'd changed since the last time they saw each other had been three years before. Going through immigration and exchanging currencies, Avery saw how coming home as a US citizen had little impact on her identity as a Taiwanese. After all, the people who waited at the terminal for her were her family and they were a hundred percent Taiwanese, no matter how far away and how long apart Avery had lived from them.

Yiwen and Avery embraced and Avery noticed how they both had aged -- slightly yet shockingly aged, as if they had to grow old before actually growing up to know how to act perfectly as adults around their next-generation relatives. How they still thought of themselves as youngsters in their family.

How they realized they were replaced by their nieces and nephews: one new generation superseded the old one to become the key players and take the center stage of the world.

Their nephews and nieces were all in colleges or graduate schools. They mastered in warm, boisterousness, and constant wisecracking as the articulate technology-savvy young people in their generation mostly demonstrated. They chattered incessantly online via social media, or face to face with their elders and peers. Avery thought to keep up with the young, but keep within her boundaries. Changeover of generations was inevitable, and preservation of her sanity, imperative.

Visit to Indigenous Villages

Yiwen, her husband Yuefeng, and Avery went on an expedition to the indigenous villages in the southeast of Taiwan. Yiwen and Yuefeng had taken days off from work just to treat Avery for a trip to see how the countryside Taiwan had changed and developed. Wide-eyed and curious, Avery couldn't wait to see her familiar yet strange homeland.

Taiwan was actually greener than Avery remembered, perhaps because she used to live in the cities. Apart from the newly constructed highways leading to all parts of the island, the trees and fields alongside were ever fresh and emerald-like. She let her memories of Taiwan sift through the membrane of time, and took in what was there to be felt as her hometown.

Yuefeng and Yiwen worked at the same automobile company in Taiwan, Yuefeng as a regional sales director, and Yiwen, an accountant. Yuefeng chauffeured them around, but never stopped talking on the phone with his staff members about daily projections and sales and so on. Avery could sense the pressure from his work, and wondered how coincidently the Liang sisters were both involved with busy men in sales.

After six hours on the highway, they arrived at the Bunun Village. The village was built and supported by the Bunun Educational and Cultural Foundation, surprisingly scenic and well-established. Yiwen had been donating money to the Foundation, and so they were treated like royalty, staying at the most luxurious cabins, served gourmet food.

Among the twelve indigenous tribes in Taiwan, Bunun was small in population, but well-known for the Hongye Little League Baseball, the team that won the world championship for Taiwan in 1968. This team was composed of Bunun tribe aboriginal students from a primary school with fewer than 100 students, located in the isolated village of Hongye in Taitung County in southeastern Taiwan. Far from elite players from around the nation, the students used pebbles to practice, too poor for real gear.

Examining the artifacts in the museum located at Hongye Elementary School, Avery was astonished by how the baseball players had lived their lives and how they had worked menial jobs after the stardom. Taiwan after all, had not the American fervor and money for sports, and the players were not supported by corporations. Their legacy however, lived on in many households of Taiwan.

Avery learned about Alex Rodriguez and Jorge Pasada of the Yankees through watching the live broadcast games with her father in her parents' living room. If Hongye hadn't made such an impact on Taiwan life, her father would have never been keen to the Yankees' winning against the Red Sox, nor would she have learned of those two fellow New Yorkers forty years later from a TV set on the small island of Taiwan. Later, she would cheer with her husband Abbey Lori's cousins, visiting from San Francisco for the Giants in their house in Las Vegas. Her homes in Taiwan, New York, Las Vegas, and various places she stayed throughout the world, were interconnected -- through sports, among other human endeavors.

Taiwan, Interconnected yet Fragmented

Taiwan, as Chinese as it could be, was always receptive to western ideas, especially those from North America. Throughout their trip to the indigenous villages, Avery, her sister and brother-in-law, for some reason, were having endless discussions about Taiwan's identity. What was Taiwan? Certainly not Thai or Thailand as many Americans could mistake it to be. Taiwan, adjective: Taiwanese. Or could it be Chinese? Or Taiwanese Chinese? Where was Taiwan headed? How should Taiwan position itself in the international forum or the world stage, out of which China the PRC always tried squeezing the island country to claim its own sovereignty?

Avery was amused by how the western media created a ripple effect on Taiwan. After Iraqi journalist Muntadhar al-Zaidi threw both of his shoes at then-United States President George W. Bush during an Iraqi press conference on December 14, 2008, Taiwanese men became very fashion-conscious when it involved footwear. "Bush shoeing incident" actually started a fad of stylish and comfortable shoes for men. And during Obama's presidency, every household in Taiwan watched the live broadcast from the white house, featuring many orations by President Obama, including the one where he dexterously snatched a fly away from his face.

With the influx of western influences, Taiwan, on the other hand, also showed its adoration of traditional or vernacular culture. The biggest hit that summer was a movie depicting rural life of Taiwan. Wang Jianmin was one super hero, not any other from the Red Sox, Yankees, Giants or Blue Jays. As trendy as Taiwanese people could be, they loved their local dialects and preserved as much as they could, their own identity and brand of culture.

What's the mix of the East and the West in Taiwan revealing? If the island country was interconnected with the world, why did its society also display prevalent fragmented scenarios? Traditional images were interposed with abstract illustrations on city murals. Political meetings or debates were interjected by dialectics on China, Asia, America, or other international occurrences. The streets of Taipei City while vibrant and developed, were chaotic with maze-like structures and crawling scooters. There was hardly any sense of integrated identity to this island; it could amount to anything, everything, or nothing at all meaningful or decipherable.

Avery thought Taiwan was a postmodern Chinese world, like no other part of the Chinese communities in the world. It's modern, it's chic, and it's alienated, like Tsai Mingliang's movies; it's simultaneously nostalgic, aged, and traditional, like the Taiwanese play "Secret Love in Peach Blossom Land" in America's Oregon Shakespeare Festival Avery and Abbey stumbled upon many years later. The unique dimension and flavor of Taiwan was domestic, traditional, and at the same time, American, trendy, and international. Taiwan had always preserved what's only Taiwan could produce, however westernized the island had become.

Avery's brother-in-law saw things more from an economic standpoint and asked what industries Taiwan could focus on in order to compete in the globalized markets. Things were no longer "Made in Taiwan" but in China, and Taiwan's service industries were on the par with other state-of-the-art

157

technologies. Perhaps medicine and tourism? However, did the island have the infrastructure or the backbone for tourism? Where and how would Taiwan fare?

With legacies variedly rooted in traditions of China and indigenous tribes, Taiwan had its own unique existence on a tiny island, thriving with sophistication. It had created a vital democracy and liberal society. Its press was raucous and vociferous, with abundant evidence of preserved traditions: worship of ancestors, respect for the elderly or authority, and encouragement of optimism and moral teachings. On the other hand, the Taiwanese people's passion for protest manifested in Taipei's Main Station on most weekends, and the free press was not refraining from stirring up more noises and clamors.

This blend of tradition, modernization, and self-reinvention was also apparent in the people's religious practice. Taiwan was heir to the Chinese traditions of Buddhism, Taoism, and Confucianism. The amorphous deities and demons were worshipped as gods. Therefore, Taiwan's culture was very distinctive and tolerant of all faiths.

Equally varied and uniquely Taiwanese was the cuisine on the island. "Have You Eaten? Zya Ba Mei" -- the phrase as a greeting showed how ritual and ceremonial eating could be. Ang Lee's "Eat, Drink, Men, Women," was a hit in the States -- the movie's theme echoed the spirit of the country and communicated its essence. The gamut of Chinese cuisines, the best Japanese outside Tokyo, and a full-house of local specialties from Hakka stir-fries and Taipei beef noodles to aboriginal-style barbecued wild boar, all were irresistible and delicious. Avery missed the night markets which served endless feasts of snacks including stinky tofu, steamed dumplings, oyster omelets, shrimp rolls and shaved ice. Fresh local juices, "bubble teas," real Taiwanese teas and gourmet coffee, were available into the wee hours. Years after this solo trip to Asia, when she took her husband Abbey to visit Taiwan, he would experience firsthand, the power of Taiwanese feasting with her family.

On the international front, Taiwan proved to have developed and would continue to strategize its relationships with China and the world. Abbey and Avery would visit Avery's oldest sister Xiangyu, who had invested in their own business in Shenzhen, China, and lived on the mainland fulltime. Tsai Ing-wen, Taiwan's first female president in 2016 took her office before Hilary Clinton's campaign against Donald Trump.

Avery's sister Yiwen said that she didn't quite understand why a movie depicting rural life on Taiwan would have turned into such a big hit in Singapore. Avery perceived that to be exactly what the world needed: imagery of Taiwan, a picture that depicted Taiwan as it was, nothing less. Taiwan, to Avery, carried a postmodern Chinese facet, full of fragments as in the movies of Tasi Ming-Liang and the productions of Lai Sheng-chuan (Stan Lai). In its fragmentation, the people struggled to pinpoint what was theirs. They lived their lives in the ways they knew how, and the island however puny, in turn, provided them with a nest they called home.

The Asia Avery visited and kept in her heart was hers, and hers alone to treasure and remember -- fondly or with agony. Her sense of Taiwan or America, or a place in the world she called home, would come complete when Abbey accompanied her back to her country of birth years afterwards. Taiwan, America and the world were hers, and she savored each and every as home.

Chapter 12. Home in America with Abbey

Their Differences and Challenges

For Abbey and Avery, there lied the intrinsic differences between men and women, and between the west and the east. Those differences caused despairs and anguishes, in more instances than desired or necessary. Abbey overlooked Teacher's Appreciation Week or any significant days, and Avery grieved that she didn't get the kind expression of love she deserved, never mind the fact that her being a teacher had little bearings on her husband's appreciation for her. Abbey drove down the freeway having a fit about how other people drove, while sitting on the passenger seat, Avery was the only person in the whole world who could hear his tirades. Abbey joked around and imitated Asian accents with the aptitude of a Thespian talent, and Avery would be amused but at times, offended and hurt because of the context of their conversations. Avery required everyone in the house to be wearing "indoor slippers," and Abbey materialized in his dusty workout shoes right after she mopped the entire house, triggering a heated debate about how insensitive men could be. Avery nagged at Abbey about his not having the habit of putting tools away after he used them, and Abbey the da-Vinci-rate mechanic and handy man fumed and seethed with an assistant of a wife tidying things up every step of the way. Avery shopped and dressed Abbey up in fashionable attires, and the minimalist Abbey stressed about the clutter and excess in his wardrobe.

Above all the petty details of daily life, the blending of Abbey's family into Avery's life proved to demand the most work. Avery married Abbey to have a life with the man she

160

loved, not to be anything else for anyone else. She had little inkling as to how disconcerting life could be for second wives of divorced men with children. Abbey doted on his kids, and at times she felt she would never be as important as those kids were to him. He was manipulated by his kids into thinking Avery was nit-picking about everything they said or did. He spent on his ex-wife and kids -- though due to orders from the court: alimony and child support. For the longest time, Abbey was paying or spending on his ex-wife and his two kids -- even when those children were grown and ready to build their own relationships and families.

Avery navigated lonelily, the uncharted and inhospitable terrain as Abbey's second wife. She didn't think she's imposed upon Abbey the same kind of toll, as her marriage with Tim was cleanly dissolved, with no strings or kids attached. She was not sure whether Abbey was inflicted with the guilt of a remarried father, but he sure went out of his way to please his kids. Avery was indignant, and was aware that experts advised couples to put their relationship first. She didn't want to feel the slightest bit selfish, but also didn't want to live a life with Abbey steered by his children. She did not sign up for all of the baggage; she only wanted to love him and build a life with him. Though he came in a package that she prepared to handle, she had no idea how it could be so draining and strenuous.

Avery even settled for the fact that fate didn't grant her any children of her own, and stopped dreaming that mom-wanna-be dream. She had too many children affiliations at school, after all. She was determined to treat Abbey's children as her very own as her mother in Taiwan advised -- only that she was excluded and rejected in every way like an outsider, or worse, as a second-class human being.

One-part Price, Three-part Happiness

So they said there's a price to everything. Avery's conjugal bliss with Abbey came with conditions she was not fully equipped to cope with.... However, for every painful occurrence her life with Abbey might contain, she enjoyed thrice as many happy experiences with him. She lived her life happily with Abbey in pursuit of a healthy matrimony together. Her quest for happiness continued as the happiness of pursuit. They traveled across the continents; they were each other's best companion and partner in life.

Las Vegas

Family therapists called it a boundary issue. In an ideal household, the adult couple operated as an integrated unit. They made decisions together and agreed to speak with one voice, resisting any given child's attempts to manipulate or to play one parent off the other to gain advantage. They also supported one another and did not share private adult business with children. Avery often felt uneasiness for not having Abbey on the same page. When the struggle was on about his children, she was bound to suffer a sense of defeat. She had not been part of his family as long as his children had been.

Avery was aware that the complexities of her marriage did not put her husband and her in a very positive statistic category. Second marriages failed at the rate of a whopping 60%. Could they improve their chance from learning the lessons of the past, or might they call it quits and simply move on once they hit any bump in the road?

Avery followed others' stories in the *New York Times* "Modern Love" column:

When I was a newlywed, an oldlywed neighbor confided: "I've never even thought about divorce. Murder, maybe. Not divorce."
Forty-five years later, my husband and I both know exactly what she meant! And thanks to admirable self-restraint, we're both still alive to tell this tale.

M. L. CHADWICK, MAINE

Married 55 years and counting. We are two strong-minded, opinionated people who butted heads many times over the years, but we are still together.
When we moved into our first apartment, my mother-in-law gave us a large Chinese evergreen plant with a zillion leaves. Kiddingly, I said that our marriage would last until that plant died. Of course, I knew that I had never

been able to keep a plant alive and healthy for more than a couple of years.

Three kids, numerous moves for job changes and 45 years later, the Chinese evergreen was still alive, although it had become noticeably thinner and had many straggly leaves. Then, you-know-what hit the fan.

I had three major medical problems within 23 months. I was depressed, more than unhappy and just wanted to run away, and I couldn't stand my husband anymore. One day, I packed up some clothes and decided to just get in the car and drive. But before I did that, I cut all the leaves off the plant, down to the stubs.

Of course, I returned home before midnight and found a distraught husband. The first thing I noticed was a bowl of water. In it were the root stubs of the leaves I had cut off. My anger and depression lifted right then and there, and as new leaves sprang forth over the next weeks, the world seemed completely right. Ten years later and now I'm his chief caregiver, as he has Alzheimer's. I still love the guy and hope to hold his hand as he takes his last breath.

RENOLADY, RENO, NV

In my long single life (only two years of it married), I've felt free to associate with whomever I choose, when I choose, for as long as I choose, and it has enriched my life immeasurably to be able to learn from a variety of people, relationships and experiences, to give to the community, to discover a range of interests and talents I never knew about myself. And I must say, the times alone, even if difficult and lonely, ended up being just as valuable, and sometimes more.

I may still marry again, if that person and I are old and in need of interdependence. But in the meantime, I can't imagine why.

GW, USA

I will never understand the part where marriage is hard. After seven years, I could never be as mad or frustrated with my wife as I am with my career, my favorite sports team or even traffic. The secret: We don't have children nor care to. Maybe marriage isn't so difficult after all; maybe it's the raising kids part that's difficult.

JOSUE AZUL, TEXAS

Now approaching Year 41 of marriage, this piece rings oh so true. Ups that lead to downs and, if allowed to carry on, lead back to ups. My parents did a lot wrong, but one thing they did right was teach me that they could have a knockdown drag-out, end it and go out to dinner as though nothing happened. Never hold a grudge, have a realistic appreciation of what marriage means, and understanding in the end that the "and yet" usually is a positive.

TED DAVID, NEW YORK

I agree with the comment that getting married should be the hard thing. Getting divorced should be easier and not seen as something to be ashamed of. I certainly don't view the divorced as failures. They are moving on to a better place. Good for them.

We fail younger people when we don't teach them our experiences in marriage. I don't recall anyone ever talking to me about marriage. You are just supposed "to know when it's right." My advice to those contemplating marriage, or better, getting engaged: What do you have in common with your significant other -- name five things you both enjoy together. Are you on the same page regarding politics, kids, alcohol, money, house chores, what to do with free time? Who's doing the house chores, cleaning, grocery shopping? Talk about everything now before you get married. Think long and hard about who your partner is, where they came from, his or her parents. Does this person share your values and what you like to do?

That's probably the best advice I would give -- when thinking about choosing a partner, be selfish. Does this person share your values, your likes and dislikes, your ideas on how to live life? Marriage deserves a harder analysis than it is given. It is the duty of those who are and have been married to help younger people make the decision which in my opinion is the greatest determinant of one's happiness.

BREAKER19, PENNSYLVANIA

Nearly 40 years along, my wife and I have reached the post-passion, post-child rearing, post-empty nest, fully conso-lidated stage of marriage. We've loved each other, hurt each other, wandered apart and then back closer again. There is something indescribably satisfying having someone continuously in your life for this long --

someone you still want to bring chocolates every time you have to be away, and who still shares them, cutting each in half carefully so we both enjoy the same flavor of life at the same moment.

STEVE FROM IOWA, IOWA

I can't imagine having to stay married just because I was too poor to get a divorce. What a terrible existence. Or living with the "dark-night-of-the-soul despair," the rage, the hatred that Ms. Calhoun describes. All because there are moments that are not that bad? That is insane.

I've been married, but now I'm single. I have no despair, no rage. I don't have to put up with someone else's mistakes, phobias, inconsistencies. There's no one I have to humor. I think too many people stay married because they are convinced that only loneliness accompanies a single life. But, I'm here to tell them that it's simply not true.

The freedom that comes from living a single life is intoxicating. Never again will I fall victim to the lie that because sometimes things are good means that the times that are bad should be tolerated. I should be tethered to some other person all my life just because he makes me laugh? Or, because we're "best friends"? Lots of people make me laugh. I have many wonderful friends.

Too many people still cling to the notion that life is better, even easier, when shared with another person. But, don't believe it. Life is so much better when it's your own.

MSPEA, SEATTLE

After reaching old age with about 40 years of marriage, may I suggest: 1) Intimacy involves conflict whether it's living with someone or being married to them; 2) Hate is not the opposite of love, apathy is; 3) Sharing your life with another, risking together, if you divorce, your emotional stability, your wealth, and your health is a deep, meaningful experience that is the right choice for a lot of people; and 4) That highly risky choice to marry might even help you both to grow emotionally if you refuse to throw in the towel in the worst of times.

BOB, SAN DIEGO

The best thing you can do in a marriage is forgive yourself. Not him; not him forgiving you; forgive yourself -- completely, totally and unconditionally. You will screw up; so will he, but it is more important to forgive yourself than to forgive him -- trust me. I wish I had done that, and I am still working on it.

SUSANN CAMPBELL

Being "newly" married at almost three years, this article hit close to home. Tragedies my husband and I went through: the death of my father, a miscarriage of our first children (twins), being financially broke at some point. Taking the anger and hurt out on each other ... basically failing. Yet, we battle through the really bad times to relish the amazing ones, like the birth of our son, who is 10 months today. Remembering that in my vows, I said our marriage won't be easy, but it will be eventful!

Even though we bicker or at times may not like each other very much, we still have a deep love that never wavers. There is no other I want to go through this life with, and I know he feels the same. Forgiveness of yourself and the hurt you may cause sometimes is paramount. Saying I'm sorry is huge! Never giving up on your marriage and each other, that is commitment and love.

MICHELLE OWENS

I was married for 21 years. My wife passed away at 49. I miss her all the time. We had our ups and downs. We have four children. Marriage is the most difficult, let's say, timeline. If you choose to marry, be committed. Not for a year or 10 years, forever. Or don't get married. It's sacred, especially when you have children. Go back and rethink it. Remember what it was that made you be together.

DENNY ROBINSON

In Zen Buddhism, meditation helps practitioners detach from the cycle of desire and suffering. In my brief stint as a religious studies major, I preferred Pure Land Buddhism, an alternate path to enlightenment for people who (as one professor told us) may find it difficult to abandon worldly pain and passion because those things can also yield such beauty and comfort. He summed it up as: "Life is suffering -- and yet."

I think about that all the time: "And yet." Such hedging, to me, is good religion and also the key to a successful marriage. In the course of being together forever, you come across so many "and yets."

But "and yet" works the other way, too. Even during the darkest moments of my own marriage, I have had these nagging exceptions. And yet, we still make each other laugh. And yet, he is still my person. And yet, I still love him.

It is easy for people who have never tried to do anything as strange and difficult as being married to say marriage doesn't matter, or to condemn those who fail at it, or to mock those who even try. But there is so much beauty in the trying, and in the failing, and in the trying again. Peter renounced Jesus three times before the cock crowed. And yet, he was the rock upon whom Christ built his church.

At weddings, I do not contradict my beaming newlywed friends when they talk about how they will gracefully succeed where nearly everyone in human history has floundered. I only wish I could tell them they will suffer occasionally in this marriage -- and not only sitcom-grade squabbles, but possibly even dark-night-of-the-soul despair.

That doesn't mean they are doomed to divorce, just that it's unlikely they will be each other's best friend every single minute forever. And that while it's good to aim high, it's quite probable they will let each other down many times in ways both petty and profound that in this blissful moment they can't even fathom.

But I would go on to say (had I not by that point been thrown out of the banquet hall): Epic failure is part of being human, and it's definitely part of being married. It's part of what being alive means, occasionally screwing up in expensive ways. And that's part of what marriage means, sometimes hating this other person but staying together because you promised you would. And then, days or weeks later, waking up and loving him again, loving him still.

Ada Calhoun

Love Interrupted and its Possibilities

Abbey and Avery's passionate love affair was abruptly interrupted when his teenage son moved to Las Vegas to live with him. It seemed all of a sudden, their love was not pure anymore when Abbey had to raise this child, and she had to worry about being next to him, about how, when and where. They needed to revitalize the true sense of wonder when they first found each other. They would not flourish, any more than a tuber, if it was planted and replanted, for too long a series of seasons, in the same arid soil, struggling for balance, for a way to incorporate what would be in their blended family. In such a reduced world, in order to blossom, they learned to contain rage and despair, and the injustice of it all. They tried to re-route, as best as they could, to their normalcy, some feel of life continuing after too many arguments about how their brand of family was and could be.

One of the amazing things about Abbey and Avery's marriage was the way it could both undermine them and keep them believing in their own possibilities, pumping them with hope. Avery knew that making it, in the terms she tried to adopt, was not only unlikely, but false and empty, no more authentic for her than trying to emulate anything other than the true her. She no longer wanted to pretend that Abbey's kids

171

could love her and see her as family. She would stay at a safe distance, and be available when Abbey needed her to "do the family thing." She no longer wanted to lose it or to have those marks of Taiwan erased. She would refuse to be discriminated, ignored or disrespected simply because she was different from the majority of Americans. She would mandate apologies when taunted and imitated for her Asian ways. She would demand to be seen as who she truly was, and have her home in America consist of a safe haven for just Abbey and her, no boundaries violated. Having re-interred her buried sense of self -- and her heart's true sanctuary, she could say what one could only say when coming to welcome and accept one's whole being: Farewell the Past; Hello Home.

Avery was quite a home-maker. The house she purchased in a down market was by no means, luxurious. She renovated the whole house, repainted every wall herself, and turned it into a lovely shelter. Abbey had lived and worked in the United States for ten years before he met Avery. He had moved away from his hometown in British Columbia, Canada, and settled his properties with his ex-wife. With Avery, he sold his old house and took the equity as his and Avery's retirement fund. They lived in that cozy house she built. They tried making the best of their life together, traveling as much as they could and saving up for old age.

Abbey's old profession of singing and playing the guitar in a band often came back to soothe him at times of both trouble and joy. On a trip with Avery to Los Cabos, he got on the stage at a local restaurant with the solo musician and instantly enraptured the whole crowd. He loved picking and plucking his guitar chords at home, and sang Avery numerous romantic songs. He was most happy singing and playing along with all of his musical brothers at a camp fire on a family reunion trip. He would sing and laugh till dawn if there's one single person in the audience.

Avery placed the elixir of plant food, a drop at a time, in the soil for the herbs transplanted into her desert garden. She would do similarly -- metaphorically for her family, adopted or not, a drop at a time. She would love Abbey consistently, whole-heartedly, for eternity. She would continue enjoying shopping, cooking for Abbey and experiencing happiness rendering the delicious recipes. The daily work that went on, it added up. It went into the foundation, into grains of life. Good things didn't get lost.

"Wear that beautiful blue dress you had on the first time we met. I remember how beautiful you looked." Abbey urged Avery on a night out in town.

"I'll gladly comply as long as you wear the shirt I got yesterday," Avery came back with a fashion consultation.

Over 6'5" tall, Abbey gave a striking impression, handsome with pleasantness. Avery loved to shop and cook for him. They were happy eating home-cook meals, and happy also to eat out and indulge themselves in what Vegas had to offer. They mostly enjoyed watching shows sharing pistachios, sweets, and Licorice Allsorts in their home theater. Their life was pretty low-key with a steady stream of visitors from all over, and frequent bike rides, excursions, and trips to other towns, cities, states, and countries.

In an email to her good friends Matt and Paula in New York, Avery wrote:

I am so happy to hear from you, as I have often thought about you and wondered how Yuelian is growing.

173

Thank you for a young woman well raised. I am very proud of her, and know that she will shine like a star wherever life takes her. All the best for her upcoming year teaching in China, and her return to graduate school in America!

My husband Abbey and I just got back from the road trip of a lifetime, through Canada and the Pacific Northwest. We are fine in Vegas, and have always been pondering which tropical locale to travel to next.

Please do come visit us in Vegas.

Warm Regards,
Avery

Matt and Paula had adopted Yuelian from China when Yuelian was three years old. They had sought Avery out to tutor Yuelian in both Mandarin and English. Avery would always cherish the time and experience with the family where she helped to bring up a little girl and watched her grow into a talented capable young woman. Avery could not wait for Abbey to meet them in New York City.

With all the travels, Abbey and Avery enjoyed their quiet yet exciting life together. One day, they would find somewhere delightful and paradise-like to call the dreamland of their own. Before that, Las Vegas was their home, not perfect or ideal, but full of possibilities.

New York

Avery had to take Abbey to return to her American home: New York City. That Big Apple of a city had a special place in her heart. She could identify herself with New York more than any other places, since that was where she studied, ventured and grew.

She remembered fondly the skyscrapers near Wall Street and Midtown, the waterways of East River and Hudson River, the silhouettes of Brooklyn Bridge and Williamsburg Bridge, and the foliage on the paths of Central Park, Bryant Park, Battery Park and countless gardens and courtyards. The irrepressible energy of New York City always summoned her to awake and revisit the dream seeker in her when she immigrated to the States decades before.

Avery returned to savor and share with her beloved Abbey how New York City's sophistication would lure and inspire her for life: culture, art, music, history, theater, fashion, media, entertainment and finance -- the city had it all. World-class museums like MoMA, the Met, the Guggenheim, and memorable landmarks like the Statue of Liberty, Empire State Building, and Chrysler Building were renowned icons that attracted people from all over the world. For Avery, the allure of the city exuded from the urban buzzes and subtle granules of everyday life: exposed bricks in trendy bars, multihued brownstones on historic streets, lovely public arts on meandering cobblestone lanes, charming ethnic eateries and exquisite upscale restaurants, assorted cultural and artistic enclaves, outdoor cafes and music lineups, and all the boutiques, booksellers, clothing stores and curio shops or galleries along the sidewalks full of street arts, music scenes and impromptu performances.

Abbey walked down the streets of Manhattan with Avery, with neon shining on their faces, and the skylight ever illuminating through the open spaces and crannies around the building blocks and high-rises.

"Oh boy, we really don't have to wait till Christmas or New Year to round up galas here." Abbey exclaimed.

"Coming here for the holidays will blow your mind. Just you wait." Avery was full of enthusiasm, with plans and ideas up her sleeves.

"What is on our list of things to do?" Abbey left all arrangement to Avery, his proud New Yorker of a wife.

"We will sit in a Moroccan restaurant to eat, warm up and watch belly dancers now." Avery dragged Abbey into the exotic establishment where patrons were laughing and enjoying the food plus entertainment.

The waitresses came by to take orders in five seconds; the Moussakas, lamb stews, and assorted appetizers arrived in fifteen minutes. Abbey had his first taste of New-York-style efficiency, all the bee's knees. However, the fast-paced establishment didn't lack laidback slowpokes, lazing and conversing about anything and everything under the sun, not heeding how time passed. Abbey learned to satisfy his need to gab with people sitting down eating, drinking and entertaining. In a matter of hours spent on the island of Manhattan, he became accustomed to not saying hello to strangers on the streets, but to engaging real local New Yorkers in stimulating discussions. He was Abbey Lori in his element, full of energy and witticism.

With the mere swipe of a MetroCard, Abbey and Avery visited Manhattan's many pocket neighborhoods: Upper East Side, Upper West Side, Midtown Theater District, Restaurant Row, Hell's Kitchen, Chelsea, Greenwich Village, East Village, Lower East Side, Little Italy, Chinatown, Soho, and the walking trails around the Financial District. Astonished by the variety of cultures and ethnicities, Abbey felt the virtues of the city: "I can see why you love New York. No wonder you want to come back to visit so badly."

"Yes I am thrilled to visit, but have outgrown the city. Too old to live here now -- unless you want to move here." Avery teased the country boy in Abbey.

"No thank you the city's 200 plus nationalities will lose me, leaving me outside my part of the Babel." Abbey was humbled by the city's diversity.

"Staying with Dave and Junko will allow you to experience New York life." Avery could not wait to get to her friends' apartment in the East Village.

When Abbey and Avery arrived, the sky started to drizzle with white new snow. Huddling together on Dave and Junko's couch, they listened to the sprinkle turning louder and louder into a blizzard, a snow storm Avery longed to experience again for nostalgia's sake. The sound of snow melded in a Jazz CD their hosts put on for them. There was a sense of consolation too delicate to describe, as if with their friends' hospitality, they could outlive any deadly storms that ever came their way. They spent the night chatting away with Dave the sound engineer about his music studio and sound projects for various theatrical ventures in the city, and with Junko about her incessant piano recitals with the New York City Symphony. The storm left the island of Manhattan rapidly after an overnight rampage, paving the streets full of granular snow for them to play with.

The next day, Dave and Junko accompanied Abbey and Avery exploring the iconic museums. They found topnotch curations of everything from primitive and contemporary America, fin de siècle Europe, ancient and modern civilizations, to Jewish tenements, New York lore, and immigrant life in the Lower East Side. They walked the sprawling galleries, shops, and restaurants, feeling sensory and epicurean joys.

"Nothing can top this artisanal excursion." Abbey appreciated everything they came across and shared.

"Not so easy -- we're going to Radio City Rockettes' Christmas Spectacular today, and tomorrow, Handel's Messiah at the Carnegie Hall." Avery had reserved the concerts three months ahead of time.

So it was with the splendid hallelujahs and the dazzling Rockettes, Abbey and Avery said farewell to the old year, and with the magnificent ball drop at Time Square, they greeted the new. They continued their show spree and attended the Late Show with Stephen Colbert at the historic Ed Sullivan Theatre. Colbert bantered lightheartedly with his virtuoso diatribes on ignorance and bigotry, well deserving the long wait Abbey and Avery had to go through to obtain the tickets, as well as the six Emmy nominations.

Statue of Liberty and the Brooklyn Bridge, New York

The Statue of Liberty was a must-see for Abbey. The ferry to Liberty Island and Ellis Island took Abbey and Avery back in time, to an era when immigrants newly arrived and went through inspection at the port like throngs of animals. To lighten the mood of the day, Avery reminded Abbey of the "Manhattan Working Girl" phenomenon: working girls would wear tennis shoes with their business attires to board the ferry to Manhattan for work, and then put their high heels on when they arrived at their offices. It was a blatant contrast of professional outfits and running gears -- the scene was amusing, almost comical.

Rockefeller Center in Midtown Manhattan was another place Abbey must visit, especially around Christmas. Matt, Paula and Yuelian were able to join them. Watching the colossal Christmas tree with their dear friends in New York, Abbey and Avery found a focal point for the massive complex of nineteen commercial buildings covering twenty-two acres. They continued on to window-shop gastropubs and restaurants, and decided Avery's favorite Village gourmet establishments were most inviting. Avery had made a reservation at Gotham on East 12th Street.

"Gotham has been luring diners for 30 years. I still clearly remembered the duck confit with foie gras I had more than 15 years ago." Avery reminisced.

"Anything new from Chef Alfred Portale?" Abbey wanted to know more about the menu.

"This Parisian brasserie always has something new and creative: food, wine and art." Their server advocated the restaurant's lively and dynamic atmosphere.

Abbey had the Seared Hudson Valley Foie Gras with blood orange marmalade, walnut granola, toasted brioche, maple reduction, and Avery, the Miso Marinated Black Cod with bok choy, shiitake mushrooms and sticky rice, soy lemongrass ginger sauce. Their dinner was sensational, the wine vintage, the spirit elevated, and the night luminously unfolding a grand stage that was quintessential New York.

New York embraced the high and the low: rock shows at bars, pubs and dives, lavish opera, music, Broadway show productions at the Lincoln Center, the Radio City Music Hall, the Carnegie Hall, the Palladium, the Knitting Factory and many more. Abbey and Avery appreciated this city of arts: painting, sculpture, experimental theater, improvised entertainment, indie cinema, literary inspirations, poetry readings, burlesque, world music, jazz, classical, pop, rock, and everything in between. Revisiting her adopted home of New York, Avery thought of the days when people smoked cigarettes at jazz clubs and piano bars, when Chinatown blew up fireworks and firecrackers during the Chinese New Year. New York City had long become gentrified and transformed. It had been jazzy, it was still fancy and lovely, and always would be, the greatest globetrotters' haven in Avery's heart.

The Road Trip of a Lifetime to Canada

Abbey and Avery were driving up to Alberta along I15. They drove non-stop through the traffic of Salt Lake City, and through the potato fields of Idaho. They drove non-stop chasing after clouds until deer on the backroads slowed them down. They stopped to gaze at the stars. Avery could not take her eyes off the thousands and millions of drooping stars seemingly whispering and gazing back at them. She had never seen anything as exquisite before. She wanted to stay there forever, right in the middle of nowhere, watching the universe coming to life.

Idaho, it seemed, especially wanted Abbey and Avery to stop over. They had a flat tire in the small town of Malad, Idaho, population 2000, but equipped with a 3'R Country Tire. The shop turned out to be a "One Stop Tire Shop" that came to their rescue.

"Let's traverse over to Boise to see a play, and then back to watch the Idaho Falls." Avery was always keen to see a play or two at Shakespeare Festivals in all cities.

"I want to get to Canada fast. But I suppose I can learn to stop and appreciate things." Abbey was adjusting to slow down a bit for Avery.

"My Fair Lady is playing in Boise." Avery had checked out the festival in Boise.

"Let's go see it then."

The play turned out to be exceptionally high-quality, much to their surprise. It was produced by a New York company and brought to the city of Boise by Shakespeare under the Stars, sponsored by the local bank called Key Bank. The play was lovely, so were the Idaho Falls and the Japanese Garden over the Snake River. Idaho was not only potatoes; it was full of charms and wonders.

When they got to Helena, Montana, they stopped to get some sleep -- Abbey at this point could barely stand. The great town of Helena happened to have its college graduation of all things. All hotels rooms were occupied with proud parents and eager friends. Abbey had to drive on to Great Falls before locating an available room -- talking about small-town America! They were troubled but amused.

When Abbey and Avery got to Calgary Canada, Abbey was feeling the landscape non-descript. Calgary's downtown industrial and urban looking buildings might as well be in Taiwan. Only when they stopped to visit Abbey's brother and sister-in-law, did Avery notice the Canadian flair.

The bi-level layouts of Alberta houses were quite lovely. They were open split-level floor plans that configured multiple compartments on various heights. The front entry was usually at ground level with a short set of stairs up to the main floor and another short set to the lower level. The entrance to an attached garage was also off the split front entry. It allowed 36" to 40" high windows in the lower level which made it as comfortable to live in as the upper floors. It's a smart design that gave room for a bonus space over the garage. Avery could picture a cozy study for that unique space. She hung out there quite a bit at Abbey's brother and sister-in-law's house. The Canadian touch was distinctive and magnificent.

Abbey and Avery had visited his Pigeon Lake cabin outside Edmonton Alberta often enough for her to appreciate the remarkable Great White North. She had acquainted herself with the wolves, the coyotes, the loons, the foxes, and the deer in the community. She had sipped Canadian Whiskies in the neighbor's garage. She had helped build camp fires and roast marshmallows. She loved singing along with Abbey when he performed for his relatives and friends, watching the northern sky turn into gray, into gradient shades of darkness, and then hues of brightness and blue-sky colorants.

Avery etched in her heart the eerie loon calls and the wild animals' footprints. She was happy to move through the Canadian Rockies to come across various gigantic snow peaks such as Mount Robson in Jasper, a massive grizzly bear, many elk, and deer on the way back to the States. Canada showed her its own version of diverse topographies. While Abbey was proud of the "Canadian water" he grew up on that endowed him with great prowess to take on expeditions on the road and in life, Avery was enchanted by the gorgeous valleys and mountains in Alberta and British Columbia. Along with the lucky four-leave clover and the wild rose they picked up in Abbey's cabin yard, they collected more memorabilia along the way: the pink fawn lilies, the rusty-haired saxifrage, the buttercups, the daisies, and of course, the pine cones, wild roses, and maple leaves.

Braden and Mary, Dan and Cloe, Abbey's brothers and sisters-in-law, joined Abbey and Avery from their homes of Huntington Beach and Sacramento on this expedition of waters and peaks. Both couples had missed Abbey and Avery's wedding reception and decided to come out of their way to show some camaraderie.

"Is Avery similar to Abbey's ex in personalities? What does she do?" Mary the travel agent and freelance detective wanted to know if Avery could be in her circle of friends, which she might as well translate into plain honest English: "Can she spend lots of money or make believe that she is a lady of richness and important stature?"

"Avery is an English teacher, and world traveler. It's hard to say. I know she loves shopping." Cloe had visited with Avery in Las Vegas and provided Mary her opinion.

"An English teacher? Isn't that odd that a farmer is hired from abroad to plant indigenous crops?" Mary insinuated

Avery's unique position and perceived the situation in a myopic, skewed perspective.

"She is quite the opposite of Abbey's ex actually. She is soft-spoken but surprisingly strong and knowledgeable about many topics." Cloe defended Avery.

"But Sally was a ten. What do you think Avery should be?" Mary went about her way of getting to know Avery from "words of the mouth," from rating newcomers to the Lori family as if they were objects with their values to be estimated.

"Oh Avery cannot be scaled. But if you must, she is definitely a ten for Abbey's sake." Cloe continued to describe how Abbey and Avery always looked out for each other and had fun together, and how they were more concerned about happiness than statuses or monetary races.

"How is Avery a ten? Abbey's kids are not close to her. They always spend their holidays with their biological mother." Mary expected Avery to win over Abbey's grown children and care for them like a traditional woman. She swore that she could detect "a rebel" in Avery and did not think that's best for the Loris.

"Well Abbey's kids have a big family on their mom's side. Don't you think it'll be hard for them and Avery to have to superfluously spend for each other during the holidays?" Cloe had more understanding of the real situation.

"But a Lori-in-law needs to meet certain expectations." Mary insisted on her pre-conception of the Lori standard.

"You're thinking for the Lori family, while I am thinking for Abbey. He married the right girl, the one who truly cares for him and can stand up for herself." Cloe saw the bright side of everything; she had mothered many of her own children and recognized the value of boundaries and restrictions.

"Abbey's family is the most important thing in his life." Mary needed to redefine and recertify the Lori clan. She was married into the Lori family, and was pretentiously outspoken and protective of every member of the Loris.

"I agree that fellowship of the Loris needs to be maintained. Avery is part of the clan. Don't you worry." Braden chimed in to mediate the gossip.

"Of course she is. I am taking her fishing. You want to join?" Dan roared with his usual good spirit.

"Oh no no, thank you. I am a travel agent and detective. I arrange travels and detect people, no wild life lessons needed." Mary stormed off to her upscale hotel lounge, as if the word "fishing" was enough to stink up the space she occupied and she had to move quickly away from it.

Family or no family, Abbey and Avery avoided the topics of politics, religions and money to make sure everyone got along, at least during the time they spent together. Avery appreciated the two couples' company and tried making the best of it.

"Let's guide her in then." Dan asked Abbey's help to launch his fishing boat for the five of them. He conferred with his brothers as to where they would go fishing and how they would cast their lines.

"Mary, watch for us in the water. It's fun." Braden still tried including his wife on the shore, knowing she would not want to be left out although she refused to ever board the fishing boat.

"Sure I will be watching. More like yep, I will be sipping my wine having fun with other guests." Mary aimed to stir the pot, which appeared to be second nature to her.

"Ok have fun. I can't wait to catch some fish!" Avery wanted to start the trip without further delay.

"No more prattle. Girls, let's go." Abbey pulled Avery towards the water.

Avery learned to use the fish finder to scope out their course. The fish she caught was indeed, precious, beautiful, and the whole fishing experience, invigorating. Avery left Mary's venomousness behind. Nothing would get to her if she would not let it.

Mary was indeed getting to many others' businesses as a secret detective undercover as a travel agent. After two many a glass of white wine, she spilled how she had traveled to different parts of the world to attend travel industry conferences, but mainly to spy on public figures, their spouses and such. Her impressive clientele included politicians and celebrities from America, Canada and the Great Britain.

Avery wondered how much of the tales Mary told on a drunken night was factual and how much was imaginative, but the detective's stories were truly entertaining.

"There was this one client of mine from the high society of the royal rich in America. Let's just call him Mr. Rich. Mr. Rich traveled outside the USA 7 times a year on business. Every time he went, he would have a new girlfriend accompanying him. His wife hired me to follow and spy on him. Guess who I found on his list of girlfriends? Movie stars, celebrity athletes, and smart ones from the President's Think Tank...." She let out the names and her audience was enthralled as how far-fetched these women could be involved in scandals like this. The renowned Dr. Shapiro certainly didn't fit the picture of an adulterer.

"One time Mr. Rich went to Paris, and unfortunately his wife and one of his girlfriends happened to hook up and followed him all the way to question him about his clandestine dealings. He had to come on French TV to get his French girlfriend to agree to a private settlement." Mary continued proudly: "I was the detective who hunted down Mr. Rich's whereabouts and adeptly arranged for the wife and the girlfriend to travel together to meet up with the French girlfriend. I enjoyed the media attention and even got the credit for the news footage. See? I can get things done."

Abbey and Avery applauded Mary's mother-hen spirit that applied to not only her own children but to everyone needing consultation. They thought compared to the differences between Mary and her husband, theirs were moderate and bearable after all.

Mary dreaded the outdoors and always hung with her fancy friends, whereas Brandon would go hunting, fishing, biking with his buddies. However, they got along so famously well that people often wondered if the opposites actually attract more than anything else.

With Brandon and Mary's synergy in mind, Avery was unwavering in dragging Abbey to Taiwan that summer. She had to show her family that interracial marriages did not imply unfathomable differences. She and Abbey had more in common than many other couples. They had similar political standpoint, moral beliefs and values. They like a lot of the similar leisure activities and events. And most importantly, they appreciated and loved each other, and could not go very long without each other's company. "Gweilo/foreigner" or not, Abbey was Avery's ideal mate.

The Road Trip of
a Lifetime to Canada

Across the Pacific Northwest

Across the Pacific Northwest, Abbey and Avery beheld the wide variety of terrains, amazed at how many more mountains and waters they had to navigate in order to visit the places they wanted to see. Washington State was incredibly stunning with volcanoes, craters, and wine vineyards. Everywhere they turned, they saw Mount Baker, Glacier Peak, Mount Rainier, Goat Rocks, Signal Peak, Mount Adams, Mount St. Helens, Simcoe, Indian Heaven, and West Crater, as if those natural wonders were playing hide-and-seek with them, one minute they were plain in sight, and next they disappeared only to resurface and parade their majesties. The mountains and valleys were huge, wide, and open to vast invasions of wind turbines comparable to an unnerving alien presence. Abbey and Avery had never seen anything so massive and bizarre. Those structures creeped up on them when least expected. They felt like they were stepping into extraterrestrial territories, too awestricken to speak about the sight.

Wineries, bike trails, beaches, and urban gardens aside, volcanic formations of Oregon were just as immense and impressive: Mount Hood, Jefferson, Blue Lake Crater, Sand Mountain, Mount Washington, Belknap, North Sister, South Sister, Broken Top, Bachelor, Newberry, Devis Lake, Devils Garden, Squaw Ridge, Four Craters, Cinnamon Butte, Jordan Craters, Diamond Craters, and Crater Lake. People of Oregon were generally liberal, friendly, and diverse. They favored environ-mental sustainability, and Portland was listed by PETA as the second most vegan-friendly in the nation, (ranking No. 1 for the number of vegetarian restaurants).

Avery loved the fact that Portlandia where young people went to retire was full of open-minded, green and friendly individuals. It was also the chichi bar capital of the nation, having more strip clubs per capita than any other city. It was home to food trucks like the ones she loved in Asia. This city was so familiar and at the same time refreshing. Avery wondered if it wasn't just a retirement place for your average Joe. Who didn't want to be able to eat healthy, vegetarian and cruelty-free food while feasting eyes on macho toys? Casa Diablo recognized that and had aspired to be the world's only vegan strip club.

Oregonians truly embodied the "live and let live" philosophy. Portland was the epitome of it. Avery chatted up a formerly homeless turned political activist sort of a person on the sidewalk, and ended up having him show her the federal building and the prison house that used clean energy and purified rain water.

"Where you are from I bet you never saw a prison house that clean and high-tech," the homeless turned active environmentalist was certain of that.

"Wow, really? It's quite different. I am from New York, Vegas, and Taiwan. You are right. I've never seen anything like it." Avery made him share more of his knowledge of the city.

"If you like, I could show you and your husband around and tell you about all the places where people used to gather for political protests and demonstrations."

Abbey put up his protector's stance, and said, "No thank you. My wife and I know our way around." Men never asked for directions, and Abbey would not allow another man to show them the city.

They could lose their way in the busy streets of Portland and end up having someone take them all the way to where they wanted to be. Whether Abbey liked it or not, the locals were just going to help. While showing them the city, a lady gave them helpful information about the housing market and population of the city. What a utopia kind of place!

Abbey and Avery ran into an outdoor concert near Main Street and the Pioneer Court House, and spent the rest of their day happily occupied with musical and artistic inspirations of the Portlanders. It was akin to being young and retired.

To its neighbors to the north, California was entirely a different world, ostentatious and hectic. Abbey's cousin in Pebble Beach invited Abbey and Avery to stay over, and so they had the chance for a look at the swanky community. While lots of tycoons and celebrities lived there, Avery could not appreciate the mentality of teaming up with the rich and glamourous just to boast prominence and success by association. Yes the hilly community by the beach was nice -- what really made Avery tick is the historic Canary Row nearby. John Steinbeck, who illustrated Cannery Row life in his lively stories, made the area most interesting to Avery. The best of Monterey hotels, attractions, and recreation, plus restaurants, convenient shopping and exciting nightlife were all there. So was the first theater of California.

Avery was delighted to move along the Pacific Coast, and saw how establishments could be so dissimilar an ocean across on the shore of the Asian Continent. While California lined up posh communities along the coast, Asia filled natural beachfronts with night markets and playgrounds. Avery recalled a story she read about affluent Californian families relying on imported household workers to maintain their life styles. While allowing the immigrant workers to live in their own homes and take care of their children, Americans had little ideas as to who the people they hired to help with their domestic arrangements really were. Every slight bit of miscommunication could cause colossal disasters and sent their whole families spun out of control. Abbey agreed that sometimes the happiest people in the world were the ones that had little.

Abbey and Avery traveled along the Pacific Ocean winding up and down the mountains. They completely forgot about the strenuous cuts and turns when they came across a whole beach of elephant seals, lying, bathing, resting, and sleeping belly-up, fetus-style, sideways, and in all sorts of manners on the shore. It was funny to see them take over the entire beach, stinking, whimpering and snoring literally like pigs.

Avery and Abbey traveled near and far. The world was their oyster; home was anywhere they found each other, sharing better versions of themselves. Their daily life together in Las Vegas had the calm and ease they desired. Their explorations of the world brought them immeasurable delight. They were blessed with all that life had to offer, happy as clams.

Chapter 13. In Taiwan with Abbey

With Abbey traveling the world alongside, Avery felt a sense of fulfilment she never had enjoyed when she traveled by herself. The world seemed so much exciting when faced together with her husband. She wondered if some of her darker memories growing up on Taiwan would be redeemed when she returned with Abbey. Avery had to show Abbey to Taiwan, and Taiwan to Abbey. She couldn't wait to show Abbey off to her family.

They spent five days in Taipei, where the city's personality matched and conflicted with Abbey's quite comically. Taiwanese were open and friendly to newcomers or "Gweilo" (foreigners). Abbey said hello and talked to everyone, being his outgoing self. Although he didn't speak a word of Mandarin or Taiwanese, people seemed happy to strike up "conversations" with him, asking where they were from and where they were headed.

"Do you have family here?" They wanted to know everything about the odd couple.

"Yes. I was born here." Avery smiled.

"That made you our country people, too." They accepted Abbey immediately.

"Do you love Taipei?"

"Loving it."

"Do you feel impaired in any way by the traffic, people, food or air pollution?"

"No, we are very comfortable here except at times we have to deal with nuisances you could run into no matter where you are."

The Good, the Bad
and the Incessant Feasting

Some troubles were actually particular to a city crowded like Taipei. Like the one big bus backing up in the small alley, completely not seeing Abbey and Avery trying to get pass the bus to the other direction. They were nearly squashed, if not for the passengers on the bus shouting for the driver to hit the brake. How could the driver not see the 6'5" Abbey and the colorfully dressed Avery? The extremely narrow alley would have to take the blame. Taiwan's plentiful narrow alleys full of kamikaze drivers in cars and scooters could precariously deliver unanticipated excitement.

One famous alley treasured in Avery's memory was no longer there to cause any trouble though. The city had changed a lot since Avery's last visit. Roads and highways were built left and right, and so the little Changes-snake alley was gone. Avery used to hang there just to watch locals and tourists take up drinking fresh snake blood newly flowing from live dissecting performances. That narrow alley epitomized a lively dimension of Taiwan, full of raw energy, unpretentious, utterly real, original, and authentic.

One thing also very apparent was the increase of imported labor and interaction with China. Southeast Asians immigrated to work as domestic caregivers, and the connection with China was ever growing. Taiwanese businesses had been a huge presence in the Mainland since the lifting of communication ban between the island and China. While manufacturers flocked into China, Taiwan became heavy in service industry, and maintained its status as one of the Asia Four Tigers

195

Hong Kong, Singapore, South Korea and Taiwan were the four Asian tigers. These nations consistently maintained high levels of economic growth since the 1960s, fueled by exports and rapid industrialization, which enabled these economies to join the ranks of the world's advanced richest nations in the 21st century. Hong Kong and Singapore became world-leading international financial centers, whereas South Korea and Taiwan were world leaders in manufacturing information technology. Taiwan was always developing rapidly, and Avery was always enthralled to visit. With Abbey by her side, Taiwan seemed to be even more captivating.

One of Avery's family traditions was to incessantly feast, especially when there were visitors from abroad. Abbey and Avery couldn't have a second of rest from one feast with her parents, before they had to go to another banquet with another group of relatives. The feasts, extravagant full-course royal Chinese festivals, were unexpectedly exciting, and at the same time, troubling and burdening them with excess of food indeed.

Abbey and Avery gained fifteen pounds easily on the island of Taiwan. They were literally burdened with too much food. They were not unappreciative, but inflated with Taiwan beers -- happily disgusted and bloated.

One thing Abbey learned and loved was the Taiwanese drinking game. There were hundreds of variations of the game, but they all simply involved using one's ten fingers, and reacting quickly and smartly to what's expressed on one's face. You held out your fingers simultaneously with your opponent, and took turns calling, singing, or rhyming depending on the game variation, a number from zero to twenty. You tried getting your opponent to lay out the exact amount of fingers that added up to the sum of your own fingers along with theirs. You won if you were quick and paid attention to how many fingers were held up. You took a swig from an array of Taiwan beer bottles on the tables when losing to your opponent. Losers were drinkers and often ended up sick with drunken symptoms. Winners, they sipped jovially at their own pace, drinking in profound inspirations from the game.

Avery made sure to take Abbey to the National Palace Museum and Taroko Gorge. She also made sure to revisit her childhood home with Abbey, and to take their pictures in traditional Chinese Qipao and Chunshan tunic. Off they went to the house with two neighborhoods. They saw Avery's cousins and old neighbors, and Abbey acquired more skills in the Chinese chess and drinking games.

They were talking to people, sitting around in the hotel restaurant next to the elongated house. (The house was a newly renovated video game arcade, but the next-door hotel stayed through plentiful changeover of ownership. So was the neighboring house with the pond.) Suddenly, it started to rain heavily. An hour before, the air had been so solidly saturated, it looked as if koi fish in the pond could jump the banks and swim onto their table. Abbey had never seen rain like that. An ominous wind was rising, and street trees were performing an ethereal tango with the wind.

Later they saw the report on ABC News:

Taiwan: 'Morakot' Typhoon Leaves at Least 108 Dead, 62 Missing

Some 14000 villagers have been rescued -- including 600 on Thursday -- since Typhoon Morakot dumped more than 80 inches (2 meters) of rain for three days this entire past weekend....

Rescuers battled Friday to save thousands of people trapped in mountain villages as Taiwan's leader warned the death toll from floods would likely top 500.

Old Skin and the Fairytale

How was it right to slither free of an old skin and walk away to wear only a healthy membrane of a hide? Avery came back to a vicious typhoon that reminded her of her old skin all too strange and familiar at the same time. She came, she experienced, she took away, and she left behind. Her survival from the anguish, torment and regret must have been unconditionally granted. She was unscathed yet again, feeling completely home with Abbey beside her -- no matter how the world would fall apart in front of her eyes.

If she had suffered from any cultural indiscretion and was fettered by her upbringing, her limbs would always bear traces of these shackles. Breaking free of Taiwan and building a home in the west and the world, what she struggled to fight off and lost was her identity, the fairytale of her young soul. She looked at the remaining traces and saw mere distortion, or at times, she blocked the marks entirely and saw nothing. Either way, she had no means to tell the story of where she came from. She only gripped her injuries, as much as her successes, and divulged them like in a storybook. And gradually and eventually, she could regain the comportment of her true self, and acquaint with the true colors of herself as well as the world around her again.

Abbey and Avery visited the destroyed villages after the disaster; they helped with their relocations and donated necessities. They felt belonged. One day, Avery would be old enough to read fairytale again.

A Sutra Difficult to Decode and
the Air She Inhaled

Every family had a "nanniande jing," a sutra/Buddhist catechism difficult to decode in others' eyes. It seemed Avery's family could comprehend her wants and dreads like no one else, because their lives were immersed in a sutra of the same precepts. It's all in the blood. Based on an official dictionary definition, Avery supposed her family, her blood, was the fluid that circulated in her heart, arteries, capillaries, and veins, carrying nourishment and oxygen to and bringing away waste products from all parts of her body. The intakes of oxygen, nevertheless, had a great deal to do with the outside world, a world that's contoured with places she had seen and people she had stumbled upon. Her schoolmates, playmates, friends, mentors, students, enemies, competitors, boyfriends, lovers, and her husband, as well as the cities she traveled to in various parts of the world, the metropolises she called home, Taipei, New York, and Las Vegas -- they devised the components of the air she inhaled. She was Taiwanese-Chinese American, also a World Citizen, pursuant to her being brought forth on the earth, her birthright.

In Taiwan with Abbey

Chapter 14. What of Step-mothering?

At home in America, daily work and routine continued. Avery's awkward situation with her step-kids remained. Like many other women, tormented by a stepfamily, Avery was not a whiner -- had just been trying to get step-mothering right. Her excitement of a new family with Abbey's kids readily being her own died down when the reality sank in. She was hardly regarded as their stepmother, but as a disrupter to their biological parents' union and intruder to their lives with their father. However wrong it was because Avery had not come to Abbey's life before he divorced his ex-wife, his children had a presumed picture of Avery that was all too unfair, biased, and prejudiced.

Miffed, Avery abhorred time spent with Abbey's children. She cried that even living separately, Abbey's kids still were first and foremost in his life. She cringed every time the phone rang and a call from Ethan or Claire would put anything Abbey and Avery were doing on hold. She recoiled every time Ethan dropped by unannounced to the house with his girlfriend in tow. Avery would greet them amiably, but she didn't want to be taken for granted to entertain or wait on the young couple. She squirmed every time she had to yet again, change her activity schedule with Abbey because of something happened in Ethan's or Claire's life.

Although Abbey assured that Avery was the unwavering focus of his life, she somehow understood that his nucleus always faltered and fumbled around his kids. Abbey, along with his children, failed to recognize the fact that Abbey actually lived with another human being who was his wife, his family in the household that he needed to contribute to.

There were external forces, most beyond Avery's control, that undermined her best intentions and good efforts with Abbey's children. They were loyal to their mother, and refused to let Avery outshine her in any area. They were jealous, and Avery was jealous back, resenting their bond. She disagreed with Abbey's propensity for permissive parenting, for overcompensating to the extent that his children would lose their opportunities to be better, grown individuals.

Avery hoped that if she was being fair, Abbey's children would warm up to her as experts advised. She did not want to fall into the trap of cultural expectations about women, content with living in conflict by proxy. She was her own person, who had so much to give and would only give so much in order to keep boundaries intact.

Kids of all ages would dislike their stepmothers no matter where Avery turned and positioned herself. Even Abbey at the age of fifty plus, still had mixed feelings about his own stepmom. Of course Abbey's ex-wife Sally would never release her kids from the tortuous loyalty bind and pave the way to a healthy relationship. She would not even look at Avery, like her daughter, Claire.

"Who was that foreign person answering the phone when I called?" Sally said to Ethan when he was still living with Abbey and Avery. As if she had no idea who her own son was living with, and she had the right to call Avery's house and made unkind comments.

Avery thanked Jesus or whatever supreme-being she could thank for Ethan's move out of her house. She stopped bending over backwards. An endearing Avery might just elicit conflicted feelings for Abbey's kids.

Teaching Others How
She Was to Be Treated

Ethan became remarkably close to his dad, and would
yearn to have Abbey all to himself. Abbey developed an intense,
peer-like relationship with his kids, having a tough time showing
how Avery, as his kids' stepmom, should be treated. So, Avery
took on the task of *teaching how she herself was to be treated*.

"I would not acknowledge anyone who does not see me
as who I am -- a person, an educated foreign person who has a
life and mind of her own. Simple." Avery said to Abbey,
refusing to join him at a perfunctory family gathering.

"Please, I know it's hard. Let's try doing the family thing
more. Things will get better." Abbey implored.

"Ok I will go for your sake. But I am not going to
please everyone or try making everyone happy as you do all the
time." Avery was no "people-pleaser," whereas Abbey was
almost obsequious when it involved his children.

"All you need to do is to show up and make
conversations as you would normally anywhere you go." Abbey
tried to make her feel more secure and comfortable.

"I can do that." Avery agreed.

"After dinner, we are all going to come home to the
house to have some together-time." Abbey loved to have them
over to hang.

"Ok, but if the house turns into a huge pigsty, messy and
disgusting as every instance indicates it will, you know I will be
mad again -- without a doubt."

"I promise to clean up." Abbey offered.

"No you promise you will demand your kids to clean up
the house before they leave." Avery taught Abbey to show

some "tough love," and to make people responsible for their own actions.

"Fair. Will do."

"And no invasion of personal space allowed. No violation of privacy."

Avery knew all too well what would happen when those kids rampaged through their entire house. She would be enraged, suffocated with wrath and resentment. For whatever reasons those grown children thought they could just do whatever they wanted in her house, and they could disrespect her as they did -- she would not tolerate or condone.

Avery needed to be seen, to be heard, listened to, and heeded with fairness and courtesy.

The question for Avery was "How do I stop hating my stepchildren?" She could not control her anger every time Abbey's kids were around anymore. She was not too cool about how Abbey frequently bought them things and treated them to fun activities, calling them "pal," "buddie," "bro," "amigo," or "sunshine bunny" and "sweetie honey." They were grown-ups, too old to be pampered like little babies.

Avery tried and tried to figure out a way to clear negative emotions. She needed to learn a better way to deal with Abbey's whole package deal. She tried ignoring the nagging feelings that Abbey's kids were always going to be more important for him.

Chapter. 15 The World with Abbey -- Continued

Avery hoped that by bringing Abbey to her home continent of Asia, he would learn more of her upbringing and understand more of her angst or desire. Besides, the rich cultures of Asian countries would blow him away.

Southeast Asia

Abbey was always interested in Asia, and was certain that Avery could lead them to the continent with great ease because she was Asian and spoke the languages. Little did he know that Asia was vast and varied, and in most Asian countries, they would see an immense variety of different peoples, hear a wide array of languages and dialects, taste assorted cuisines, and experience wide-ranging geographical features.

The Ever-Welcoming Smile of Thailand

Thailand was the first Asian country outside Taiwan Abbey and Avery visited together. Thai people were friendly and fun-loving, with an ever-welcoming smile. The good nature of its citizens exuded a national characteristic, exotic, tropical, as well as cultured, and historic. From its shimmering temples to tropical beaches and resorts, Thailand offered comforting and appealing retreats for tourists worldwide.

Abbey and Avery felt less like tourists staying with Josh and Pensri, who became Avery's long-term friends since her previous travels in Asia. Josh and Pensri had settled in Mae Sai near Thailand's northern border with Myanmar. Josh, a British national, had started a family and business with his Thai wife Pensri, and never left the country. Their charming guesthouse in Thailand' rural heartland was surrounded by a mix of rice paddies, tropical forests, and lovely villagers' gardens along the Mae Sai River. The meals they cooked up revealed fundamental aspects of Thai culture: generous, warm, refreshing and relaxed. Each dish relied on fresh, local ingredients -- pungent lemongrass, searing chilies and plump seafood. Abbey and Avery enjoyed everything and everyone. They were happy to see another interracial couple had successfully built a relationship and raised great kids together (their son Bill was a marketing manager at a corporation; their daughter Hom helped run their guest house and was prepared to manage the whole operation.) They adored the quiet and relaxing way the villagers went about their lives, they loved the open and curious minds of the tourists visiting there, and they learned the Thai culture by mingling with both the locals, the expats, and the travelers from all over the world.

Traveling south to Bangkok, Avery urged Abbey to see Thailand's floating markets and try Thai street foods. Damnoen Saduak Floating Market was within reach right outside the city of Bangkok. Its fluid charm seemed to be forever enchanting tourists, colorful and lively, full of boats selling food and fruits.

"Sawadika! How much is the durians?" Avery had to introduce the strange-smelling yet delicious fruit to Abbey.

"200 Bhat a pound."

"How about the rambutans?" The gorgeous looking litchi-like fruit was Avery's all-time favorite.

"Same same."

Avery was aware that the prices were hyped for tourists, but the experience was incomparable. Abbey and Avery went on to Soi 35, Bangkok's street food doyenne, where a leafy, pleasant avenue lined up vendors of excellent Thai dishes of all kinds. During the day, the street markets bustled with local shoppers and workers from nearby government offices on their lunch breaks. Abbey was thrilled by the exotic views and tasty foods. They even found a traditional shop where a cobbler made shoes for the royal palace. They also witnessed deep-fried cockroaches sold as snacks by a street vendor. The street foods proved to be irritating Abbey's stomach, and neither Abbey nor Avery would ever touch any roaches on a plate. Nevertheless, they had a ball sampling the authentic Thai flavors.

From the local foods to nightlife on Royal City Avenue, and to sleazy sex shows on Patpong Road, Abbey and Avery selected what was appropriate for their age and taste in the city, and took away a street-party kind of vibe that was uniquely Thai.

Heading further south, Abbey and Avery returned to natural wonders of Thailand, to watch scraggly limestone cliffs poking out of the cultivated landscape in mainland as well as the small islands scattering along the coast. They were breath-taking like prehistoric skyscrapers. After Bangkok's cluttered streets and party scenes, these cliffs were sacred, echoing the colorful and ubiquitous religious temples framing both the rural and modern landscape. The long coastlines and jungle-topped islands anchored in azure waters, making Thailand a picturesque paradise, breathtakingly beautiful. Krabi, Ko Phi Phi, Ko Samui, all those lovely islands and resorts gave Abbey and Avery plenty of fond memories and unprecedented merriment. How could anyone not love Thailand back? They would definitely revisit the country someday.

Laos' Remote Charms

Laos, a forgotten backwater, had a fairytale landscape with jagged limestone cliffs, brooding jungle and the snaking Mekong River continuing from northern Thailand as a backdrop. The Lao people were also wonderfully welcoming as their natural charms, among them Avery was most overwhelmed by Vieng Xai Caves.

Vieng Xai Caves seemed underdeveloped for a tourist spot. Much of the country's economic and social issues were revealed on the streets of the surrounding villages. Abbey and Avery were bewildered by the sight of street children alongside street dogs and cats. Dogs and cats lived on the streets of many third-world countries, but children on the streets, depicted a picture too appalling and disturbing to behold.

"Food for me, sir?" Two scrawny children looking to be under the ages of fifteen and ten begged of Abbey for something to eat.

"Is there some place to eat around here?" Abbey asked.

The boy pointed to a wooden structure hidden along the curve of the road and looked on expectantly. He was hoping Abbey and Avery could take him there to eat.

"Come on. Let's go get something to eat." Abbey and Avery were ready for a random act of kindness.

The boy devoured a whole bowl of noodles in five seconds and stared at Avery for a second helping. He then, turned to his little sister and shared with her some of the vegetables in his food. Akamu told Abbey and Avery his and his sister's story, after he ate enough and had the strength to try speaking in English, communicating with gestures and with the eatery owner's help.

Akamu and his sister Aelan had been "working" for a living since they were five, sifting through garbage for metal or plastic scraps to sell. Their buyer gave them next to nothing and always asked for more recyclable materials from them. They ended up having to roam the streets because their parents left the village to search for work. And, there was nothing to eat unless they sold whatever they could find on the streets to anyone willing to pay or exchange for food.

Abbey and Avery learned that Laos took 25th place on the Global Hunger Index, and seemed to be the only country in Asia where the hunger situation was rated alarming (orange tone). Its infrastructure was underdeveloped, particularly in rural areas. There were no railroads; the road system was rudimentary, and external and internal telecommunications, limited. Japan and China were supporting the Laotian government, sponsoring major improvements in the infrastructure. Although visible results would take time to come, it was a start.

On the plus side, Laos still retained much of the tradition that had disappeared in a frenzy of bulldozers and reality TV elsewhere in neighboring countries. Village life was refreshingly simple, and this sort of languid riverfront life even existed in the capital city of Vientiane. Abbey and Avery embraced the quiet before they were headed for another city's sensory overload.

The Asserting Vietnamese

Unforgettable experiences could be found everywhere in Vietnam. Abbey and Avery gazed over a surreal seascape of limestone islands from a junk yard in Halong Bay. They took ten minutes just to cross the street through a tsunami of motorbikes in Hanoi. They watched a moped loaded with honking pigs weave a wobbly route along a country lane. They observed solitary graves of tens of thousands of war victims. They got lost while exploring the cave systems in Phong Nha-Ke Bang National Park, spending a whole day trying to exit the park. They tasted the Vietnamese subtle and diverse cuisine, while interacting with the energetic, direct, sharp, and resilient locals. They respected how driven the people were, and at times, taken aback by their fierce assertiveness.

"This table is for 5 people dining." A bartender at a trendy place commanded.

"We're about to order food." Abbey responded humbly.

"We still need 5 people for this table. Or you order enough food for 5 people."

Abbey and Avery consumed five-people-worth of food at the Vietnamese French establishment, feeling exploited. They also noticed that the street peddlers would not leave them alone unless they bought more than several items. The Vietnamese people were determined to profit from tourists, and their country had commercialized a great deal with Americans' sundry businesses and undertakings.

As a matter of fact, a population boom at the end of the war called for a closer look at the aging infrastructure and worsening environ-mental conditions. Poverty lessened, but living standards remained low especially in rural areas. Increasing urban affluence stimulated migration from rural provinces into the cities. Wages were low and jobs, scarce. Abbey and Avery's hotel front-desk helper, Ngoc, was a single mother of three. She could barely survive, let alone keep up with the pernicious excesses and indulgences of globalization.

"I have to go home to my children. Can't work evening shifts." Ngoc wished Abbey and Avery a fun time at the hotel's Entertainment Night while she was leaving work for home.

"Joining us for a cocktail?" Avery invited her cordially.

"If your husband is buying, I will stay." Ngoc liked to flirt with men, including the married ones, including Abbey who had his wife alongside him.

"Sure we can do that." Abbey was amiable as always.

"I love you. You're the best!" Ngoc crooned in a scratchy high-pitched voice, and went on to narrate her life story including how she was a high-society girl turned sort of poor because of her many pregnancies during her teenage years.

Avery eventually told Ngoc to hurry on to her children at home, and to leave her husband alone. Amused by the situation, Abbey comforted Avery that they could really start their own evening fun, since Ngoc was no longer welcome. They went on to sing their best karaoke selections. Abbey got standing ovations, and Avery, a calm peaceful evening with her husband holding her all the time while he was singing.

Cultivating Cambodia's
Killing Fields

Cambodia was an empire of temples, with a history both inspiring and woeful. Angkor Wat was the world's oldest Buddhist temple, treasured as the eighth wonder of the world. The glorious empire's Tuol Sleng Prison incarnated, on the other hand, the terror of its rule during the horrifying Khmer Rouge era.

Years of bloodshed, poverty and political instability, however, had not broken the Cambodian people's spirit. Their infectious optimism prevailed from Siem Reap to Phnom Penh. Abbey and Avery visited the thousands and thousands of skulls lying at a local school turned war museum. They observed in awe as to how with the Killing Fields bygone, the country could remain so unbelievably endearing and steadfastly welcoming.

85% of Cambodians were farmers. The main crop of rice was not profitable because of monsoons' poor effects on crop quality and quantity. Again, rural people moved to the city or neighboring countries where jobs were hard to come by. Life in Cambodia was difficult -- in comparison, the average life expectancy of a Japanese person was 83, and a Cambodian's, only 56. The situation was ever dismal because education was not readily available, with only one university in Phnom Penh within the entire country. In rural areas, there were hardly enough schoolhouses.

Examining the thousands of mystifying Buddha sculptures on the stone structure of Angkor Wat, Abbey and Avery could attest to Cambodia's rich culture. The images were sacred and the site, serene. They struck up a conversation with a school boy selling water to tourists. With a fellow tourist functioning as a translator, Abbey and Avery were able to converse with the boy.

"I must walk 3km to reach my school." The boy muttered when Avery asked why he was not in school.

"How brave of you! You must love school." Avery encouraged the boy.

"Right. I don't like missing school."

"How's school when you do go?"

"I read books translated from other countries; they are ok. But I'd rather have something more fun."

"You must read anything and everything that comes your way."

"Yes, ma'am. My mom also told me to have an education so I can get a job and stop selling water or picking through garbage."

Avery left the ancient temple of Angkor Wat feeling the immense potential of the country and its people. Cambodians should build their schools, process their garbage, and reconstruct their nation with the same kind of optimism and strength she saw in that school boy. She hoped that the world would help cultivate and get to see a restored Cambodia, with the grim wartime pictures replaced by a robust image of revival.

Back to Civilization in Malaysia

Crossing the border to Malaysia, Abbey and Avery returned to the hustles and bustles of modern civilization. Kuala Lumpur offered them the comfort and luxury of a cosmopolitan city, yet still showed them a historic side of the country. They sat in a café built in the colonial age sipping coffee watching the city people going about their daily lives, and the shimmering Petronas Twin Towers, once the tallest building in the world.

Malaysia had two faces, cleaved by the South China Sea. Peninsula flaunted lively cities, colonial architecture, misty tea plantations and exotic tropical islands, while Malaysian Borneo housed wild jungles of orangutans, granite peaks and remote tribes. Abbey and Avery delved into the impressive variety of microcosms, from the high-rises of Kuala Lumpur to the traditional longhouse of Sarawak. The diverse pockets of ethnicities, religions and landscapes were intriguing, and the Malaysian people, pragmatic and down-to-earth.

Abbey and Avery were able to discern the competitive edge of the country and its people. Malaysian tourist industry workers showed them the efficiency and ethics rarely found elsewhere in Southeast Asia.

"We have to change our flight to Indonesia to a later time. Can you help?" Abbey inquired.

"We can check the system. Just a moment, please."

"Anything after 8:00 pm is fine."

"I found this flight via Malaysian Air, not Jakarta Airlines. Is it ok? It will get you there before midnight. "

"Ok but we have to check out."

"No problem. It's safe here. We will store your luggage, and get you a van to the airport in time."

Abbey and Avery got to spend the waiting time in the hotel lounge munching on the appetizing dishes of various origins. They could see how and why the Resorts World in Las Vegas that was under construction was funded by a Malaysian corporation, Genting Group. They looked forward to experiencing what a mega resort built by such efficiency of the Malaysian corporation had in store for the world back in their home city of Las Vegas.

What They Did for the Hodgepodge that Was Indonesia

Indonesia was made up of thousands of volcanic islands, with hundreds of ethnic groups speaking many different languages. Abbey and Avery had heard about the country's beaches, volcanoes and jungles sheltering elephants, tigers and Komodo dragons. Their flight into Jakarta though, was nothing characteristic of natural adventures or wonders. Javanese, Malay, Chinese, Arab, Indian and European -- had influenced the architecture, language and cuisine of the city. The hodgepodge made it crowded, polluted, and more industrial looking than any others they had visited in the region. They were prepared to leave the sprawling capital on the island of Java, for the exciting beaches in Bali after an overnight stay.

Denpasar, the capital of Bali, was located in the southern part of the island. Abbey and Avery found many beach lovers from all over the world, bathing, frolicking and surfing in tropical delights. Avery took her first outdoor shower in a charming guest house, where the garden was designed with stalls of cement enclosures open to the sunny blue sky. She felt herself merged with the nature, as if the water could cleanse her soul and took her flying, away to infinity. She fell in love with the huge geckoes on the bamboo ceiling of the bungalows, ever peeking at the roomers in their non-menacing way of parading across the spaces. She found the sculptures of the Indonesian god called Geruda enchanting, and bought too many pieces of wooden artwork, including a chess set, where the kings, queens, bishops, knights, rooks, and pawns, all came vividly alive through the ingenious carvings of their sculptor.

Abbey paid more attention to the fact that Indonesians were more into political interests than to socio-economic recovery. He saw many unsolved serious social problems, and was agitated by unrest and conflict in some areas of the country, concerned about human rights violations, corruption, nepotism, collusion, scandal, and poverty. He read in the news:

A series of explosions has rocked the Indonesian capital, Jakarta, with gun battles on the streets.

The blasts were centered around Thamrin Street, a major shopping and business district close to foreign embassies and the United Nations offices. Police say the situation is now under control, with five suspected attackers among at least seven people killed.
The so-called Islamic State (IS) said it carried out the attacks, a news agency linked to the militant group said.

Separately, Indonesian police said they suspected a local group linked or allied to IS was to blame.

Indonesian President Joko Widodo described the attacks as an "act of terror".

"We all are grieving for the fallen victims of this incident, but we also condemn the act that has disturbed the security and peace and spread terror among our people," he said.

While reading the paper, Abbey engaged the locals in discussing the incident. Suhendra was an advocate for economic recovery, and complained to Abbey about the Indonesian government: "It failed to keep its promise. There was no improvement in living condition of approximately 40% of the population who were living below the poverty line."

Suhendra's wife Inge had worked alongside her husband to urge critical awareness of people and expression of ideas. "We want a new Indonesia," said Inge earnestly.

Inge enlisted Avery's participation in the conversation and stressed the issues of refugees and violence against women. Citing the examples of female leaders in Southeast Asia, such as Aung San Suu Kyii, State Counselor of Myanmar known to have been in house arrest for years, Inge insisted that women played the most crucial roles in solving the country's pressing issues. She favored Megawati, the first woman president and fifth president of Indonesia, who replaced the impeached incumbent in July 2001. She had high expectations of women to carry out good deeds and change the system for the better.

Inge detailed the country's dilemma:

"There's no improvement in poverty, education or women's rights. Conflicts and refugee issues unsolved. The number of people living in refugee camps increased. Unfair distribution of wealth by the centralized government created huge gaps among regions in terms of welfare, development and accessibility. The majority of the refugees, women and children, lived in inadequate refugee camps spread across 19 provinces in Indonesia. They were victims of several conflict areas including West and Central Kalimantan, Central Sulawesi, Aceh, Maluku and others."

Inge went on to tell tragic stories of women, as a domino effect of social economic problems. She depicted how violence against women increased dramatically, many suffered from domestic violence or became rape victims. Girl children of young age, many of whom Inge tried rescuing, were sold to sex and entertainment industries.

"I wish I could save them all. There are many sold in my country, and the ones shipped abroad I have no means to set free." Inge fumed about the injustice and cruelty of it all. "Avery, maybe you could somehow help me stop this clandestine trade," added Inge with heartfelt urgency.

"Yes definitely. I will see what we can do from North America. My sister-in-law might be able to help." Avery was thinking about Abbey's brother's wife Gena, who had worked for unions all her life before she retired, and had close ties with people in the NGOs.

Later Avery did work together with Gena and Inge to identify a few cases and petition for international assistance. Two girls were rescued from the brothels in the West; they got to return home to their family. Five criminals were charged with smuggling of under-aged migrant sex workers. And the rescuing team of the three women, Inge, Gena and Avery, vowed to keep acting as the advocates of human rights as well as social justice.

Abbey and Avery feared for the country of Indonesia and hoped that the process of decentralization could give each region the autonomy to manage and control their own area and

217

resources. If each region could regulate and set rules based on traditional and customary laws, it might just stabilize the turmoil and get down to the root of the problems. If each region could incorporate necessary modernization tailored to local situations, it might just find the keys to unlock Indonesia's social and economic impasses.

East Asia

The Wacky, Cute and Advanced Japan

Japan brought about contrasts of traditional and modern, the West and the East, and created a national spirit that was strong and incredibly distinctive. Abbey and Avery tasted the delights of Japanese cuisine, and were impressed with the details, rituals, presentations, and the fine ingredients. It was worthwhile to just visit Japan and stand with the locals at a counter to have a quick lunch with two rolls of sushi, two cold beers, and continual muttering of "oishiis" to boot.

The Japanese people showed a personality in the fashion of how they prepared food, how they were dressed, how they conversed and ran daily routines: meticulous, reserved, particular and careful.

"Would you mind if we sit next to you?" Abbey asked a single young Japanese girl who sat alone at a dinner table.

"No not at all." She nodded, smiled, and waved her hand rapidly to express how she would not mind.

"What is good to eat here?" Avery tried a friendly chitchat with her.

"Oh, I don't know. You ask the chef." She giggled and covered her face as if she was ashamed of her own opinions.

Later during the visit, Abbey and Avery ran into many people that showed similar traits as the girl sitting next to them at the dinner table. They seemed welcoming, but were extremely reserved and watchful. Perhaps that was why some travelers to Japan always found themselves entranced by a culture and people that was unfathomable and downright peculiar in their ways of social interactions.

Avery took Abbey to a ryokan (traditional Japanese inn) that was utterly traditional and different from modern-day Japan. They wore robes and sat on a tatami (woven floor matting inherited from the Chinese Tang dynasty), eating raw sashimi and mountain vegetables. They watched a Kyoto geisha dance, whose dancers transformed into modern women with dynamic fashion tastes and veracious appetites for pop-culture right after the show. The dancers revealed their true looks: chic sleek get-ups pocketed with iPods and all sorts of other devices that emitted electric dance music, popular songs and beats. The transformation was uncanny.

Tokyo especially vibrated with its traditional culture and passion for everything new. It had everything in spades: a rich, cosmopolitan dining scene, more shops, cafes and bars than you could visit in a lifetime, clean and efficient public transportation, pretty grassy parks and cozy Japanese gardens. It was a contemporary bustling city built on old souls -- Abbey and Avery looked and found the contrast of old and new everywhere. Next to the skyscrapers they found anachronistic shanty bars and quaint alleys. Besides the neon-lit avenues of Shinjuku they found raucous traditional festivals and lantern-lit yakitori (grilled chicken) stands.

Abbey was much amused by Japan's "little girl's pop culture." He commented on the saucer-eyed school girls and the ubiquitous Hello Kitty with bewilderment:

"How the girls and kitties travel so far and wide, all the way to my niece's bookshelf and school bag in Trenton, New Jersey, I could not fathom."

"It's not all about little girls, not really. Look at the giant robots they have, too." Avery tried pointing out the abundant pop icons and assorted idols of the country.

"That's like the Wonder Woman among the male heroes. When you think of Japan, you think of the little girls. And when you think about heroes, you mention Superman, Iron Man, Batman, Spiderman, Captain America...." Abbey was determined to name Japan a land of little-girl sensation, too cute and bizarre.

"It doesn't matter what gender the pop icon is, Japan is strong, progressive and has super smart technology like no one else." Avery advocated for the Japanese valor.

"Yes very interesting." Abbey agreed but remained a Marvel and DC Comics fan.

Marvel or not, Abbey and Avery enjoyed watching the top pop stars projected on the massive video screens in Shibuya, as well as the trendiest anime or manga popping up in every corner in the electric town of Akihabara.

Japan was no doubt, wacky, cute and advanced. Abbey and Avery wowed how the densely-populated, earthquake-prone land was pushing the limits, adding ever bigger, taller and loftier malls and buildings. Tokyo Sky Tree was a twisting spire that blinked and stretched into to the night sky. Much of Japan's conceptual art was intertwined with technological installations. Cutting-edge technology was predominantly a Japanese lifestyle, weaved into people's daily life.

Abbey and Avery skipped the hurly-burly of Sinjuku nightlife, and preferred the lilies, orchids, and the cherry blossoms in the green houses all over the city of Tokyo. They had seen enough Japanese singing and gambling, as well as Japanese urbanites popping their heads along with EDM back home in Vegas casinos, Karaoke places, and dance clubs. They didn't come to Japan for more of the same, but were much amused and enthralled by the irreplaceable experience of the Shibuya crossing.

Rumored to be the world's busiest, this intersection in front of Shibuya Station was touted as 'the Scramble'. Abbey and Avery stood and inched forward among the crowds in front of giant video screens and neon signs.

"It's quite a spectacle, isn't it?" Someone struggled to make room for them, and attempted friendly conversations.

"Yes, wow, we're pressed to move but can't even look one foot ahead." Abbey observed. "Be careful, only my wife can touch me, nobody else can." He added jokingly.

"I feel like we're going to be squashed." Avery stretched her neck to gain a clearer view of the people and objects around her.

"There's got to be over a thousand people trying to cross this street with every light change. You need to sit on my shoulders to be safely transported, shorty." Abbey's usual comicality came out at situations like this, making the absurdity bearable.

Avery was not sure whether to laugh or to come back with similar banters, but managed to dodge human bodies with nonchalance and agility. She would not pass this prime photo opportunity, and insisted that they went to the Starbucks on the 2nd floor of the Q-front building. Finally seated, Abbey relished the view in a great mood:

"Look at all the colorful people pouring out of the station in their finest ensembles."

"The teenage girls in high-heel boots are coming. Quick, get out the camera. They have orange, purple, or red hair…, and the young men, the tousle-haired gyaru-o, are quite amusing." Avery observed while snapping pictures of the incredible scenes. She was typically Asian when it came to picture-taking. She took too many pictures everywhere she traveled, and called herself a photo journalist.

Avery's enthusiasm was contagious. Abbey even took over the picture-taking responsibility after a couple of light changes. He was apparently impressed by the city dwellers' skillful parades across the intersection, as well as their sleek, flashy "costumes" that they wore as regular attires.

Abbey and Avery concluded their trip to Japan with the ancient sanctuaries and mesmerizing summits in the region surrounding Tokyo. They climbed Mt Fuji, the symbol of Japan 110km west of the city. They followed the pilgrim trail up to the peak and watched the sun rise from the snow-capped cone. Avery recited some Haiku poems she remembered about the sacred mountain:

>The wind from Mount Fuji
>I put it on the fan.
>Here, the souvenir from Edo.
>-- Basho Matsuo
>(17th century)

>Seek on high bare trails
>Sky-reflecting violets...
>Mountain-top jewels
>-- Basho Matsuo
>(17th century)

Abbey tried imitating the Haiku master but claimed his soul of rock and roll would fare better when sticking to his familiar way of song-writing for the guitar. Haiku or rock and roll, Abbey and Avery captured the uplifting moments on the peak in their own ways, and each conceived renewed appreciation for the wonderful world. They couldn't imagine any better way to understand the fascinating country of Japan.

Traveling Korea Gangnam-Style

"Gangnam Style" was released as a single by the South Korean musician named Psy in 2012. It became a worldwide hit, and the first YouTube video to reach one billion views. Avery's students in America were among the Gangnam-Style fans, intensifying her interest in the lifestyle associated with the Gangnam District of Seoul. Though Psy's dance moves were too funny and bizarre for Abbey or Avery to master, they did follow their curiosity to the trendy, hip, and classy parts of South Korea. They understood the parody the song intended, on posers of the style, and appreciated the no-nonsense, practical way the Koreans went about their lives.

"The Korean Wave sure was taking off in the West." Abbey attested to a Korean pal named Jong back in Las Vegas.

"We make music and live life. We do our best." Jong reflected on his home country.

"Korean soap opera is very popular outside the country, too. Have you noticed?" Avery asked, thinking about the marathon-watches her relatives undertook when gluing themselves to Korean TV.

"We have 5000 years of culture and history, similar to our Chinese counterpart. We have the resources and know certain things." Jong offered the explanation.

Work hard, and play hard. The Gangnam Style can-do spirit resonated with Abbey and Avery. They hit the calendar of festivals and events in South Korea: Boryeong for its mud festival, Gwangju for its annual salute to kimchi, the pickled vegetable dish too foreign for Abbey's taste. The Korean people were always promoting their traditions and culture, and they had successfully mixed up temples, palaces, natural landscapes with dynamic city rhythms to formulate constant K-POP beats in everyday existence.

"This is a 24/7 city. I am thrilled we can visit a temple at any hour of the day." Abbey noted with surprise.

"You can sip tea or go gallery-hopping at any hour, too." Avery agreed.

"They also have your favorite night markets. You see?" Abbey promised to visit and try the local snacks.

Abbey and Avery wandered the streets of the Korean cities till dawn. They were as free as the wind. They let their hair down to enjoy what the country had to offer, and in turn, they often felt like royalty at a readily accessible banquet or on a seemingly important social occasion. It was the comforting effect of this country and its people Abbey and Avery would keep warmly in memory. It was tender, lovely, and most definitely smile-inducing.

Adventures in China

Imperial Bejing
and its Slanderers

Avery was always ambivalent towards China, a country so big, diverse and fast changing that she often caught glimpses of her ancestral roots in the philosophical and ideological frames of its people. On the other hand, she was also frequently appalled by how differently and afar China veered from her birth country of Taiwan. For one thing, China was known for centuries to assume the role of a "big brother" and oppressed the island of Taiwan. And many of the human-rights violations Avery witnessed while touring China were flabbergasting enough to lead her to think that, China's antiquity or autocratic mindset was hindering its progress and modernization. No matter how breathtaking and opulent the land was, the country had a lot to catch on.

Boy oh boy, wasn't China grand and soul-inspiring? The world's oldest continuous civilization was bountiful in historic and geographic wonders. It encompassed a riveting jumble of dialects and climatic and topographical extremes, out-of-scale differing and vast. The resources and means of the country were second to none. However, government bureaucracy as well as three decades of continual development and socialist planning had taken their toll. The riches were accompanied by out-of-the-blue shanty towns far and wide in the cities and villages of the country. Amidst the new was plenty of the old run-down side. Avery had traveled to China previously, and warned Abbey to prepare wayfaring gear, as they were about to journey into this conundrum of a country where adventures and surprises awaited.

225

Beijing, Shanghai, and Hong Kong portrayed a modern China that was ambitious and trailblazing. Abbey and Avery arrived in Beijing and stayed at a high-rise hotel above a network of city roads and freeways. The city showcased a plush window of travel arrangements and merchandise for them to pay higher prices than the locals. When the un-Chinese-like Avery actually spoke Mandarin to the residents, they were often astonished and changed their course of bargaining with them.

"Please take us to the Great Wall. How much will it cost?" Abbey asked a taxi driver on the roadside, seeking more comfort than the local transportation offered.

"Get in; get in. I will do it cheap. By meter." The driver assured them.

After they took many turns around winding city streets, the Great Wall was still nowhere in sight.

"Ni Rao Quanzi. You took the long way circling around." Avery pointed out in Mandarin with a stern look.

"Duibuqi. Sorry. I took the wrong turn." The driver tried saving face.

"Koudiao. Deduct the cost from the fare," insisted Avery, looking even sterner.

By the time they got ready to climb the Great Wall, the sun was high and the heat was on. Abbey was almost jogging every step up the majestic structure, while Avery carefully balanced herself and watched the tumble-down part of the site unfold as they got to the less touristy spot.

"He who has not climbed the Great Wall is not a truly good man," claimed the former Chairman of China Mao Zedong. The construction was indeed, China's greatest engineering triumph. It twisted haphazardly from its dispersed Manchurian remains in Liaoning Province, to windswept rubble in the Gobi Desert, and to scarce traces in the sands of

Xingjiang Province. Undulating over the peaks and hills of Beijing municipality was the renowned chunk of the Wall. Although better maintained compared to other sections, the Beijing segment already revealed the dreary contrast of the great wonder and its inevitable deterioration.

Abbey and Avery called themselves "truly good men" after a day of climbing the Great Wall. They returned to the city for the lavish Peking duck and many other gastronomic treats, such as Wujing Changwang, an intestine dish stewed in a pot, Yanwogeng, bird's nest in a soup, and Hehua Daxia, lotus flower and shrimp. Abbey was aghast with too many unfamiliar dishes on their dinner table:

"What is this pot? I am not eating intestines." He objected and frowned.

"It's delicious. You will have to try it." Avery wanted to broaden his tasting horizon and knowledge of the diverse Chinese cuisine. "Wait till you get to the south. There are spicy but heavenly dishes you have to try."

"Like what?" Abbey asked dubiously.

"Like Sichuan's Fuqi Feipian, Husband and Wife Lung Slices, Anhui's Huangshan Dunge, Yellow Mountain Stewed Pigeon, Zhejiang's Xihu Cuyu, West Lake Vinegar Fish, or Fujian's Hongshao Yuchi, Braised Shark Fin, and so on."

"I can't wait," the wide-eyed Abbey announced cheerfully.

"China has delicacies in every province. Starchy in the north; spicy in the south. They are so widely differing -- like countries apart." Avery described her previous dining experiences traveling in China.

"They all sound very exotic. Not sure if my stomach can take it." Abbey was not used to too many "strange" flavorful ingredients in his diet.

"Wait till I take you to the back alleys and see some real street food. You will know what's exotic." Avery saved the best for later.

When they ambled down the winding narrow alleys at the back of the towering skyscrapers, they came to an area where food vendors dominated the streets and local Beijing people liked to hang out: Wangfujing Snack Street. Avery told Abbey that this was the place to see how the Chinese in the city really lived. She pointed out the oddities like the barbecued scorpions and starfish.

"I can't even look at the food, man." Abbey was too stunned to stay adventurous.

"There are many delicious snacks to try. We can stay away from the insects. I promise." Avery encouraged him to be open-minded and try new things.

"Like what?" Abbey was intimidated.

"Like barbecued meats on sticks and buns and dumplings. Like Bingtanghulu, the Sugarcoated Haws."

She continued to explain: "Bingtanghulu is traditionally made with hawthorns on a stick. You dip them in sugar syrup. The sugary shell resembles ice, giving its literal name 'iced candied hawthorn.' Sour fruits such as hawthorns bring a contrast to the sweet coating. Many other fruits are often candied to make Tanghulu: strawberries, apples, mandarin oranges, and pineapples."

Avery was enticing Abbey's sweet tooth, grinning cheerfully with persuasion.

"Sounds like it'll give me heartburn." Abbey challenged.

"How about Ludaguner Rolling Donkeys, over here. These are glutinous rice rolls with sweet bean or soybean flour. The name comes from the appearance of a donkey rolling around in dust. It is like a cake roll. It tastes not too sweet, with about three layers of bean paste." Avery was unwavering about their dessert choices and was determined to have Abbey try.

"Yes, this sounds more doable. We'll try this. Give us two orders." Abbey bought the Rolling Donkeys as a heroic deed. He was convinced that there were no donkeys in the cakes, or any concoctions Avery suggested.

The evening out turned even more farfetched for Abbey when they entered a Beijing disco out of curiosity. They saw young men and women dancing around shaking their heads. The women especially made a spectacle, jiggling their long silk black hair left to right, right to left, rapidly following the music beats, in tandem alongside each other. The line of dancers looked to have put themselves into a trance. Rumored had it that these partiers were on some sort of performance enhancement chemicals called "Yaotouwan, Head-shaking Pills." Abbey and Avery were hugely entertained. They deemed the trip worthwhile and concluded their night with a couple of nightcaps in their safe hotel room.

The next day, Abbey and Avery joined a tour group to the Forbidden City, China's largest and best-preserved collection of ancient buildings. Listed a UNESCO World Heritage in 1987, the enormous palace was the largest of its kind in the world. The tour guide led the group of five people, including Abbey, Avery, another couple and their ten-year-old child. They entered through Meridian Gate, a colossal U-shaped portal at the south end of the complex. Mr. Huang, the tour guide, informed them:

"We are entering through the gate formerly reserved for the sole use of the emperor. Gongs and bells would signal imperial comings and goings, while the military used the west gate, civilians the east gate. From this gate, the emperor also inspected and reviewed his army personnel, passed judgement on prisoners, oversaw the flogging of misbehaving subordinates, and announced the coming year's event calendar."

"You'd better behave or else you might get a beating." The wife of the other couple admonished her son.

"I didn't do anything. Corporal punishment is illegal in the States." Little Johnny was in every way, an American boy, the conviction in his tone, poignant.

"You're in China now. So beware." The father went along with his wife's scheme.

"Up there is the Meridian Gate Gallery. It houses temporary cultural exhibitions of Chinese or foreign origins." Mr. Huang interrupted them and continued to give information about the Gate.

"The courtyard here has five marble bridges spanning like a bow across the Gold Stream. This courtyard is so enormous; it can hold an audience of 100,000 people."

The group continued walking through the yard to visit the Calligraphy and Painting Gallery inside the Hall of Martial Valor, and the Ceramics Gallery inside the creaking Hall of Literary Glory.

After the art galleries, they reached the Three Great Halls, a three-tier marble terrace with balustrades all around. Mr. Huang continued to explain:

"The Hall of Supreme Harmony is the most important and largest structure in the entire Forbidden City complex. It was built in the 15th century and restored in the 17th century. Ceremonial occasions took place here, such as the emperor's birthday, the nomination of military leaders and coronations."

"Wow, it's so spacious and beautiful." The group of five exclaimed in unison.

Mr. Huang led them to the stately chair, "You see the Dragon Throne? The emperor sat there for trembling officials to worship. The entire court had to touch the floor nine times with their foreheads in the emperor's presence. The custom is known as kowtowing, bowing with respect." He finished with a reverential smile, as if he was paying tribute to the emperor.

Little Johnny knelt down in front of the Throne and started playing kowtowing. The adults watched Johnny with affection and were reminded of the mindless ebullience of children -- they could have fun anytime, anywhere, with anything they had in their possessions. Wouldn't it be perfect if grown-ups could recall some of the innocent joviality of their youth once in a while?

"Let's get close to see the back of the throne. It's decorated with a carved picture of Xumishan, the Buddhist paradise or heaven. This signifies the throne's supremacy." Mr. Huang further specified.

They proceeded behind the Hall of Supreme Harmony and came to a smaller Hall called Middle Harmony.

"As the emperor's transit lounge, it had everything he needed to make last-minute preparations, rehearse speeches and receive important ministers." Huang explained the function of the hall.

"What are those sedan chairs for?" Abbey was mostly intrigued by the royal contraptions.

"The two Qing-dynasty sedan chairs provided the emperor's transport around the Forbidden City. Puyi, the Last Emperor as we called him, used a bicycle and altered the palace ground surfaces to make it easier to get around." Huang expounded in response.

Now the group arrived at the third of the Great Halls, the Hall of Preserving Harmony. "It's used for banquets and later for imperial examinations. The emperor used to be carried over the carriageway at the rear of the hall in his sedan chair as he ascended or descended the terrace." Huang supplied further detail: "The buildings surrounding the Three Great Halls were used to store imperial treasures."

On and on they walked through seemingly countless buildings and houses: the Palace of Heavenly Purity, the Hall of Union, and the Palace of Earthly Tranquility, as well as other numerous gardens and palaces, all had important functions and special significances. By the time they finished their tour in the Imperial Garden, they were too fatigued and awestruck to criticize any of the harems or evidences of corruption they observed on the way. China was too excessively clandestine for the world to find its faults. Everything and anything under the table didn't count. Culpabilities didn't matter -- on the grand scale of the national identity, dissidents or critics had no place, and were generally accused as slanderers or criminals.

Shanghai, Once Not for
Dogs or Chinese

Contemporary Shanghai was born in the concession-era when westerners invested in the port and created the Bund, the city's Wall St. A towpath for barges of rice prior to the international trade, the Bund (an Anglo-Indian term for the embankment of a muddy waterfront) was transformed into a focal point for heated trading, for the making or losing of huge fortunes. The most powerful banks and trading houses took over the city of Shanghai, and its Huangpu Park, could only be accessed by certain subjects, not for dogs or Chinese. Avery made a point to enter that park and museum with dignity and pride -- as a defiant Chinese descent, not to be wronged.

Abbey and Avery meandered through the Bund, contrasting the backbones of the past with the futuristic cityscape of modern-day Pudong. The majority of art-deco and neoclassical buildings here were built in the early 20th century and presented a westernized skyline that was un-Chinese but striking. They browsed the designer shops and upscale boutiques, and hotels. They viewed the 128-story Shanghai Tower, and chuckled about the way the world competed in building skyscrapers. Once the tallest building to supersede other countries' constructions, it was now surpassed by Dubai's Burj Khalifa, a 160-story building.

After Shanghai, Abbey and Avery took a train all the way to the south of China. The train ride was exhilaratingly new to them since the US lacked a comprehensive railway system like the Euro Train. Even the Chinese were more sophisticated in "the train culture." Avery reckoned that there was too much money in the car industry in America for the country to build a railroad system all over the map. What a shame -- it's so pleasurable and relaxing to be able to take a train anywhere and everywhere one wanted to go.

The ride to Guangzhou supported travelers with bunk beds to sleep, and the dining facilities looked appetizing. Abbey and Avery were so pleased about the experience, that they tipped the conductor for no reason. They were happy to get away from the big cities and rock away in the train's rhythms to the interior of China. The scenery of the countryside on the way was soothing, with green rice paddies and mountain ridges extending endlessly to the misty and enrapturing distance, soaring and flying freely in perpetuity.

Rat Restaurants Featuring
Super Deer in Guangzhou

Guangzhou in the province of Canton was China's third largest city, and the busiest transport and trade hub with a long history as a strategic port to the South China Sea. Abbey and Avery appreciated the tree lined streets among the city towers, but were stupefied to see cages of rats along some sidewalks of this international trade city.

"What are the rats for?" Avery wanted to find out.

"To kill them, I guess." Abbey was thinking along the line of rodent extermination.

"Let's ask this lady over there." Avery decided to find out about those creatures.

She approached the friendly-looking woman and inquired in Mandarin. It turned out the woman only spoke Cantonese, like most people in Canton. Avery indicated that her Cantonese was very limited: "Suisui, sinting emsingong. A little bit of Cantonese. I understand but can't speak it." She signaled and pointed at the rat cages. The lady was kind to give her a newspaper ad to explain what the rats were for. It was an ad to Mr. Wu's Rat Restaurant in downtown.

Staggered, flabbergasted, Abbey and Avery had to visit Mr. Wu's Rat Restaurant now. In the heart of Guangzhou, they found the family business of Mr. Wu and were surprised to see many patrons there for the gourmet delicacy of rats, "super deer" in its euphemism.

"My restaurant was struggling before I found this Super Deer delicacy. Now we're doing really really great." Mr. Wu informed Abbey.

"How does it taste?" Abbey controlled his grimaces, and addressed Mr. Wu politely.

"You should try. These rats were caught in the countryside. They are not of the sewer variety." Mr. Wu clarified proudly.

"How do you cook them?" Avery chimed in to ask.

"Roasted, kebabs, stews, or stir-fried. Field rats have become known in Taiwan and Africa. They are very good for your health." Wu further enlightened them.

Abbey and Avery could not make up their minds. It was too tormenting to put the pieces of rat meat anywhere near their mouths. So there were limits and boundaries they would not cross, in life and in diet as well. They opted to continue their adventure in Guangzhou's famous classical gardens without actually eating the super deer. Perhaps with more exposure to the city, they would become braver, bolder, and as daring as the local Chinese people.

Abbey and Avery arrived at the graceful garden, regaining their cool and composure once inside the elegant property. It was built in 1871 by an official of the Qing court who incorporated the landscaping styles of Suzhou and Hangzhou, of beautiful Jiangsu and Zhejiang provinces. The refined architecture of Lingnan (South of the Ridge) highlighted a photogenic collection of halls, pavilions, terraces, bridges and lakes. Avery and Abbey observed the colorful birds flutter about in the garden. They were lucky to have escaped the rats to this much more esthetic setting.

After coordinating with her oldest sister Xiangyu, who lived in Shenzhen, Abbey and Avery would head west of Guangzhou first to visit the legendary Guilin and Yangsuo in Guangxi Province. They would move east to Shenzhen, Canton or Guangdong, to stay with Xiangyu. Avery was very excited about seeing Guilin and Yangshuo, and she was even more eager for the time to come when she could take Abbey to reunite with Xiangyu and her brother-in-law Qiang.

Guilin and Yangshuo of
Poetry and Art

Chinese proclaimed "Guilin's landscape to be the best under heaven, with Yangshuo outshining Guilin." The two stunningly beautiful towns of china could only be captured in poetry and art. Their natural endowments amazed Abbey and Avery, but they could discern how China had exploited resources and overdeveloped the area. The hyped-up ad-mission prices to the sites as well as the street vendors ballyhooing their cheaply-made souvenirs were signs the towns were losing their natural charm to man's greed.

Setting aside their aversion to the peddlers, Abbey and Avery visited the 1000-year-old village of Jiangtouzhou, tucked away among farmland 32km north of Guilin. They rented a bicycle to soak up the rustic charm on the two-hour ride, and went sight-seeing along the cobblestone alleyways and ancient homes from the Ming and Qing dynasties. They continued bicycling to Yangshuo's dramatic karst mountain landscape. It was the pinnacle of Bilian Feng (Green Lotus Peak) that caught their eye and blew them away. Standing on the west bank of Li River, the peak resembled a budding lotus bloom with many pavilions, inscriptions and stone statues carved on its cliffs. The scenery was simply marvelous.

"What does that character mean? That's not a statue, but a huge Chinese character with bunch of characters beside it, right?" Abbey was impressed by the cursive calligraphy about 6 meters high and 3 meters wide (19.7 by 9.7 feet).

"Yes, the brochure here has the story. It's a huge character that composes a poem of eight Chinese characters. The character 'dai' means 'area' or 'generation'. So it's playing with the homophones to convey the duo messages of the eight-character poem." Avery explicated.

"Which means...?" Abbey couldn't wait to know.

"Yi dai shan he, shao nian nu li which translates into a message, 'As the area of rivers and mountains unfold their greatness, the young generation should work hard to contribute.'" Avery appreciated the subtlety of it all, and hoped that she did a fine job translating for Abbey. She read on and found more information, "this was inscribed by a Yangshuo mayor in the Qing dynasty; and it's been preserved until this present day. It's very famous and significant."

Abbey also wanted to know who the giant statue was inside one pavilion. Avery stated her findings: "The Peak has a long history. One of the first known people to stay here was the famous monk or Buddhist called JianZhen. JianZhen lived from 688 to 763 AD in the Tang dynasty. He was originally from Yangzhou in Jiangsu Province. Japanese scholars Rongrui and Puzhao invited him to visit Japan. He tried six times to travel to Japan without success. During the fifth attempt in 748 AD, he got lost in a storm and the boat was driven to Xijiang. In Guilin, he took a boat to Yangshuo to visit the Jianshan Temple. He taught Buddhism there, and tried again to go to Japan. In 753 AD, he succeeded. He lived for 11 years in Japan and was an ambassador for the Sino-Japanese relationships."

Abbey and Avery were mesmerized by the historic stories, by the rivers, mountains, and villages. They extended their stay in the area and could see why some westerners never left the town of Guilin or Yangshuo. By the time they picked up to leave for Shenzhen, they were two days late to visit Avery's oldest sister Xiangyu and her husband, Qiang.

The Wealth of Shenzhen
with a Sister's Blessings

One of China's richest cities and a Special Economic Zone (SEZ), Shenzhen attracted a mix of business people, investors and migrant workers to its wealth, including Avery's oldest sister Xiangyu and her husband Qiang. More than fifteen years before, Xiangyu and Qiang moved to Shenzhen to operate their own business. They became Shenzhen's permanent residents, and it was never easy for the American Avery, the Taiwanese sister Yiwen, the Shenzhen sister Xiangyu, or any relatives spreading over the world to see each other.

Xiangyu and Qiang took Abbey and Avery to a myriad of public squares and theme parks in the city. The luxuriant markets and shops were impressive. Avery was exultant to see Xiangyu and was pleased to learn that her sister's business thrived and she lived comfortably and prosperously in this special city of China.

"Where do you go see art or culture in Shenzhen?" Avery wanted to see other aspects of Shenzhen other than shopping and dining.

"The OCT-LOFT."

Abbey and Avery received the warmest welcome from Xiangyu and Qiang, and were now on their own to explore the sprawling OCT_LOFT complex. Converted from austere communist-era factories, the complex housed contemporary art, which appeared to be even more commercial than artistic. Large exhibition spaces and private galleries had cafes and restaurants with exposed ventilation ducts, peculiar fashion boutiques, excellent bookstore, and expensive fashion outlets.

Abbey and Avery watched the happy-go-lucky Chinese local shoppers and tourists. They perused replicas of celebrated world monuments at Window of the World. Abbey was mistaken as one of the famous athletes associated with the exhibit, and forced to have his picture taken with Chinese strangers and foreign travelers alike. He was semi-famous when finally yanked away by Avery to a safe cozy café.

China Folk Culture Village introduced to Abbey and Avery, about two dozen faux minority villages complete with minority-culture demonstrations. On a mini-monorail run by the Shenzhen Happy Line Tour Co, they toured around the complex and were becoming "culture-weary" when they returned to Xiangyu's place at nightfall.

Hong Kong's Star Ferry
with Sagacity

Xiangyu and Qiang accompanied Abbey and Avery to visit Hong Kong which was only one hour away from Shenzhen. It was a blessing to view the city island's iconic skyline from the mainland with their beloved sister and brother-in-law. Indeed, Xiangyu and Qiang frequented the lush city and indulged themselves in the luxury every two weeks or so, and were able to take Abbey and Avery to legendary kitchens and must-see sights.

"The Star Ferry will take us to Hong Kong in one hour." Xiangyu expertly boarded the boat, holding Avery's hand.

"You can see the glass and steel buildings from this side already. It must not be too far." Avery gauged the distance and happily announced.

"Underneath Hong Kong's commercial persona you can find Chinese roots and colonial connections. They're intertwined and constantly inventing new things." Qiang as a descent of Hongmen, was always interested in how historic roots generated new voices and grew organically. He had explained to Abbey and Avery how his family evolved in present-day Taipei, Shenzhen, Hong Kong, and other parts of the world:

"My father was an important leader in the Tiandihui organization, also called Hongmen. Literally the name means Society of the Heaven and the Earth, and its purpose was to revolutionize a corrupt China. Our family was oppressed and spread to different counties and provinces in the Qing dynasty. Many of our fraternal members started their own branches of the organization, and some became criminal in nature and were collectively named Triads. They are now illegal here in Hong Kong. But don't be scared, I am no Triad or criminal. I am only sticking to the principles of righteousness, patriotism, and loyalty. So you know I will take care of you no matter what. You're my brother and sister."

In reality, the Hongmen in Taiwan was not only legal, but politically and monetarily influential. Sun Yat-sen, father of the Republic of China on the island of Taiwan, was a senior figure within the Hongmen, as was the first nationalist president Chiang Kai-shek. Qiang's family in Taiwan was sustaining the Hongmen traditions, and they always showed camaraderie for their family and friends far or near.

Together, the four of them went exploring Hong Kong's culinary repertoire, and their gastronomic desires were incredibly satiated with freshly steamed dim sums, warm and juicy pineapple buns wedged with butter, sweetly spiced prawns, as well as the exclusive recipes of the latest celebrity chefs. They took a historic double-decker tram to tour the city streets and travel up to the tallest point in Hong Kong, Victoria Peak. Standing at 552m-height of the Peak, they viewed the vibrant metropolis, gleaming and beckoning with its neon on tall towers. The tram up to Victoria Peak was a 125-year-old gravity-defying device, making the vertical Avery scream and squirm all the way. Fortunately, she had three dear family members to fight the dinosaur funicular clanks with. Its trip up the hillside was most fun and exciting. It was even more enjoyable because her oldest sister Xiangyu gave her approval of Abbey, watching how he protected and shielded Avery on the tram ride.

Over 70% of Hong Kong was mountains and sprawling parks. It was surprising considering all they could see on the street level was the neon shining, the cars crawling, and people inching about the city. They escaped the city limits on a smooth transport system and spent their day wandering in a Song-dynasty village. They returned to the waterfront to take a Harbor Tour from Tsim Sha Tsui, coursing along Central and Wan Chai.

They learned that the Star Ferry was founded by Dorabjee Nowrojee, a Parsee from Bombay. Parsees believed in Zoroastrianism, and the five-pointed star on the Star Ferry logo, an ancient Zoroastrian symbol. Interestingly, the symbol was the same as the one followed by the Three Magi to Bethlehem in the Christmas tale that Avery used to teach her students in Las Vegas. The Magi might have been Zoroastrian pilgrims who abided by teachings of the prophet Zoroaster in ancient Iran approximately 3500 years ago. Fire was considered a medium of spiritual wisdom, and water, the source of that wisdom. The knowledge of the Star Ferry logo imparted profound meanings on their tour, as if the water was sacred, a source of wisdom.

At the end of the tour, it was apparent that Hong Kong's complexity defied categorization. It was Chinese, Cantonese, western, oriental, new, old, busy and tranquil all at the same time. The four of them, Xiangyu, Qiang, Abbey, and Avery, embraced the sagacity that was gained from the time and the trip together with gratitude.

Abbey and Avery saw Xiangyu and Qiang off to the mainland of China -- four of them bid their farewells and gave each other blessings. Their journey to Asia was brought to a close in the way that they could ever wish for: with love, with care, with support, and with boundless tenderness and sympathy towards the world.

From Mainland China to Hong Kong

Chapter 16. The Price of Happiness

To live was to discern. To live was to change, to reflect and acquire the words of a story, and that was the way Avery knew to observe her journey of life. In immobility, there's only woe and stagnation. Much of the taciturnity of Avery's disposition was to be attributed to the condition that her life had turned, to a great extent, from passion and emotion, to contemplation and deliberation. She had traveled far and wide to celebrate beauty of the world. She had found happiness in pursuing what she enjoyed most and being curious about in life. She had found happiness in doing. However, she had not yet, sorted through and processed the price of happiness.

Her Favorite Place in the World

Avery always knew before her jaunt around the world, that whatever place she traveled to or lived in, she had one constant in her life. She always knew and felt that her favorite place in the whole world was not some exotic deluxe villa, or some glamorously outlandish estate. Her favorite place had always been and would always be: the safe and snug world in her husband's arms. With Abbey, she had everything to gain, and much more to discover about life.

The Price of Happiness to Pay

So Avery accepted the fact that she was married to a great man with kids. So after casting serious doubt on their marriage on exasperating occasions, Avery reinstated Abbey's significance in her life. She attended more kids-father-stepmom get-togethers.

Eventually, Avery adjusted her own mindset to believe that if both of Abbey and her asked themselves "what more could I do" at all times -- if they could consistently and unfailingly considered for each other, they would find more assurance and love in each other.

Eventually, Abbey transferred more responsibilities to his children about their own lives and finances.

Eventually, Avery became more willing to support Abbey's needs for a closer brand of family, or for keeping his kids close.

Eventually, Claire graduated college, and started talking to Avery. Eventually, Ethan would come ask for Avery's help when he needed guidance, like the time when he was applying for colleges.

And hopefully, the two grown children would one day, make fewer demands on the people around them, and Abbey would, in turn, not cater to every whim and desire they threw out to make him feel guilty, liable, accountable and answerable.

In a letter for Ethan's college application, Avery wrote:

Dear Admissions Team:

I am privileged to write in support of a very promising young man, Ethan Lori. Ethan came to Las Vegas as a high school sophomore, full of drive and music talent. Being a secondary English Language Arts teacher in the local school district, I witnessed a keen sense of curiosity and ambition rarely found in his peers. Ethan comes from a very musical family, learned the guitar from his father at three, started to DJ publicly at fourteen, and has strived to expand his knowledge on various topics pertaining to music production, song writing, and the music industry as a whole. He has had great industry exposures and Grammy winning contacts, earned and well-deserved because of his skill, diligence, persistence, hard work, and his ever-lasting love for music.

Ethan's father and I married when Ethan was seventeen. I had the opportunity to watch him learn the valuable trait of positive human interaction, and to appreciate his inner ability to shine through change or adversity. I applaud his tremendous growth and development. The development comes not only in the area of career achievement, but in maturity and character.

Ethan is currently working at a major casino in Las Vegas, meanwhile taking the initiatives to advance his music credentials and production skills. He continues to grow in the music industry, and shows adamant desires to pursue a college music program. Ethan has always demonstrated the motivation and independence needed to be a successful learner. His personal preferences, work habits, and learning attitudes all show that he is likely to do well at college. He manages time well, researches and asks for help when he needs it. He is proficient at technology, his environment is conducive to learning, and he is equipped with great interpersonal skills that enable him to effectively discuss and collaborate with his professors and fellow students.

The college's world-renowned faculty and lifelong learning opportunities can provide Ethan with invaluable fulfillments. I trust that Ethan will perform well, and recommend him to your program with absolute confidence. He has made me proud as his stepmother, and I am sure will continue to do so as he grows in your program and beyond.

Thank you for the opportunity of correspondence,

Sincerely,

Avery Liang Lori

On the Same Team for the Beauty of Daily Existence

Avery had talked frankly with Abbey about launching his kids towards maturity. Abbey had successfully retained their affection. Abbey and Avery were on the same team, and continued to face challenges together to shift their relationships with the two grown children to a more comfortable and positive status.

In the end, everyone's needs could be met, and the Lori family met enough of the time and not too much of the time for life to feel at ease. Avery put behind all the scary thoughts and dark emotions, and conversed with Abbey honestly. Through communication and adjustment, and compromise, everything could be worked out, life could be adapted -- but love would not be sacrificed.

Aldous Huxley, the acclaimed author of *Brave New World*, named a price to happiness, his dystopia arraying appalling inventions of an overturned order:

> Actual happiness always looks pretty squalid in comparison with the overcompensations for misery. And, of course, stability isn't nearly so spectacular as instability. And being contented has none of the glamour of a good fight against misfortune, none of the picturesqueness of a struggle with temptation, or a fatal overthrow by passion or doubt.
> Happiness is never grand.

Avery realized that her life was unlike most people's. Her happiness, in the subtlety and beauty of daily existence, served her purpose, a journey self-piloted, full of lessons.

Every attempt at repair could bring new wounds that lacerate and bleed. Avery could try to heal the wound with fresh wounds, and once, twice, three times, she tried and tried and tried and didn't give up until she had nothing to lose. Every attempt at repair could open new doors that gyrate and rotate. She could try to turn the door with fresh outlooks, and once, twice, three times, she tried and tried and tried and didn't give up until there's everything to be regained and much more to learn. As the adage from her country of birth clarified for her, "While the mountain will not turn, the road will turn, and if the road will not turn, the mountain climber turns." Avery turned and modified her life for Abbey and his family. In turn, she gained a magnificent viewpoint to value life as it unfolded. The beauty of daily existence was after all, hard earned, significant, remarkable, and far from predictable.

For every painful occurrence Avery's life with Abbey might contain, she enjoyed thrice as many happy experiences with him. She lived her life happily with Abbey in pursuit of a healthy matrimony together. Her quest for happiness continued as the happiness of pursuit.

It was in the journey of pursuit that she attained possibilities of joy -- rather than giving up on a quest, she searched, aimed, fired, killed what's detrimental, and experienced destruction akin to death, in order to resurrect herself to new forms of happiness. It's what went on in the world, and on the journey of pursuit that gave her peace, that turned the death of her old self into a rebirth, into the un-death of her.

Willa Cather once explained how it happened. When she found out how to take her journey, or to let her journey take her, she told stories about herself:

> If there is one thing one can always yearn for and sometimes attain, it is human love.... You get to find your own way to dig out a heart and shake it off and hold it up to the light again. We all are.... Trying to invent our version of the story. All human odes are essentially one. "My life: what I sole from history, and how I live with it."

Like a story Avery told herself and the world, like a story unfolding in a book -- with luck, life came true.

Chapter 17. Multiple Frames of Reference

Back in Las Vegas, Abbey and Avery stopped feeling they were mere transplants. Las Vegas was home after all the travels, sweet to its core. Abbey continued his busy days with his demanding job, with a newly acquired sense of satisfaction. Avery's colleagues and students continued their gossip about celebrities and TV shows, but seemed not so irritating as before. Abbey and Avery's visits with family became less tiresome for the anti-social side of Avery. Even the knocks on their door from various religious missionaries became utterly tolerable, and the noises of gamblers and drunkards in the city, customary. Abbey and Avery found gems everywhere they turned in their home city.

Fangzheng looked and acted as square as his name, which literally meant "square" in Mandarin. Proud of being a missionary of the Las Vegas Chinese Christian Church, he took time to knock on Chinese people's doors and tell them about the Lord. Along with Fangzheng, came Victoria and her husband Edwin Taylor.

Victoria was from Avery's birth country of Taiwan. The two women quickly formed a bond that did not need to be explained or conditioned. So the two couples double dated though they were nothing alike.

"We had a miracle when I threw my back traveling to Taiwan. Usually my back would take longer than two days to recover, but I got well because our prayers were answered." Edwin narrated an incident with great stamina and enthusiasm.

Abbey and Avery glanced at each other, not saying a word to contradict. It was beneficial for Edwin to believe and enjoy good health. So they let Edwin believe and have faith.

They were not about to argue that his belief was false or unscientific. It was wiser to set aside differences and get along. It was more sensible than having a divided world or a civil war. Abbey and Avery avoided rebutting and accepted their friends as they were.

Abbey took Avery along for a staycation when he had business associates in town. His colleagues Kenneth and Emma visited Las Vegas often for trades shows and meetings. Emma was quite a southern belle and often crossed the line to entice her male coworkers to drink a tad too much after work hours.

"Come on, live a little bit." Emma hollered at everyone and drank incessantly.

"We are entertaining our clients, not ourselves." Someone explained and tried redirecting.

"You're here, and she's here, and I am here. Let's drink up!" She was forceful and aggressive, wanting all the attention.

Abbey sipped his drinks and stayed focused on business issues at hand. He and his clients usually ended a day with productive results, with or without Emma urging everyone to revel with her. Avery had to order more drinks for the drunken Emma who spilt her beverages all over; a coworker of Abbey's took Emma to the dance floor to placate her craze. With a happy Emma diverted, Abbey's team usually completed a work day with missions accomplished. It was wiser to set aside differences and get along. It was more sensible than forming a squabbling team. Abbey and Avery avoided disapproving and accepted their colleagues as they were.

Abbey's cousin Kevin and his wife Betty were hard-core Republicans. Kevin doubted everything the Democratic government had to offer. Betty would not care to discuss how people had no water and suffered in Africa or any other part of the world. If it's not American, it's not her concern.

Abbey often got into heated discussions with Kevin, debating the best course of action on various instances.

"God dame it, you Democratic tree-huggers are just not seeing the point of opening up the oil pipeline." Kevin yelled.

"Well there's more to it than the environment vs. money."

"What else is there to think? Business means business. If I run a corporation, I want profit, and that's the end of the story. Period."

Abbey and Avery stayed away from politics, money, and social standing with this couple. If the prevalent desperate-housewife dream could bring esteem, why bother to kill the vanity? It was wiser to set aside differences and get along. It was more sensible than having a quarreling family or a feud. Abbey and Avery avoided refuting and accepted their relatives as they were.

In Vegas, Abbey and Avery learned to have multiple frames of reference. They settled to a population consisting of all sorts of people from all over the world, the urban dwellers, the suburban rich, the famous, the almost-famous, the wannabes, the dangerous, the riffraff, and the people-like-you-and-me trying to get through life. They were happy that Ohannes and Taguhi, their Armenian friends from Budapest, moved to Vegas after listening to Abbey describe how fabulous and yet challenging the city of Las Vegas could be.

And, Abbey was happy and busy with work, gratified that he could have Avery's company traveling on business or for leisure most of the time during the summer, whereas Avery, happy learning from the world, or spending time with her challenging teenage students day in, day out, rolling and rising with adolescent whimsies:

One minute they would love her and admire her, calling her the smartest and the most beautiful. Next minute, they would gang up on her, making racial and disrespectful comments. Avery recognized, and acknowledged, her students' developmental processes, full of angst, lacking developed emotional depth. She only hoped that some of them could learn to love stories and grow wiser with reading. Although teaching the public schools was far from being lavished with wisdoms of all the classics and great works she grew up with, Avery urged her students to convert their love of digital games into understanding of intrinsic benefits of the language arts and literature.

Avery understood the needs of her underprivileged student population. She came to acquire teaching aptitudes similar to parenting skills, where encouragement and redirection of behavior worked far better than punishment. She stopped sending students to the Dean's, and instilled in them that she would never ever quit on them. However challenging her students were, she was determined that each child could be reached and taught. She would do whatever it took to get them where they needed to be.

Abbey and Avery relished the home they built, and took in the world as it came.

Chapter 18. Aware and Alive:
the Un-death of Me

Before Avery moved to Taipei, she had lived in the house with two neighborhoods. It had been an elongated, rectangle-shaped house full of her childhood memories. She had been the center of attention, and the "school flower" who boys vied for and adults doted on.

"You need to pull your shirt down so you don't show your belly before you go on the parade." Avery's mother had cautioned her and commanded her to dress properly.

"I am fine. Not enough time to get my baton shine...." Avery had been stressed for time with her duty of a commander for her school marching band.

"You need to prepare better next time."

"Ok if you allow the boys to help me."

It baffled Avery why she was not allowed to even talk to boys from school. She followed her parents' wishes and focused on her school work. She learned how important education was, and it was fine to do in Taiwan as the Taiwanese did.

Before Avery moved to New York, she had managed to open an English school in Taipei and earned enough money to go to Columbia University. It had been a rewarding endeavor watching adults and kids learn.

"You and Robert can form a study team. I will have Mr. Ibsen help you." Avery had grouped her adult students to do partner work.

"Mr. Ibsen is not here today. Could you help our class?"

"Sure, I will be right with you."

Although Avery hired native speakers to teach classes in her private school, she oftentimes had to be the classroom

253

teacher herself. She ran a tight ship and planned every detail herself. She learned how crucial it was to be hands-on and ready to undertake any task, and it was fine to do in Taipei as the Taipei people did.

Before Avery moved to Las Vegas, she had lived in apartments in Midtown Manhattan and the Village. Those had been efficient spaces for her to soak up New York City and embarked on her own coffee business.

"You need to make sure there's crema in the drinks. It makes all the difference." Avery had told her baristas to heed qualities of the coffee beverages.

"Sometimes, there's not enough time to wait for the crema to form."

"Customers have the events to attend to in our lounges, and are not in a hurry. We should give them the best."

Avery had all the ideas for an ideal creative space, but was not funded in ways she would have liked. She let her ex-husband's parents run the show and take over her business. She let Tim be the business operation chief and lost her business to various lawsuits. She learned that life could twist and turn, and it was fine to do in New York as the New Yorkers did.

Before Avery bought the house she lived in with Abbey, she had been upside-down like everyone in Las Vegas. It had been an upscale house where the master-planned community association had a say about everything in people's houses.

"You need to paint your door again. You can't change the color of your door." A vicious property manager visited and bared her teeth at Avery like a beast.

"Oh why? But I do own this house." Avery objected.

"Don't you know what a home owners association does? You have to follow our HOA rules and regulations."

"Does that mean I don't get to design my own house?"

"You can't change the color of your door, period. End of discussion."

It did not make sense to Avery, though she complied and repainted her door. She learned how the America outside New York worked, and it was fine to do in America as the Americans did.

Before Avery met Abbey, she had sought out wrong men and fell hard for her mistakes. She had experienced lonest moments in her life when predators tried squeezing money out of her, for any amount in any shape or form that helped during the downturn in the economy.

"Ding-Dong" sounded Avery's doorbell. She jumped three inches out of her chaise lounge, stirred by the sound.

"Who is it?" She had hardly any acquaintances who would call up without advanced notice. Could it be another summons serviced by some lying processor?

"I am not going to live like this the rest of my life!" She told herself, keeping quiet and waiting the person at her door to go away.

She sold the upside-down house to a lawyer who had a beautiful wife and two lovely daughters. She learned to short-sale the Vegas way, and it was fine to do in Las Vegas as the Las Vegans did.

After Avery bought the house she lived in with Abbey, things started to take a turn for the better. The house was in an old cozy neighborhood where Avery got to design it anyway she liked without an HOA looking over her shoulder. She even took her bicycle and motorcycle out for a spin around the park near her house.

"Those dirt bikes of yours look pretty cool. Did Avery always know how to bike?" Neighbors would comment.

"Yes, she scootered around in Taiwan as a teenager, and of course I trained her how to be a real biker." Abbey said.

"We need to go biking together in the mountains." A new neighbor suggested.

"Sure, we are in. We also have regular bikes to muck around on if you prefer."

Abbey and Avery got to travel around using various types of transportation: dirt bikes, regular bikes -- in cars, in their motor home, on cruises, and on countless airplane rides. Avery was exploring and enjoying ways of lives, learning lessons along the way, and it was fine to do in the world as the world did.

After Avery met Abbey, things started to take a turn for the better. Her house was bought outright, without creditors or predators calling or visiting out of the blue. She got used to the unannounced Lori children and their friends or enemies.

"I have three hours to kill before my studio time." Ethan showed up at the door.

"Ok are you hungry? Want a sandwich for lunch?" Instinctively, Avery had to offer.

"Sure, can I have Cody over too? He's working with me on a project right now."

"All right, a quick jam session and you're on your way." Abbey set the limit.

Abbey and Avery had companies from many places: Ethan, Claire and their buddies, Abbey's siblings and in-laws from nearby cites, Avery's nephews and nieces studying, working or living in the States, and Abbey's and Avery's friends and colleagues from past and present. Avery was learning to mix and hang, and it was fine to do at home as the kinfolks did.

A Limber and Supple Life

Avery nurtured and transformed herself, and learned to grasp life as it was. Her life became limber and supple. Happiness -- it was a garish color picture of a place Avery had not seen in years before Abbey came along. After that, happiness lived in the possibilities.

Memory ran along fixed directions in her brain, like electricity along its conduits; only a cataclysm could make the electrons charge up in shock and spin over into another channel. Avery ceased to be doomed in believing that where she had been was the only possibility, the only path to happiness. Her world shook and jarred for possible outlets and media to paint that bright color picture of a place, where she was aware and alive, reborn and declaring to the whole world --

"the Un-death of Me."

Epilogue

It was in the journey of pursuit that Avery attained possibilities of joy, of happiness -- rather than giving up a quest, she searched, aimed, fired, killed what's detrimental, and experienced destruction akin to death, in order to resurrect herself to new forms of bliss. It's what went on in the world, and on the journey of pursuit that gave her peace, that turned the death of her old self into a rebirth, into the un-death of her.

Willa Cather once explained how it happened. When she found out how to take her journey, or to let her journey take her, she told stories about herself:

> *If there is one thing one can always yearn for and sometimes attain, it is human love.... You get to find your own way to dig out a heart and shake it off and hold it up to the light again. We all are.... Trying to invent our version of the story. All human odes are essentially one. "My life: what I sole from history, and how I live with it."*

Like a story Avery told herself and the world, like a story unfolding in a book -- with luck, life came true.

Thank you for reading!

Dear Reader,

I hope you enjoyed *The Un-death of Me: Life of an Asian American Woman*. I have to tell you that I really learned a great deal from the characters in this book -- in writing this "fictional memoir" of mine, I have grown wiser and happier.

All the characters mentioned here in the book, true or imaginative, have contributed to the world I construct, and have their own voices. I created them with the purpose of illustrating a world that hopefully can be rid of injustices or biases.

I plan to write my next book using one of the character's viewpoint (probably a male character), to narrate the intricacies of human relationships. Our complex yet beautiful world has so much to offer, that it's hard not to explore as many aspects as our time allows us to.

Finally, I need to ask a favor. If you are so inclined, I'd love a review of *The Un-death of Me*. Your honest review is the most precious feedback I could have.

You, the reader, have the power to make voices heard and change our world for the better. Please find below a link to my author page on Amazon:

http://amazon.com/author/aliciasulozeron

Other platforms where you could communicate your thoughts about my book are as follows:

http://www.aacs.website/en/membership/featured
https://www.facebook.com/people/Alicia-Lozeron/100013834032346
https://www.facebook.com/aliciasulozeron
http://www.aliciasulozeron.com
https://plus.google.com/108984032785909720247

Please make yourself heard by voicing your opinions. Thank you so much again for reading *The Un-death of Me: Life of an Asian American Woman.* I look forward to reading your review.

Sincerely,

Alicia Su Lozeron

Discussion Questions:

1. Do you think this "fictional memoir" is more fictional or autobiographical? To what extent is this book a cross-genre endeavor?
2. Does the book start in a disoriented way with a purpose? What purpose does it serve? Reflect on the narrator's state of mind and how "stream of consciousness" brings out her stories.
3. What kind of character is Harry? When the narrator says she needs to teach people how she is to be treated, including adults and children, do you think she has this man and her students/step kids in mind? What other characters might be included in this list of people that need to be taught about cultural competence?
4. Do you think the character of Avery Mingli Liang is well developed? How has she changed throughout the book? What kind of realizations does she experience? To what extent is her isolation self-imposed? Does she establish true connections with her husband Abbey Lori? Or is it another quandary?
5. What kind of character is Tim Rosenberg? Abbey Lori? How are they similar or different? Why do you think these two men

become the most important influencers on Avery's life?

6. Do you think you can be truly empathetic of Avery's immigration life and experience? Based on your own upbringing and heritage, can you picture what Avery has to undergo in order to find her niche in the American society?

7. How sympathetic are you of people of foreign origins? Do you think they should all go home to avoid struggles in their adopted countries? Or, what do immigrant experiences like Avery's teach you?

8. What is your favorite part of the book? Why?

9. The differences and similarities among nations are nuanced in this book. Compare and contrast. Give examples.

10. The prologue/epilogue of the book draws out the same topic of quest and life fulfilment. To what extent do you think the implications change although they both employs very much of the same narration?

THE UN-DEATH OF ME

Life of an Asian American Woman

Author: Alicia Su Lozeron

About the Author

Alicia Su Lozeron is the author of numerous news/magazine articles and short stories. Born in Taiwan, she moved to New York City in the 1990s and subsequently became a US citizen. She holds two Master's degrees in English and Comparative Literature, respectively from National Tsinghua University and Columbia University in the City of New York. Her debut novel, *The Un-death of Me*, depicts an immigrant woman's life in a fresh light. It is a fictional world full of contemporary and global resonance; it is about many subjects: alienation, individuality, self-doubt, self-discovery, complexities of love and marriage, quests of fulfillment/happiness, (in)justice, cultural diversity, discrimination, and mankind as a whole. Its subtle yet intense emotions detailed in the many characters and locales, render a visionary sense of humanity, gratifying and unforgettable in their own rights.

www.ingramcontent.com/pod-product-compliance
Lightning Source LLC
Chambersburg PA
CBHW030411030726
47497CB00002B/564